WORLDS WITHIN VERONA'S WALLS

Vivienne Raffaele

WORLDS WITHIN VERONA'S WALLS

Part I – Autumn Term

Meanwhile the sun paused ere it should alight,
Over the horizon of the mountains; Oh,
How beautiful is sunset, when the glow
Of Heaven descends upon a land like thee,
Thou Paradise of exiles, Italy!

Percy Bysshe Shelley

CHAPTER 1

Clare stood at the bus stop in Verona in the pouring rain, trying to make some sense of the timetable. A summer storm was underway and water was not so much trickling as flooding down her back, infiltrating freely between her rucksack and anything but impermeable anorak, seeping unpleasantly and relentlessly into the t-shirt underneath. People always moan about British weather, she thought, but although it may rain frequently it's usually a question of a brief ten minute shower or a gentle drizzle that allows you to go about your business relatively unaffected. In Italy there are no half measures. One moment the sky is blue, the sun is shining and all's well with the world. A few minutes later dark clouds gather ominously, the wind builds up and before you know it, the heavens open and in two minutes you find yourself completely soaked from head to toe. Clare was so wet that she might as well just have dived directly into the fountain in the middle of the nearby square. In the rain Verona had undergone a transient dimming of light and colour, melting into monochrome greyness, whereas just a couple of hours earlier it had shone with the brilliance and vibrancy of Mediterranean countries.

She hunched her shoulders and pulled up her collar, peering at the tiny print and trying to interpret the symbols, perplexed by the distinction between 'festivi' and 'feriali'. In any case there did not appear to be another bus for Mantua for at least an hour, so she was looking around desperately for a bar when she noticed that there was an English school just opposite. She toyed with the idea of going in and asking for a job. After all who could possibly resist someone just out of university with no teaching qualifications, who couldn't speak Italian and looked like a drowned rat? Of course logic would suggest that it was not the best moment, and that she would be far better off coming back the following day having dressed more appropriately, but today was Friday, she was planning to spend the afternoon in Mantua and the school would probably be closed over the weekend, while on Monday she would already be on her way to Florence.

Clare did in fact have a job more or less lined up in Naples, but having spoken to several people who had been there, she was having doubts about whether she really wanted to live in such a chaotic city. So she had decided to buy an Interrail pass and spend a little time travelling around Italy first. If all else failed she would still be in time to take the job in Naples, but on the way down she would have a great holiday and maybe even be lucky enough to find work somewhere attractive en route. Stuff it, she thought, what did she have to lose? Verona was beautiful, the bus wasn't for another hour and there was a fair chance she might even get a cup of decent tea in an English school.

Italy might be famous for its espresso coffee and wonderful food, but Italian bars had not yet grasped the concept of tea, Clare thought. They tended to give you a small cup of lukewarm water and a selection of cheap fruit teabags. If you were really lucky you got a tiny half-full teapot. It was already astonishing that anybody bothered to produce teapots that small, she reflected, but you'd think they could at least manage to fill it.

She dashed across the square, putting one foot in an enormous puddle on the way, and heaved a sigh of relief as she made it under the shelter of the stone archway and out of the rain. She walked damply up the impressive stairway to the first floor, where she could see the reception desk of the school. Behind the desk there was an intimidatingly well-dressed middle-aged woman with bright pink lipstick, huge gold earrings and a mass of red hair. In fact she looked so intimidating that Clare seriously considered turning around and making her way back down the stairs, but at this point she had already been spotted and it was too late.

Clare approached the desk. "Uhm, Ciao, Buon giorno, Hello, I'm afraid I don't speak Italian."

"No worry, I speak very well English" replied the woman briskly. "Can I help you?"

"Well, uhm, ah, I've just graduated and I was passing and I thought I'd pop in and ask whether by any chance you might be needing an English teacher", Clare tried to stop herself babbling incoherently, but with little success.

There was a slight pause, while the woman looked her very quickly up and down. "Oh, excellent, we have emergency, maybe we have job for you." "My name is Ursula. What is your name?"

"Clare".

"OK, so now you speak with the teaching director and she say me if you are OK. Please remove your coat, you are leaving the floor all wet. Why you have no umbrella?"

"Oh I'm so sorry", said Clare. "I was caught out unexpectedly." She hung her anorak on the coat stand by the desk, where it dripped into the designer wastepaper basket, and smoothed her lank hair back from her face.

"You teach English before?"

"Well, not really", admitted Clare.

"Is no problem, and you don't speak Italian?"

"No".

"Is no problem. You wait here."

Ursula strode down the corridor, her high heels making an incredible racket on the stone floor, and disappeared into the room at the end. Meanwhile Clare looked around desperately for a bathroom so that she could at least attempt to tidy herself up. She tentatively opened the nearest door, which led into what was clearly a classroom, with lines of desks and a large whiteboard at one end. There was another door behind the reception desk, but she didn't dare explore any further in case Ursula returned, and she certainly didn't want it to look like she was nosing around without permission. She contemplated wringing her hair out in the umbrella stand but decided it would be too embarrassing if Ursula were to reappear.

The phone on the desk started to ring. It seemed to go on forever but nobody came out to answer it. Clare shifted uncomfortably from one foot to the other, feeling uneasy and in some way guilty, as though she ought to answer. It finally stopped ringing and at that moment Ursula emerged from the other room and motioned for her to come over. As she walked down the corridor Clare was very conscious that she was in fact squelching at every step, the left foot notably more so than the right, and every sound seemed to be magnified by the stone floor and high ceiling. What's more the bottom of her jeans had obviously trailed in the water and the damp was now steadily seeping upwards, as if she had blotting paper wrapped round her legs.

Ursula seemed to be getting impatient. She had the air of someone who is perpetually in a hurry and she looked at Clare as if she was taking an inordinately long time to arrive. She showed her into the room and presented her to a very English-looking woman in her 30s sitting at a large desk stacked high with piles of papers.

"She is Janet. She is Clare", Ursula stated succinctly. "So now you talk and then we speak", after which she turned on her heel and clattered her way back down the corridor.

Janet was tall and slim, with short brown hair and a fraught but friendly expression.

"Hello, do sit down," she suggested, pointing at the chair opposite her. "I gather you're looking for a job", she began.

Clare perched herself self-consciously on the edge of the seat. "Yes, well I wasn't really planning to call in, as you can perhaps guess, but it was a spur of the moment decision. I've just graduated and I'm planning to spend a year abroad. I have actually been offered a job in Naples, but to be honest I'm not really sure I want to go there. I know it seems very presumptuous because I don't have any experience and I can't speak Italian, but I thought I would drop in and ask whether you were looking for teachers."

Janet was looking at her thoughtfully. "Well, the Italian doesn't really matter because we are only supposed to speak English during the lessons", she said. "The lack of experience is a bit more problematical, but frankly we are pretty desperate because one of our teachers walked out yesterday and we absolutely have to find someone to replace him immediately. You realise that most of the lessons are in the afternoons and evenings, don't you?"

"Oh, that's not a problem."

"And would you be willing to teach both children and adults?"

"Absolutely. I'm happy to take on anything. I've never done any teaching but I've worked with children before and I'm a quick learner!"

"I would need you to commit for the whole of the academic year, so up to the end of June. I don't want to be looking for another teacher in the middle of the year and the students don't like it if their teacher changes half-way through the course."

"Of course, I realise that and I would certainly stay for the whole year."

Janet relaxed back into her chair. "So what's your degree in?"

"Drama", replied Clare. "I studied at Birmingham University."

"Well, that helps a bit, I suppose. You'll just have to pretend you know what you're doing. You're an attractive girl, which always goes down well, you've got a degree and you speak English without a marked regional accent. I think you'll have to do. Could you start next week?"

"Good grief", said Clare, "I suppose so, but don't you have to carry out background checks and things like that?"

"Ah, now you're displaying your ignorance about Italy! There can be the most absurd bureaucracy about unimportant things, but in many other ways it's very laid back. This is a private language school, so we can take on whoever we like and the boss isn't bothered who I hire so long as the students don't complain. At some point it would probably be a good idea if you had a copy of your degree certificate sent here, but that can all be sorted out later."

"But are you really sure I'm suitable? I know absolutely nothing about your teaching methods and I can't speak any Italian at all."

"Oh, you'll learn soon enough. I'll give you some books so that you can keep one step ahead of your students. That's what everyone does at the beginning. They're nearly all adults and most of them are beginners or pre-intermediates, so it's not particularly demanding."

"Isn't it more complicated with beginners? Surely I would need to know at least some Italian?"

"No, not really. Our method is based on teachers communicating only in English, at every level. Of course we all cheat a bit now and then, but in theory you should never say a word in Italian during lessons! I'll tell you what, I'll go and speak to Ursula and sort out all the details. You can wait for me here. If you need a bathroom by any chance, there's one next door. I'll be back in 5 minutes."

Janet left the room and headed off towards Ursula, while Clare decided to take advantage of the bathroom. She started at herself in the mirror, pushing her lank locks back from her face. "Blimey", she thought "I didn't expect it to be that easy. They must be really desperate. I wouldn't have hired me. I look like someone on the run from a serial killer in the woods." Shell-shocked, she made her way back to Janet's office.

Janet reappeared with Ursula, who looked her up and down critically.

"OK, now you go change and then this afternoon we go to offices to make documents. You come back at 4 o'clock, yes?

"Uhm, yes, OK I suppose", said Clare. "I was meaning to go to Mantua but I can put that off."

"Where you stay?"

"At the Hotel Verdi, but I've only booked until tomorrow, because I was expecting to move on."

"Is OK. We put you in one of the apartments for the students", said Ursula. "I organise everything. You come back this afternoon, yes?

8

"OK then, I'll see you later."

Ursula escorted her to the top of the stairs and watched as Clare made her way back down the steps and towards the exit. In the meantime the rain seemed to have stopped and Clare gazed out at the street in a bemused fashion. "I didn't even think to ask what they would pay me, or what the hours are", she thought. Still she could hardly run back up the stairs and say "oh, by the way what are the working conditions?" So she squelched out into the street and looked for a bar. "Sod it", she exclaimed "they didn't even offer me a cup of tea."

CHAPTER 2

Vanessa ran over the bass part for the fifth time in succession. As usual the basses behaved impeccably when singing on their own but when brought together with the rest of the choir would sneakily join the sopranos one by one, perhaps feeling that it was more fun singing the tune, or more worryingly because they didn't even realise they were doing it. Vanessa tried standing alongside one of the slightly more reliable men and screaming his part into his ear, hoping he would then pull the others along with him. Up to a point this worked quite well, but was clearly not a viable solution as it made conducting impossible.

There were only three rehearsals left until the concert and of course following the summer break most of the choir had completely forgotten their parts. Vanessa made a mental note not to schedule concerts for September again because there simply was not enough time to rehearse after the holidays, added to which everybody was still in that relaxed, happy-go-lucky frame of mind associated with August in Italy, not conducive to getting any work done.

For the umpteenth time Vanessa wondered why she continued with the attempt to create a choir with twenty-five assorted Italian plumbers, teachers, mechanics and housewives, only two of whom could read music and only about five of whom could actually sing. She could not bring herself to exclude anybody, as the choir was essentially a social occasion, allowing people to get together once a week and do something different, providing frequent excuses for celebrations with home-made cakes and a couple of bottles of good wine. On the other hand, she felt, it was essential to make at least a token effort towards improving the quality of the singing and producing something which sounded more like music.

If nothing else at least it made the church services slightly less dreary. Last Christmas, after tense negotiations with the parish priest she had succeeded in eliminating some of the grimmest pieces and doubling the speed of old classics such as 'Oh come all ye faithful', making them a little less funereal. Not that they would normally be so solemn, at least not in Britain, but if you perform anything at the pace of geriatric snail it tends to lose some of its appeal. She still had to keep her eye, or rather her ear, on the organist, who tended to revert to the old speed given half a chance. He reminded her of one of those old clockwork toys which has to be wound up every few seconds, otherwise they gradually grind to a halt.

On this occasion they had been called on for a wedding and given the chronic dearth of available keyboard players Vanessa had decided to use pre-recorded backing tracks. On the one hand this avoided having the complication of having to find a decent accompanist, but on the other it offered scope for a whole range of possible disasters. She vividly remembered a previous occasion when the choir had got completely out of sync with the track, falling gradually further and further behind while she gesticulated like a lunatic trying to speed them up, waving her arms around frantically in a desperate attempt to catch up with the music, surrounded by total cacophony. On terminating there had been polite applause from the audience, thankfully mostly made up of friends and relatives of the choir. In general if you start together and end together you can get away with a lot in the middle, but there are times when even the least musical realise something is wrong.

Since then Vanessa had developed specific techniques for managing the choir and always made sure there was a speaker pointing their way so they could hear when things were getting out of hand, but there was always a degree of risk involved. The wedding was to take place in a church they had never sung in and she had no idea what the acoustics were like. Cheap amplification equipment and the lack of a sound technician made it very difficult to ensure the quality of the music, even when the choir was on its best behaviour. However, Vanessa trusted their enthusiasm would make up for the inevitable defects and ensure that the bride and groom were happy, which was all that mattered in the end.

She decided to bring the rehearsal to a close. While some of choir, especially those with young children, headed off home, the rest made their way to the local bar for the most popular part of the evening – a beer, or coffee or coca cola, depending on your taste, accompanied by a good hour of serious gossip. It was a pleasantly warm evening, so they sat outside, enjoying the last days of summer and one of those magnificent starry evenings that appeal so much to those who have grown up in colder northern climes.

As she sat down to enjoy a cold beer, well-earned in her opinion, Vanessa's cell phone began to vibrate in her pocket. She had that immediate sinking feeling that always came to her when her phone rang so late in the evening, as she could never rid herself of the fear that it meant bad news. At best a call from home at this hour usually meant there was some minor domestic disaster, probably requiring her urgent presence, as her family generally avoided ringing her when they knew she was at choir practice. She glanced at the number and was relieved to see the call was from Janet, moving away from her choristers to answer.

"Hello Janet. What can I do for you?"

"Hi Vanessa, I'm sorry to call you at this hour, but I knew you were at choir practice and I wanted to contact you before tomorrow morning."

"Don't worry", is there a problem at the school?"

"There have been nothing but problems at the school since Jim walked out last week after that massive row with Ursula", Janet pointed out. "But there's some good news. We've managed to find a new teacher and she's starting on Monday. She's got absolutely no experience, so we need to sort out which classes I can give her and which ones do ourselves. Do you think you could possibly make it into Verona tomorrow morning? Of course I could arrange everything by myself, but it would be really helpful if we could talk about things face to face."

"I think I can manage that", said Vanessa. "Frankly I'm just relieved you managed to find someone, because nobody who knows what Ursula is like would touch the job with a barge pole and it would have taken ages if we had had to advertise. In the meantime there was no way I was going to get stuck with doing all Jim's lessons! Three days a week is more than enough for me."

"Anyway the new teacher's called Clare", explained Janet. "She's a drama graduate and seems smart enough, although frankly I would have taken her even if she had had a third class degree in mechanical engineering from some polytechnic in New Zealand. Beggars can't be choosers! I think we'll give her the children's courses, and she can definitely have the traffic wardens, because I've had enough of them and it's impossible to teach

13

them anything anyway. We can sort out all the details tomorrow, though. Can you come in for 9 o'clock?"

"Yes, that's fine", answered Vanessa. "That way I can take my daughter to school first and drop off some stuff at the dry cleaners on the way. I'll see you there at 9."

"Great", I'll pick up a couple of cakes at the bakers' and we can have breakfast in my office. Ursula is at some meeting, thank God, so she'll be out of our hair."

"Perfect. I'll see you tomorrow. Bye for now."

"Bye then."

Vanessa rang off and returned to the table, where three of the choir members were involved in animated discussion about the new rules for differentiated waste collection. Even after all these years, it never ceased to amaze her how much noise Italians make when having perfectly ordinary conversations. When she had first arrived, almost twenty years before, she hadn't been able to speak any Italian at all and it had often seemed to her that people were arguing, when actually they were just talking about the weather, or complaining about their husbands. But that is just part of the joy of Italian life for the English, she thought. We love Italians because they are loud and friendly and hospitable. You couldn't imagine sitting on an Italian train for three hours without speaking to anyone, whereas in England people hide behind their newspapers or look away hastily, terrified that some strange loony may start chatting to them.

At least that's what it was like twenty years ago, she thought. Maybe times have changed. She had lived abroad for so long that when she returned to England she felt a bit like a foreigner. When she paid in shops in the UK she would examine the coins in her hand carefully like someone on holiday abroad, or pensioners when the decimal system came in decades ago, she thought. Vanessa was still just old enough to remember shillings and pence when she was a child, just as more recently she had seen the transition from the Italian lira to the Euro.

Vanessa sat for a few minutes listening to the others chatting, before deciding it was time to make her way home. She wished everyone goodnight and walked back through the village, glancing up at the stars now and again in mute appreciation. The older and more characteristic rural buildings were mostly situated along the main road and on the hill leading towards the cemetery, situated away from the residential area, as always in Italy, while newer houses had sprung up relentlessly in the last few years, sprawling out in every direction. What had once been a small hamlet with just a few families was now a thriving community made up of local people, recent immigrants and outsiders buying second homes in an area close to Lake Garda, but just far enough for house prices to drop considerably. The ten minute stroll was a sort of feeble attempt at physical exercise, given that her job was about as sedentary as you can get. When translating she spent all her time at the computer at home, so she didn't even have to get to the office, whereas on her teaching days she drove into Verona and parked just outside the school. Of course this wouldn't have stopped her going to the gym or doing sport, but she had decided long ago that exercise was not for her. She liked dance, but the only courses available locally were ballet and hip hop classes for children, while aerobics and kick boxing classes seemed understandably to be frequented mainly by anorexic young women and fitness freaks.

When she arrived home the house was in darkness, so obviously everyone had already gone to bed. She tiptoed up the stairs, nearly tripping over the dog's ball, and headed as quietly as possible for the bathroom. As she looked at her reflection in the mirror, she thought over what she needed to the following day. It was a hassle having to go in to town, but at least it was a relief that another teacher had been found, otherwise Ursula would have given her no peace. The woman was so insistent that in the end it was almost always simpler to give in and do whatever she wanted. Why is it, Vanessa thought, that unpleasant people always seem to get their own way? I suppose because they know what they want and will do anything to get it.

She turned off the light and crept into bed.

CHAPTER 3

Janet set off from home at half past eight, walking briskly towards the city centre over the monumental Castelvecchio bridge. She had always been an active person, so she enjoyed the daily walk to and from school, which always took her across the medieval fortified bridge in red brick, faithfully reconstructed after the Second World War, when it had been blown up by retreating German troops. It had originally been built in the 12th century by Cangrande II della Scala as an escape route from the castle in the event of rebellion or unrest, a pretty impressive emergency exit Janet had always thought. At this hour there were only a few tourists about, standing on the walls in front of the M-shaped merlons to take selfies of themselves against the backdrop of the river.

Janet had initially considered living in the country, attracted by ideas of bucolic bliss, but in the end her pragmatic side had asserted itself and she had decided that the city had more to offer a single woman. One of the great advantages of the small but well-equipped rented flat she had found was that it was only 15 minutes on foot from the school and the historic part of the town, while living in the centre saved her money on transport, as she hardly ever used the car. Nevertheless she still sometimes dreamed of living in an isolated farmhouse, surrounded by nothing but vines and olive trees.

She made her way past the imposing castle and stopped off at the bakery to pick up a few biscuits and small cakes, as she had promised Vanessa. It was a beautiful sunny day, with that clear blue sky so typical of southern Europe and so rarely seen in northern England, where she came from. The climate had been one of the chief reasons for her decision to move to Italy, along with the end of an unsatisfying relationship and the need to start anew. She had paged through the ads, looking for a job abroad, and when the position as Director of Studies had come up at a school in Verona she had seized the opportunity to live in one of the most romantic cities in northern Italy. Maybe she would get lucky and find the man of her life, she thought.

That had been three years earlier and though she had had a couple of boyfriends, somehow the perfect partner had not yet materialised, attractive, intelligent, witty, single men of appropriate age being hard to come by, as women in their thirties all over the world are aware. She was now 35 and her biological clock was ticking so loudly she wondered that people didn't hear it as she passed, like the crocodile in Peter Pan. She had never been a particularly maternal type, but now she was surprised to find herself increasingly obsessed with the idea of having a baby. After years of thinking that such things were not for her, she now desperately wanted to give and receive that unconditional love that only seemed to her to exist between a parent and child. She would look at families around her in the streets, at the supermarket and playing in the parks and wonder what it would be like to have her own child, to create another human being from scratch. She hadn't yet got to the stage of going into shops and looking at baby clothes, thank God, but she thought about motherhood more and more. Men are lucky, she thought, they can still be fathers right into their fifties and beyond. Even if things don't work out first time around, they often get a second chance after a divorce, so it's easy for them to procrastinate about children. Women, on the other hand, have to cram everything into a much smaller space of time. When you're twenty you don't even consider the issue, the number one priority being simply to enjoy yourself. Then you're taken up with your career and all of a sudden you find yourself at the age when you have to make a decision – now or never.

She was torn between envy for Vanessa's life, which revolved around her husband and two children and their various commitments, and the fear of giving up the freedom which goes with being single. The older you get the harder it is to adapt to someone else's needs, she thought. Vanessa had been lucky to find someone to share her life with when she was young, marrying in her twenties and having a few years to spend with her husband alone before deciding to have children.

She and Vanessa were complete opposites in so many ways, and yet since Janet had arrived in Verona they had become good friends. While Vanessa was easygoing and optimistic, extrovert and sociable, Janet was quieter and more introverted. Her tendency to analyse everything and evaluate people critically often led to her being considered cold and somewhat sarcastic. She preferred not to show her emotions, not because she had been brought up that way, but just because she was intrinsically a very private person. However, despite their differences, or perhaps because of them, Vanessa and Janet had got on immediately. In many ways they were complementary, and each of them respected the other's qualities.

Janet was so taken up with her thoughts that she was very nearly run over by a bus. She had rashly stepped onto the zebra crossing without looking and as the bus screeched to a halt, the driver gesticulated at her angrily, his comments fortunately inaudible. Janet in her turn theatrically indicated the black and white bands on the road and holding her head high crossed over the road with studied calm, her heart beating very loudly in her ears. Pedestrian crossings in Italy are not to be taken seriously, she thought. It is unwise to assume that any motorists will actually stop at them, with the possible exception of German tourists. And if anyone does stop, you risk being run over by a car overtaking on the other side. Initially when she was driving in Italy she had responsibly halted at crossings, only to find that local pedestrians were so surprised that they lingered in perplexed fashion at the side of the road, wondering what she was doing or whether she had stopped to ask directions.

She arrived at the door of the school and got out her keys, letting herself in but closing the door behind her so that she wouldn't have to deal with people wanting information about English courses. Ursula was not due to arrive until midday, so she would have plenty of time to sort things out with Vanessa, and they could then present Ursula with the fait accompli. Janet went into her office, resting the tray of cakes on the table before nipping into the bathroom to fill the electric kettle and rinse a couple of mugs. As she came out the door bell rang.

"Is that you Vanessa?"

"Yes, it's me."

"Come on up then, but don't leave the door open", said Janet. "I want an undisturbed breakfast."

Janet would have recognised it was Vanessa in any case from the noise she made clomping up the stairs. I wonder if there is a clumsy gene, she thought to herself, but if there is Vanessa must undoubtedly have it. Of all the people she knew, Vanessa was the one who could be most relied on to drop things, walk into inanimate objects or trip over rugs. If an obstacle existed, she would find it, but even in the absence of apparent risks she could find a way to make day-to-day life unduly complicated.

"I brought biscuits", Vanessa announced, dropping them on the desk "just in case you forgot. I can't resist the temptation of something sweet and at home the family have decided that I'm too fat. Everyone keeps watching me when I open the kitchen cupboards to check that I'm not eating anything sugary, so I have to take advantage of the situation when I'm out of the house. The other day I ate a whole packet of biscuits and then had to carefully hide the evidence under the other rubbish".

"Don't worry", replied Janet. "I picked up some cakes at Luigi's on the way. I know how uncooperative you are if you don't get a sugar fix."

"I'm not uncooperative, just distracted because I'm hungry!"

"Whatever; enjoy your cake so that we can get down to business."

Vanessa carefully selected one of Luigi's delectable strawberry tarts, following it up with an exquisite mini cannolo filled with ricotta cheese and garnished with candied orange. She let out a sigh of satisfaction and relaxed into her chair.

"OK, so tell me all about the new teacher. How did she turn up?"

"She just suddenly appeared out of the storm. A gift of God, I guess. To be honest she didn't look terribly promising, dripping with rain and dressed in jeans and an old sweatshirt. It shows how desperate Ursula was if she immediately sent her in to see me. You know how fussy she is about what people wear. Anyway, I'm sure she'll be fine. She's called Clare. Quite pretty really, and nicely spoken, as my mother would have said, so realistically what more can you ask for if you need someone so urgently?"

"We could have asked Ashley the American."

"No way, she refused to come back after Ursula failed to pay her for some teaching she did in the summer."

"I never understood exactly what happened there", commented Vanessa.

"Oh well, she went over the number of hours established for the course, but as Ashley pointed out, if nobody told her how many she was supposed to do how could she be expected to know? Anyway, Ursula wouldn't pay her for the extra hours and Ashley was so pissed off that she swore she never wanted anything to do with the school ever again."

"I'm not surprised she didn't want to come back. I would have been pretty fed up myself!"

"She got her own back by keeping all the school's books, so in the end Ursula was irate, everyone was unsatisfied and we lost another English teacher!"

"So what are we going to give Clare?" asked Vanessa. "Has she got any experience?"

"None whatsoever."

"OK, so she had better not have the advanced courses, not that there are many of those anyway. Everyone tends to be lower-intermediate. Besides, as the last one to arrive it's only fair that she get the naff groups!"

"Well, as I said on the phone, I thought she could have most of the children's courses, and the traffic wardens of course. They'll like having someone young and pretty. There's also a new intermediate course starting from 8.30 to 10 on Tuesday and Thursday evening. Do you want that?"

"Absolutely not", said Vanessa. "I'm already doing 5 hours on Thursday and I don't think I can stomach any more than that. And the late evening courses are a pain anyway. It's more complicated with the family." She hesitated for a fraction of a second. "Are you going to eat that last cake."

"No, go ahead and have it." Janet barely had time to respond before Vanessa had disposed of the last pastry with almost orgasmic fulfilment. Fortified, she sat back in her chair and turned her attention fully to the question in hand "OK, let's try and sort out this timetable then."

They settled down to discuss the finer details of the programme and the changes in the forthcoming academic year. Four cups of tea and half a packet of biscuits later they had finally arranged everything to their satisfaction, so they agreed to adjourn.

"What time is it", asked Vanessa.

"Quarter to twelve."

"Oh God, I want to get out of here before Ursula arrives and tries to mess everything up."

"Well, it is her school", Janet pointed out.

"I don't care. We make all the money for her anyway. All she does is sit around and complain about everything. The only reason she's the boss is that she inherited this amazing building bang in the middle of the city from her parents, so she doesn't even have to pay rent."

Vanessa stood up, pushing back her chair and grabbing her bag.

"Anyway I must dash. I've got to go to the chemist and the post office, and what's more I still haven't found the last school books for Elena. It's astonishing how expensive they are here. When I was at school in England everything was free! It's not surprising that Italy now has practically the lowest birth rate in the world, even if it is a Catholic country; it's so hideously costly to have children."

"Don't start that again. You made your bed, so now lie in it! Anyway it's always the richest families that have the fewest children, in fact wealth seems to be inversely proportional to the number of kids." She paused. "By the way you've got icing sugar all down your front!"

"Oh damn, I can't understand how people manage to eat these cakes elegantly. I always make a tremendous mess". Vanessa ineffectually tried to brush the icing sugar off her t-shirt, before getting up and heading rapidly towards the door. "I'll see you on Monday afternoon then. Have a nice weekend."

"And you. Bye for now."

Once the door banged shut and the noise of Vanessa's footsteps gradually diminished, Janet settled down at her computer to draw up a hopefully Ursula-proof timetable.

CHAPTER 4

Ursula had arranged to meet Clare outside the school so that they could go and see the flat that was destined to be her home for the coming months. As well as providing English courses for Italians in the afternoons and evenings, the school also offered Italian language courses for foreigners in the morning, and the apartment they were going to see was used to house some of the foreign students.

Clare and Ursula had spent the previous afternoon sorting out all the bureaucracy linked to the hiring of the former by the latter, and Clare now had her own 'codice fiscale', which as far as she could understand was the equivalent of a national insurance number, and was apparently necessary in Italy for any and every kind of contract, service or transaction. Clare had then placed endless signatures on various sheets of paper put in front of her. Of course she hadn't understood a word of what she was signing and Ursula had not wished to waste time in explanations, so Clare had simply signed on the dotted line when requested to do so, hoping that she was not selling herself into slavery for the next seven years or drawing up a pact with the devil.

Everything had taken place so quickly that she couldn't quite believe it was happening. She had rung her mother the previous evening to let her know that she would be staying in Italy for a few months at least. While surprised that she had found a job so rapidly, her mum sounded genuinely delighted that she would have an excuse to visit her in a place as attractive as Verona. Her father had never been particularly keen on travelling, preferring to sit in front of the fire with his feet up, immersed in a good book, forcing her mum to seek out every opportunity to go and visit friends and family anywhere in the world.

Absorbed in her thoughts, Clare didn't even notice Ursula arriving , which was in itself an achievement, as with her high heels and bright red hair Ursula was pretty noticeable.

"Come, we go to see the apartment", she announced, immediately setting off at a rapid pace down a narrow side street. Clare was amazed that anyone could move about on heels so quickly, as she found it difficult to walk in them at all without looking like a drunken robot, but clearly years of practice had given Ursula an enviable ability to cover large distances on smooth marble pavements without giving it a second thought. They weaved their way through the backstreets of Verona and after about ten minutes arrived at a slightly dilapidated building with an old stone portal and a surprisingly modern glass door. Ursula pulled out a large bunch of keys and opened the door, which led into a high-roofed hallway with a stone staircase.

"We go to top floor", explained Ursula. "There is no lift but you are young so is good for you and near the school for evening lessons."

"I'm sure it will be fine."

When they reached the fourth floor (great when you're carrying up suitcases or shopping, Clare thought to herself), Ursula stopped and opened up another door on the left-hand side of the landing.

"Here there are three bedrooms. This one is occupied by two Swedish girls, this one by two American students and here is your room." Ursula led the way into a small, darkish room with sloping ceiling, equipped with a single bed, desk and wardrobe. On the plus side, there was a pleasant view over the roofs of the city from the window. The ceramic tile floor was not exactly stylish, but nevertheless functional and cool for the summer.

"This will be OK for the moment, I think", Clare commented "but maybe later I will look for something a bit bigger."

"It is very good. You are lucky to find something in the centre at this price. You pay 300 euro a month including bills, plus one month's rent as deposit."

"I can manage that, I think", commented Clare, as they made their way around the rest of the flat.

There was a largish shared living room with a kitchen area, and a massive bathroom with spectacularly hideous brown tiles and avocado green bathroom suite. Why would anyone, in any era, possibly want to have an avocado green toilet? Clare pondered. Presumably it was just as cheap to have white one, but no, someone had deliberately chosen avocado green.

"Good, so now we go back to the school and you sign contract for apartment. I give you key and you can move in from hotel. Now we go shopping."

"Shopping?" asked Clare. "Shopping for what?"

"Clothes. You cannot possibly dress like this for school."

"Like what? What's wrong with my clothes?"

"You look like English student. Always jeans, trainers and t-shirt. No style."

"I don't imagine my pupils will be that bothered by what I'm wearing! Anyway, by the time I've paid the rent I won't have any money left to buy clothes."

"I give you advance on your pay. You need proper clothes now. So now we go and I show you what to buy. Come."

Ursula shepherded Clare out of the flat, locked the door behind her and headed rapidly down the stairs. She clearly considered the issue had been decided. Slightly irritated, Clare nevertheless thought it was probably not a good idea to antagonise her employer before she had even started work, so trotted meekly after her.

There followed an hour of intensive shopping, during which Ursula picked up armfuls of clothes and pushed a protesting Clare into the changing room. She would then duly emerge, looking hesitant and uncomfortable, and Ursula would pass judgement on the suitability of her outfit for the required purpose. In the end they left the shops with two pairs of trousers, two blouses, one navy blue dress, a jacket and a lambswool twinset. Clare had the distinct feeling that rather than being dressed like her mother, who dated back to the transition between the hippy and punk generation, she was dressed more like her grandmother, who always made her think of Jaeger and 1950s style jackets. The only moment she succeeded in putting her foot down, quite literally, was when Ursula tried to impose stiletto heels to go with the outfits. Clare at this point had had enough and flatly refused to consider anything over 3 inches. They eventually compromised on one pair of pumps and one pair of shoes with 3 inch block heel. Ursula was plainly not completely satisfied, but despairing of ever getting Clare into anything more feminine, had decided that this was the best she was going to be able to do with a clearly hopeless case and abandoned the struggle.

"I cannot understand why you English always dress so bad. What is wrong with you?" remarked Ursula as they made their way back towards the school.

Clare, who by this point was tired and deeply fed up with her employer's comments on her taste in fashion, had to forcibly restrain herself from replying sharply, although she secretly had to admit that there was an element of truth in it. Why did French and Italian women always seem so stylish as compared to the Brits? Why was their hair and make-up always perfect, whereas in Britain girls seemed to be divided into those, like Clare, who wore no make-up and dressed primarily for comfort and practicality, and those with fake tans, false eyelashes, half a ton of make-up and dressed to kill?

"I suppose we just like to be comfortable", she admitted blandly.

Ursula snorted with disapproval, expressing her complete contempt for the concept of comfort in comparison with the evidently superior requirements of fashion.

"If I want to be comfortable, I stay at home in pyjama", she retorted.

Clare decided that any further discussion was pointless and that it was better to save her energy for the walk back to the school, laden with shopping bags. Ursula clearly did not feel the need to offer any help, although in the end she did pick up one small bag which Clare kept dropping, sighing at the clumsiness of her new employee.

On the way back to the school Clare realised that they were quite close to her hotel.

"If you don't mind, I'll leave all these bags in my hotel room, rather than taking them to the school and then having to haul them all back again to the flat. We can meet up at the school in half an hour, if that's OK with you."

"Alright, but please be rapid. I cannot waste all afternoon to organise your accommodation", Ursula replied, before handing over the shopping bag she was holding and speeding off in the direction of the school.

Clare watched her as she marched away, with the unmistakably self-assured air of those who have money and authority and no wish to hide it.

"I haven't even started and I already hate the bloody woman", she thought "I just hope the other teachers are nice." She sighed as she tried her best to push open the large glass door of the hotel while simultaneously manoeuvring the plethora of shopping bags.

"Room 24." She smiled at the receptionist before taking the lift up to her room, where she could finally dump all the bags and sit down for a moment. She felt as if she had just been for a 2 hour workout, rather than on a shopping spree. She took a few deep breaths and relaxed back into the plush armchair, kicking her shoes off and switching on the TV. Fifteen few minutes later she felt sufficiently refreshed for the next encounter with Ursula.

CHAPTER 5

On Sunday morning Vanessa got up later than usual. Surprisingly the dog had not woken her up by whining next to her bed, eager to get out for his walk. He could usually be guaranteed to make himself heard within around ten minutes of 8 o'clock and was infinitely more reliable than any type of alarm clock. Vanessa opened one eye and glanced up at the ceiling, noticing that the clock was instead projecting a time of 9.10, so she immediately stuck her head over the side of the bed to look at the dog's basket, suddenly terrified that their rather ancient Jack Russell might have died during the night. He was now 15, and although still very active he was largely deaf, partly blind and suffered from an enlarged heart, requiring complicated manoeuvres in order to ensure that he took his daily pill. This was no easy task, because he would suspiciously examine any food potentially capable of hiding a pill, rolling it around in his mouth and spitting it out if it was not heavily disguised. Lately Vanessa had taken to inserting it into a macaroni tube, then carefully closing both ends with left-over meat sauce or cream cheese. It seemed like a lot of effort just to make the dog take his medicine, but as a mother she had long experience of uncooperative patients.

There was no sign of the dog, unimaginatively named Spot by her daughter, after the books she used to read her when she was a little girl, in the same era that they had acquired the said dog. There were however suspicious noises coming from the kitchen below. Vanessa got up, put on the first clothes she could find in the dark, as her husband was still asleep and she didn't wish to wake him up by putting the light on, and made her way downstairs. She groaned when she reached the kitchen, as somebody had obviously left the cupboard door open under the sink and the dog had managed to pull out the organic rubbish bin, scattering potato peel, coffee grounds, old tea bags and leftover bones all over the floor. Being deaf, he had not heard her come down the stairs and was happily chewing on an old bone in the midst of complete mayhem, rather than escaping to his basket in the utility room, as he would have done in the old days.

"Spot", she shouted "get away from there, you wretched animal." He looked suitably guilty, but she couldn't bring herself to be really angry, so she shooed him out into the garden while she cleaned up the kitchen. Free access to the organic waste bin was simply too much of a temptation for any dog, and she was really more annoyed with whoever had left the door open. However, she decided not to give him any food, as he had obviously already had breakfast. Before having her own, she took him for a brief walk down to the field and back and then settled down on the sofa with a cup of tea and a slice of strudel.

Breakfast had always been her one moment of true relaxation during the day. Once her husband had left for work and the children for school (or now university), she could enjoy the one time of day when she was on her own, not working, cooking, shopping or attempting to bring some kind of order to the house. Spot would cuddle up beside her on the sofa and she could watch the news on BBC World, or perhaps a TV costume drama, without any interruptions, blissfully free of family commitments for a brief moment. She sometimes wondered if she was fundamentally anti-social, as there were occasions when she couldn't wait for everyone to go out and leave her on

32

her own. While she enjoyed being with people, she was perfectly happy to spend an evening on her own, reading or watching a film. One of the things she had found most difficult when the children were young was the impossibility of ever having any time to herself, something which had never seemed to bother her husband. They had no relatives close by, so they had never been able to leave the kids with grandparents, nor at the time had they been wealthy enough to afford a babysitter. Now they were more comfortably off, and of course the children were older, so the situation was very different, but she still savoured those moments of blissful solitude.

The summer holidays were now over and the language school would open the following day, meaning that Vanessa would be teaching three days a week until June. She had fallen inevitably into English teaching when she had come to Italy with her husband, whom she had met in England. She was not sad at having come to live near Verona, after all it was a beautiful place, but sometimes she missed her homeland, even after all these years, or perhaps more so after all these years. She missed stupid things, like cheese and onion crisps and Indian takeaways, pubs and English supermarkets. She missed the tongue-in-cheek humour, the understatement and the freedom that goes with being able to dress how you like without anyone noticing or commenting on it. She missed being able to speak all the time in her first language, however good her Italian was, being just part of the scenery, rather than a foreigner. Of course she realised that like many people who have lived abroad for a long time, she would forever be a foreigner. She would be a foreigner in Italy, because she had never managed to completely lose her accent, and because she had grown up in England, with the British culture, a British education and British traditions. But even when she returned to the UK in some ways she still felt like a foreigner, because she had lived away for so many years that she had lost track of what was happening and was out of touch with life in modern Britain. Even the language had changed to some degree, while she continued to speak as she had twenty-five years ago. Americanisms and idiomatic phrases that would once have been considered unacceptable were now in common use, while for some reason other people seemed to see her as much posher than she remembered being, after all she came from an ordinary middle-class family. On her last trip to London her friend had accused her of sounding like the Queen, something rigorously denied by Vanessa.

In any case, sounding like the Queen was not considered a disadvantage for teaching English. Vanessa didn't always enjoy teaching, in fact at times she found it rather tedious. Giving English lessons tended to be the inevitable fate of married British women living abroad, because it fitted in so well with having a family and because there was such high demand, but Vanessa had long ago realised that twice-weekly lessons after work were not the best way of learning a language. When she had first come to Italy she had made rapid progress and after six months she was already fluent, while her students seemed to have learned little. Initially she had asked herself whether this was just because she was a useless teacher, but later it became increasingly clear to her that learning a language quickly really does require full immersion. It needs to become an obsession; you have to speak, think and dream in the language for it to really become a part of you. In subsequent years she had improved her vocabulary and extended her knowledge of the Italian language, but she had learned most of what she knew in the first few months. Now that she was older, strangely, she almost felt as if she were going backwards. She was more likely to make mistakes when under pressure, or absentmindedly insert an English word, or even just the root of the word, in the middle of a sentence.

"Oh my God", she thought "senility is already setting in. Maybe in another twenty years I'll have completely forgotten my Italian and reverted to English. Perhaps I should retire to an English-speaking country just in case!" This would presume, however, that her Italian husband was first of all willing to move away, and secondly not suffering from the same problem himself, given that although he spoke English well, he was not as confident as she was in Italian.

At all events, she tried her best to make sure her students were able to communicate in English, but most of them came in the evenings, after a long day at work, and although they always started the year with the best intentions, experience had taught her that after the first two or three weeks they usually gave up doing any exercises at home and just turned up for lessons, hoping that this would in itself be enough to ensure progress. The end result was that many of them remained forever bogged down at lower intermediate level; they could communicate at basic level, obtaining information, buying a ticket, ordering a meal or booking a hotel room, but they couldn't really participate in a proper conversation, at least not with native speakers.

Periodically, Vanessa would consider giving up teaching and doing something else, but there were few alternatives available in a city the size of Verona. She could perhaps find a job in an office, dealing with correspondence in English, or she could concentrate on translating, although given the high taxes and national insurance contributions for the self-employed it was difficult to make a living out of it. She did take on occasional translation jobs and on the whole enjoyed it, although it was demanding having to deal with fields as diverse as Copper Age burial rites, trout farming or bottle-washing machines. In any case, translation had contributed considerably to increasing her vocabulary, in both languages.

One good thing about teaching, on the other hand, was that it gave her the chance to get of the house and meet people. Vanessa had every respect for those who dedicate themselves to homemaking, but personally found it very hard to get excited about the joys of cooking and cleaning. Housework reminded her of Sisyphus, condemned to roll an immense boulder up a hill, only to watch it roll back down again. What is more, although she adored her children, she did not feel that she had a particularly strong maternal instinct, and although she made every effort to be a good parent, she sometimes asked herself whether she was about as effective a mother as she was an English teacher, a discouraging thought. If somebody were to assess her parenting skills in the style of an old school report, it would probably read something like "Tries hard, but could do better".

Anyway, teaching gave her the chance to come into contact with different kinds of people, and she liked the relationship that usually developed between colleagues. Tomorrow she would meet the new English teacher for the first time. Vanessa really hoped that she was a strong enough character to stand up to Ursula and that she would settle in well. Obviously, all the teachers worked with their classes individually, but it made a big difference if they got on and could count on each other for emergencies. The new girl was more or less the same age as her son, so they were unlikely to become bosom pals, but with a bit of luck they could still be friends, and it was always nice to have someone to speak English to properly, rather than having to concentrate on speaking slowly and enunciating clearly, using simple vocabulary as if speaking to the intellectually challenged.

Vanessa recognised the sounds of people starting to move around upstairs and realised that it was unlikely that she would be allowed to watch an episode of The Tudors in peace, deciding to reserve this minor pleasure for the following day, when with a bit of luck everyone would be out of the house early. Reluctantly, she got up and started unloading the dishwasher.

CHAPTER 6

The first week of the academic year was always fairly chaotic. While Ursula was busy registering new students and dealing with the financial aspects, Janet was responsible for assigning students to courses of an appropriate level, which was not always as straightforward as one might think. While some people were overly confident of their own ability and demanded to be put in a higher group, despite the entrance test results, others with low self-esteem preferred to join a course that was really too easy for them, so that they would not feel embarrassed if forced to speak during the lessons. Left to her own devices Janet would have favoured a rigid approach and insisted on putting everyone in the correct level anyway, but as a businesswoman Ursula would tend to try and keep everyone happy, regardless of the educational objectives.

"It all depends whether the goal of the school is to make money or actually teach people something", Janet had remarked acidly to Vanessa "but I think we all know where Ursula's priorities lie".

Janet usually also tried to put people of similar ages together so that they would feel more comfortable, and thus there were teenagers' courses, as well as courses for 'mature' adults, which basically meant anyone over 50. In Italy, a country where young people often live at home until they get married and spend years trying to find a stable job, you are considered 'young' until well into your thirties, and Janet often heard people in their 40s referring to themselves as 'ragazzi'. You knew you were moving into the seriously adult sphere when people started addressing you as 'Signora', Janet thought. At the moment she seemed to be in a transitional phase, in which she was still considered a girl by those older than herself, while at the same time being seen as totally decrepit by those of school age. All in all she considered herself to be fairly well-preserved, and did her best to keep fit by running and going to the gym two or three times a week, in contrast with Vanessa, whose idea of exercise was walking from her home to the cake shop and back.

Just as this thought was passing through Janet's mind, Vanessa appeared at the door.

"OK, so remind me what I've got at 4 o'clock then."

"Teenagers intermediate."

"Great, as if I didn't have enough to do with bloody teenagers for the rest of the week. I thought we gave that one to Clare."

"No, she's got teenagers lower intermediate, followed by the traffic wardens, so have pity", Janet commented.

"Oh God, traffic wardens on her first day?"

"I'm afraid so, they always start on Mondays."

"Oh well, baptism of fire I suppose", Vanessa commented "anyway, I'm sure they'll love her. Where is Clare, by the way? I haven't met her yet."

"She should be here soon, although her first class isn't until 4.30. I told her to come half an hour early so that I could explain a couple of things. Oh look, that's her coming through the door now."

Clare was wearing the dress that she had bought with Ursula, together with flat pumps. She had tied back her long blonde hair in an effort to look neat and tidy and even made an effort to put mascara on.

"Hello Clare. You're looking very posh. Has Ursula been on at you? Anyway, let me introduce you to Vanessa, one of our most long-serving teachers."

"Long-serving? What you mean is oldest, surely. Anyway, nice to meet you. Is this your first ever experience teaching?"

"I'm afraid so", commented Clare "in fact I'm feeling a little bit anxious."

"Oh, don't worry. It'll be fine. If anyone asks you a question that you don't know how to answer, just say it's something you will be looking at in the next lesson and then move on rapidly. That way you can go and look it up in the grammar book! You have no idea how many times I have had to do that", confessed Vanessa. "I could barely distinguish a noun, adjective and adverb when I started teaching. Janet here, on the other hand, has proper teaching qualifications."

"Not that they have ever really been any use at all to me, but then qualifications are rarely useful for anything other than getting your foot in the door. So don't worry; most of our teachers wandered into EFL teaching by chance."

"Well, that's certainly true in my case. I'm only here because I missed the bus to Mantua!"

"I'm here because I happened to go to a dinner party in London where I met my husband", responded Vanessa.

"And I'm only here because in a moment of depression in England I happened to pick up a newspaper and see the ad for this job", added Janet.

"Well that's it, we were obviously all meant to be here. It's fate", concluded Vanessa. "Ah, the fickle finger of fate...."

At this point Ursula, who had been on the phone at the other end of the office, emerged from behind the desk and came over to the group of women.

"Ah excellent, I see you have all met". She looked Clare up and down appraisingly: "Much nicer, but is better with tights."

"Tights? You must be joking. It's incredibly hot, even if it is the end of September" protested Clare.

"Is more elegant with tights. Next time you wear tights."

"Oh come on Ursula, give the girl a break. I think she looks most appropriate, and quite charming." Vanessa smiled at Clare, doing her best to make her feel at ease. Over the years she had fought many battles with Ursula over every possible matter, from dress and teaching style to pupil assessment and wages. By now they had reached an uneasy truce, but the possibility of a definitive divorce still loomed fairly large. Periodically Vanessa threatened to resign and even more regularly Ursula threatened to get rid of her, but ultimately Ursula couldn't afford to lose an experienced teacher, while Vanessa needed the money, so they made the most of an unsatisfactory relationship.

"Is nearly time for your class", Ursula remarked pointedly. "Perhaps you go to start preparing now?"

"I was indeed just about to go and start organising the classroom. Thank you so much for reminding me. I might have forgotten." Vanessa could not keep the sarcastic note out of her voice, although sarcasm was usually lost on Ursula, it being unclear whether this was because her English was not perfect, or because she carefully chose to ignore it.

Ursula always preferred to address her teachers in English, on the theory that this would improve her knowledge and understanding of the language, but Vanessa had noticed little or no progress over the many years that she had known her. Ursula had no trouble understanding anything and seemed to have a bionic ear, homing in when anyone was talking about her or anything that concerned her, but her spoken English was still littered with the classic mistakes made by Italians and Vanessa was convinced that by now no amount of interaction with her teachers would change that. She nevertheless retained a disarming, or annoying, confidence that she spoke English practically perfectly and was even given to making corrections to the material produced by Janet in English.

"I think maybe it sounds better so", she would comment.

"It sounds better to you, because it's more similar to the Italian translation", Janet would reply "but the scope is to not to make English sound more like Italian, but simply for it to sound right to English speakers." She found this intensely irritating and would usually end up by rejecting most of the changes, retaining one or two just to keep her boss happy. Nevertheless, every now and again Ursula would discover a typo and could not conceal her joy at discovering an error that had escaped an English native speaker. Consequently Janet made every effort to ensure that everything she wrote was faultless, at times checking things that she knew perfectly well were correct.

"I'm so obsessed with mistakes that I think I'm developing OCD disorder", she had said to Vanessa on one occasion. "Sometimes I review e-mails over and over again, before and after sending, and I have even been known to open sealed envelopes just to make sure there are no mistakes. I end up by second-guessing myself completely."

"I have a similar problem with translations sometimes", Vanessa had confessed. "I keep rereading them because they don't seem to sound right, or I use a word and then suddenly wonder whether I have just made it up or whether it actually exists. On occasions my brain seems to go into Italian mode, and after I have written something I realise that it sounds like complete rubbish because the sentence structure is all wrong. It's one of the side effects of living abroad, perhaps. The first few years I was in Italy I deliberately spoke Italian all the time so that I could continue to improve, but now I have taken to watching British TV and reading books in English, to make sure that I don't forget how to speak my own language!"

Under Ursula's eagle eye, Vanessa gathered up her things before turning to Clare.

"Well, nice to have met you Clare, albeit briefly. I probably won't see you later because I think I finish earlier than you, but hopefully the three of us can meet up later in the week for a chat. And don't worry, it'll all go swimmingly."

She headed off unenthusiastically towards the classroom, almost tripping over the belt of her raincoat, which was trailing along the ground.

"Swimmingly?" Ursula looked puzzled. "What has swimming to do with it?

"It means without difficulty, with ease", explained Janet.

"Ridiculous expression," muttered Ursula. "Anyway, please show Clare where to go for the first lesson and give her the textbooks for the students. I need to return to reception." That said, she turned on her heel and made a beeline for two middle-aged ladies who had just come through the door, with a huge phoney smile stamped on her face.

"OK, come on Clare. I'll show you where you will be teaching this afternoon. With the teenagers you'll probably want to spend the first lesson just getting to know them a bit. The traffic wardens may be a bit more challenging because they are usually all more or less beginners. You know how the English tell jokes about the Irish and the French about the Belgians? Well, the Italians make fun of the Carabinieri, and here at the school we traditionally joke about the traffic warden's class! There's no reason why they should be any worse than any other group of beginners, but somehow they always seem to include a few individuals of spectacular ineptitude. Some of them have done the beginner's class three years running by now."

Janet showed Clare into a largish room looking out onto the main street. The sun was streaming in through the glass, lighting up the white walls and the elaborate pattern of the ceramic floor tiles. There were a series of maps and drawings on the walls and three rows of modern desks set out formally in front of the teacher's desk, with the whiteboard behind it.

As Clare scrutinised the classroom, the reality of the fact that she was actually going to have to stand up in front of a group of strangers and attempt to teach them something finally began to sink in. She took a deep breath and thought of drama training; "OK", she thought "It's Showtime".

CHAPTER 7

Her first lesson had gone pretty well, she thought. To be honest, practically the whole time had been taken up with checking the register, distributing the new text books and getting to know a little about the students. A fair number had turned up late and being adolescents, they did not seem to be particularly anxious to start doing any work. For many of them, the afternoon course was just one of a series of recreational activities organised for them by their parents, who had decided that it was indispensable for their children to have a head start in life by learning English and were willing to pay handsomely to ensure this. The pupils had seemed pleasantly surprised to find a teacher so near their own age, and were curious to know more about her, appearing to consider her more as an interesting stranger than as someone responsible for imparting knowledge.

In any case, Clare now felt more relaxed and was less anxious that at any moment she would be revealed as an imposter. As the teenagers left, clucking away noisily like a group of angry hens, she pulled out the flashcards she had been told to use for the next course from the cupboard. Fortunately for Clare, the teaching method adopted provided for the teacher communicating exclusively in English, which was just as well she thought, as she knew no more than a couple of dozen words in Italian. She could run to 'vino bianco', 'vino rosso', a few more food terms and a bit of musical terminology remembered from piano lessons: 'allegro', 'lento', 'forte' and 'con brio' etc., but she suspected that this would not take her very far in a conversation.

She put her head around the door to see whether anyone was arriving and saw Ursula speaking to a group of four people at the reception desk. Apparently they were some of the participants in her next course, because at that moment they turned and looked at her, as Ursula pointed towards the classroom. The three men and a woman strolled leisurely down the corridor, smiling and chatting. When they arrived at the door the older man held out his hand towards her and said something to Clare, presumably introducing himself she thought, although given her knowledge of Italian he could just as well have said "I have come to arrest you for being a complete fraud" or "I am a serial killer and I look forward to cutting you up into pieces and dissolving you in an acid bath."

"I'm sorry. I don't speak Italian, at least not yet. My name's Clare. Please come in."

"Hello, my name is Fabrizio." At this point he seemed to have exhausted his vocabulary because he lapsed back into Italian, before gesticulating at his companions, who appeared to be called Maria, Marcello and Michele.

"So, the 3 Ms", smiled Clare.

"Sorry?"

"The 3 Ms: Maria, Marcello and Michele."

"Sorry?'"

"Ms."

There were more blank looks, so Clare wrote the letter M on the whiteboard and then pointed at the students. "Maria, Marcello and Michele. One, two, three."

This was followed by more gesticulation and discussion, before they all exploded into laughter as if she had told some huge joke. In the meantime several other students had come into the classroom and began to sit down at the desks. A couple of them were rather chunky, Clare noticed, and seemed to have some difficulty fitting into desks that had probably been designed with older children or slender teenagers in mind. There were more men than women, belonging to a reasonably wide age range, the youngest perhaps being in their late twenties and the oldest around fifty.

"Hello, I'm Clare. What's your name?" she asked a man in the front row. He looked puzzled, so she repeated the question very slowly. "What's your name?"

Beaming with pleasure at having understood the question, he replied "Giorgio."

Clare wrote on the board "My name's Giorgio. I'm Giorgio". Then she pointed at him, "What's your name?"

"Giorgio."

Clare pointed at the board and repeated slowly "My name's Giorgio. I'm Giorgio." Then she pointed at him again hopefully, "What's your name?"

"Giorgio."

There were loud protests from around the classroom. The man who had introduced himself as Fabrizio appeared to be insulting poor Giorgio, who looked duly embarrassed and eventually turned to Clare and said apologetically "My name's Giorgio. I'm Giorgio." This was greeted by a round of applause from the other students.

Relieved to have come out of the impasse, Clare directed her attention at an older man in the second row.

"What's your name?"

"My name's Giorgio. I'm Giorgio."

This evoked general laughter around the class. At this point Clare was beginning to despair. Were they having her on? Was it a conspiracy? Or was it genuinely possible that they were both called Giorgio?

Fabrizio smiled broadly, doing his best to resolve the situation.

"Giorgio and Giorgio. Your name Giorgio and your name Giorgio. 2 Giorgio!"

It appeared that they really were both called Giorgio. Still slightly concerned that they were taking the piss, Clare nevertheless proceeded to question the other students. Having gone round the whole class for names, she then moved on to the first flashcard. This showed a room with a table, two chairs, a number of objects on the table, a dog under the table, two windows with a clock between them on the wall and a door.

"What's this?" she asked, pointing to the book.

"It's a book", she answered herself, feeling like a complete prat, but following the instructions in the teacher's book.

Then she turned to Fabrizio, who appeared to be one of the most promising students.

"What's this?"

"It's a book."

Confident that she was finally getting the hang of this teaching business, Clare introduced a few other objects and did the rounds, asking various students the same question. When she got to Giorgio number 1 she had a moment of hesitation. Deciding to play it safe, she pointed at the book.

"What's this?"

Giorgio stared at her blankly so Clare carefully repeated the question. He then turned to the woman sitting next to him and appeared to be asking her for assistance. After an inordinately long whispered dialogue, having apparently grasped the concept, he beamed at Clare and said "E' un libro."

"I know it's a 'libro' Giorgio" Clare tried to keep her calm, "but in English, in English please – It's a ....?" she paused dramatically, turning the palms of her hands towards him.

More discussions with Giorgio's neighbour ensued, during which Clare clearly heard her whisper the word 'book' to him, after which he turned triumphantly to her and announced - "book".

"Well done Giorgio, so what's this?" she repeated, hoping beyond hope that he would pull out the whole phrase. He looked confused.

"Book", he shrugged, as if to say "But I just told you."

Clare couldn't resist glancing at her watch. To her horror only twenty minutes had passed. Given that the lessons lasted seventy-five minutes; that meant that she still had fifty-five minutes to go. How on earth was she going to fill up another fifty-five minutes?

She decided to give the students the task of acting as teacher, and abandoning Giorgio I to his fate, she started by calling up Fabrizio to ask the questions using the flashcard. He came up somewhat smugly to the front of the class, perhaps feeling that he had taken on the role of teacher's pet. Once he had asked a few questions, Clare called on a couple of other students, before dividing everyone up into pairs to work together. Despite her best efforts, time seemed to pass with staggering slowness, and she was hugely relieved when the bell marking the end of the lesson finally sounded.

The traffic wardens gathered up their things, chatting amicably to each other and trying to make conversation with Clare, which was somewhat difficult given the communication problems. They all appeared to be very friendly, insofar as she could judge without understanding a word of what they were saying, but they all smiled at her and said thank you before leaving, so perhaps it had not been a total disaster.

Once they had all left she dropped heavily onto the chair and sighed. Was she really cut out to be a teacher, she wondered, or does it get easier with time? She had taught only two classes, for a total of two and a half hours, but it felt more like eight. She rested her forehead on the desk for a moment, wondering whether the whole idea of spending a year abroad was a terrible mistake. It was difficult to leave all your friends and family behind you, to move to a place where you couldn't speak the language and didn't know anyone, but she had decided that if she didn't try now, she never would. She jumped up, slightly embarrassed, when she heard the classroom door open, but was relieved to see it was Janet, who stuck her head around the door and grinned.

"How did it go?"

"Not great, I think."

"You're wrong. I heard some of the traffic wardens saying to Ursula how charming you were. So whatever you did, it was fine."

"We spent the whole lesson asking 'What's your name?' and 'What's this', so I don't think I they have made huge progress in acquiring language skills."

"Oh, don't worry about that. For a start it's only the first lesson! Anyway, the municipality pays for the course, meaning the participants don't have to pay out of their own pockets, so they're not that bothered about learning anything. They liked you; that's all that's important."

"OK, that makes me feel a bit better", said Clare. "What's next?"

"I'm giving you a guy that I taught last year. He's a doctor and he prefers to come for private lessons. It's just an hour, after which you've finished for today."

"So why have you given him to me if you taught him last year?"

Something in Janet's manner suggested to Clare that she was not entirely comfortable.

"Well, he's a fairly advanced student and he basically just wants conversation classes, but I felt we weren't really getting anywhere, so I thought it might be good for him to have some new input."

"OK, so what should I do with him?"

"I suggest that today you concentrate on getting to know him, and then perhaps read a magazine or newspaper article together. You'll find plenty of material in that cupboard over there. I'll send him in as soon as he arrives", said Janet, before heading back towards the reception desk.

Clare walked over to the cupboard and started pulling out a few potential magazines. There was a range of stuff going from Time and National Geographic to cookery and women's magazines. Discarding the women's magazines, she paged through National Geographic, looking for something suitable. There was an article on climate change that she thought might do, of course depending on what his interests were. In any case, she picked out a couple of periodicals and was looking at another, when she heard a knock on the door.

"Come in", she said, turning as the door opened to see an attractive man in his early thirties making his way into the room. He was tall and clean-shaven, with dark wavy hair, but she was struck particularly by his eyes, which were an amber colour with a coppery tint.

Clare had the pleasant sensation that perhaps things were looking up.

CHAPTER 8

Janet, Vanessa and Clare had decided to meet for an early afternoon cup of tea at a cafe near the school before they all started teaching. At this time of day in mid-October it was still warm enough to sit outside the sun, and like most northern Europeans they never took sunny days for granted, determined to make the most of the trail end of the summer. The temperature came down rapidly as soon as the sun went in, of course, but as most of the courses at the school were in the afternoon and evening, there was time to enjoy the warmest and brightest hours of the day. Janet and Vanessa had taken a leisurely stroll through the main piazza, one of the largest squares in Italy, although given its shape it could not realistically be described as a square. It rejoiced in the name of Piazza Bra, often a source of amusement for English speakers, although pronounced with a shorter 'A' sound, as in bag. The piazza was dominated by the Arena, a Roman amphitheatre built nearly two thousand years before and now incongruously adopted for pop and rock concerts, as well as an internationally renowned opera season. While it now hosted crowds of up to 22,000 people, apparently it had originally been built to seat no less than 30,000.

Vanessa and Janet wandered past the cafes and restaurants lining the piazza, taking a side street in order to make their way towards a quieter bar in a small square nearby. They had arranged to meet Clare there directly, as she lived nearby, and it was also conveniently placed for the school. By now, the autumn term had been running for about a month and things were getting into a routine. Clare seemed to have settled in well, but the two older women thought it was a good idea to meet up

53

outside Ursula's earshot and in a neutral setting to see whether she had any concerns, and of course to exchange all the latest gossip. When they reached the bar, a bar in the Italian sense, serving both alcohol and coffee and tea at any time of day, Vanessa pulled one of the cast iron chairs around so that it was facing the sun and plumped herself down comfortably. Janet also drew up a chair, but preferred to face away from the sun, as she had forgotten her sunglasses and would otherwise have found herself squinting uncomfortably. The waiter came over almost immediately and Janet ordered a cappuccino, while Vanessa chose tea as usual, accompanying it with the inevitable pastry.

They sat there contentedly, enjoying the warmth of the early afternoon sun and watching people going about their business. There was a mixture of both local people and tourists, Verona being a city that attracted visitors throughout the year, not just in the summer months. Out of the corner of her eye Janet spotted Clare sprinting up the side street and turned to greet her.

"I'm sorry I'm late. Have you been waiting long?" asked Clare.

"No, we've just arrived. Sit down and relax. Ten minutes doesn't even count as being late in Italy!" Janet waved to the waiter and when he came over Clare ordered a cappuccino and a pastry to keep Vanessa company.

"So how are things", asked Vanessa. "Are you enjoying being in Verona?"

"Oh, absolutely. I can't believe how beautiful it is, and I just adore this extended summer."

"Well don't get too excited; it's not always this warm in October. In fact it can be very wet indeed, so prepare yourself. What's more it gets pretty cold in the winter" Janet remarked.

"I know, but in the meantime I'm making the most of it. It's just so wonderful to be able to sit outside in such an amazing setting, appreciating the sunlight and at the same time enjoying the views. There's so much more to Verona than Romeo and Juliet!"

"Well that may be true, but the city certainly makes a fortune out of the story, despite the fact that there's not a lot of evidence that the couple ever existed", said Janet. "Juliet's house must be the most popular attraction in the city, and it's packed with couples of all ages photographing the balcony, or taking selfies in front of the wall covered with graffiti left by past visitors."

"I occasionally get paid to act as an interpreter for weddings organised in the Franciscan monastery that is supposed to house Juliet's grave," said Vanessa. "The hall is beautiful, but you would think that the site of Juliet's tomb was a singularly unpromising place to hold a marriage ceremony, given that the protagonists of the story only spend one night together and both commit suicide within 24 hours of getting married! However, for some reason people seem to think of it as the ultimate romantic location."

"I've always thought of Venice as the most romantic city in Italy", Janet commented. "It's something to do with the water and the gondolas, I think. Have you been there yet Clare?"

"Yes, I went there last Sunday with one of the girls I live with and two Italian boys she introduced me to a couple of weeks ago. They delight in teaching me swear words in Italian and then laugh at my pronunciation. The first things I learned when I got here were profanities, and things you can see around you when you're sitting in a bar, like cup or spoon. I had terrible trouble with the word for teaspoon, 'cucchiaino' at first; altogether too many vowels! Anyway, everyone thought it was absolutely hysterical as I tried to get my mouth around cucch – i – a – ino. But I get my own back at school when my students are trying to pronounce crisps, or thirty-three."

"So did Venice have the desired effect and lead to romance?" asked Vanessa.

"No, Giulio and Sergio are just friends, but Venice was beautiful. The only person I'm at all interested at the moment is Marco, the doctor who comes for private lessons on Mondays and Wednesdays. He has the most beautiful eyes, but he is quite a lot older than me. He invited me for a beer last Wednesday evening after the lesson."

"Ah, well perhaps you should be a little careful there," suggested Vanessa, looking sideways at Janet. "It can be a bit difficult if you get romantically involved with your students."

"I don't see why. It's not as if I'm a therapist and he's my patient, and what's more he's older than me, not vice-versa, so I can hardly be said to be taking advantage of him!"

"Well just be careful, that's all," Vanessa said rather lamely. "It might create problems."

There was a slightly uncomfortable moment of silence, then Janet turned to Clare:

"What Vanessa doesn't want to say, but I might as well tell you as it's bound to come out sooner or later, is that I went out with Marco for a few months last year. It's all over now and it ended perfectly amicably, so there's no reason why you shouldn't see him outside school if you want to."

"Oh, I'm sorry. I didn't realise. That is a bit embarrassing, even if absolutely nothing has happened between us yet". Clare wanted to ask whether Janet still felt something for Marco, but didn't think it was appropriate given that she was effectively her boss, so ending up by blurting out "Are you sure you don't mind?"

"Of course not. He's not my property, although perhaps you should be aware that there is also an ex-wife on the scene."

"Yes, I gathered he was divorced. He can't have been married for very long."

"No, only two years. His wife left him for one of his colleagues. It was all rather complicated and unpleasant, I believe."

"Divorce is rarely pleasant," said Vanessa. "Several of my friends have got divorced and in no case did it end pleasantly, whether after one or thirty years, and of course if there are children involved it's even worse."

"How long have you been married?" asked Clare, keen to change the subject.

"Twenty-seven years. I suppose I can consider myself a success story, given the statistics, although like most people I couldn't say my marriage is perfect."

"My parents have been married for thirty years and their marriage isn't perfect either, but they're good friends. They have their own interests and whenever my mother is really fed up she goes off a holiday with some girlfriends and comes back rejuvenated."

"Sounds like a good solution to me," said Vanessa. "Perhaps I should do that more often. There are certainly times when I feel like escaping from everyone. I don't really understand why Italians are so reluctant for their children to leave home. There are times when I can't wait!"

"I couldn't wait to leave home and be independent," confessed Clare "but now that I have, I sometimes miss being able to rely on someone to sort out my problems. In some ways I feel like I'm pretending; pretending to be an adult, pretending to be a teacher. I have had a very confrontational relationship with my parents in the past, but now that they're no longer close at hand I'm actually quite surprised to find I miss them."

"Well, if you need a temporary substitute Mum you can always come to me," said Vanessa. "It's so much easier to give advice to other people's children, and what's more they are often much more willing to accept it."

"Thanks Vanessa. I may even take you up on that."

Janet cleared her throat, "I think I should be getting back to the school. I'm teaching at 4 and I wanted to do some photocopies first. But please stay here and enjoy the sun for a while. I know you two don't start until 4.30."

She fumbled in her bag looking for coins, but Vanessa pre-empted her, "Oh, don't worry I'll pay. We'll see you back at the school shortly."

"Thanks, it's my turn next time then."

Janet buttoned up her jacket and headed briskly down the road. For some reason she had an unpleasant feeling in her stomach that she couldn't quite explain to herself, but she felt the need to be on her own for a while. She couldn't quite work out whether it was because of Marco, or because she was slightly envious of the relationship that Vanessa and Clare seemed to be developing. In either case, they were feelings that did her no credit whatsoever. She had chosen to break up with

Marco, because she it was abundantly clear that he was not ready for another serious relationship, so she could hardly behave like a dog in the manger just because somebody else was interested in him. Nor should she be any less than delighted that Clare seemed to get on well with Vanessa, after all the two of them had deliberately decided to meet up with Clare to see whether she was settling in well.

The problem, Janet felt, was that she seemed to be neither one thing nor the other. She was no longer young and carefree, like Clare (although carefree is a silly expression, she thought; nobody is immune from worries, and young people have their own concerns just like anyone else), but nor was she the sort of person that people turned to for motherly advice, and it was looking increasingly likely that she would never have children of her own to advise, or to worry and complain about. She was in a sort of spinsterish limbo.

Being an analytical sort of person, she could see perfectly well that her reaction was unproductive and inappropriate, but that didn't help her to feel any better, so she decided simply to ignore it and get on with her daily routine. She stopped just outside the school, took a couple of deep breaths and then marched up the stairs, ready for another day's teaching. There was nothing for it but to concentrate on a job she loved and take life as it came.

CHAPTER 9

Despite the age gap, over the past few weeks Vanessa had increasingly come to appreciate her younger colleague's company. They would quite often meet up before work for a tea and in Clare Vanessa had found someone who shared her passion for cakes, chocolate and anything sweet in general. Janet was a good friend, but she belonged to the category that essentially considered food as fuel, rather than one of the joys of life, and Vanessa always had the sneaking suspicion that she considered her fondness for sweets as a sign of irresponsible behaviour and lack of character. Clare, on the other hand, was an ally, although her slim lithe figure belied her love of sachertorte.

The week before Vanessa had introduced her to a cake shop specialising in sweets from Sicily and couldn't believe that she had never eaten a cannolo, the quintessentially Sicilian tube-shaped shell filled with creamy ricotta and garnished with candied orange.

"Oh my God, you haven't lived until you've eaten a proper cannolo," exclaimed Vanessa. "It's like a sort of cylindrical cheesecake. Pure bliss!"

"I thought it was called a cannoli, rather than cannolo."

"No, that's actually the plural form. The singular is cannolo. It's like panini, which always seems to be used in the plural in the UK, whereas the singular should be panino. Italians find that hilarious when they go to Britain, although they're hardly in a position to gloat, given that they massacre the English language on a daily basis!"

Today Vanessa had invited Clare to visit the village close to Lake Garda where she lived with her family, on the occasion of the local festival. Traditionally held over the 3rd weekend in November, it dated back to the times when shepherds used to bring the livestock back down from mountain pastures to the lowlands for the winter. Needless to say, over the centuries the fair had changed radically, but was still seen as an important event by local people, and was one of the few occasions when the village was crowded with people, making their way on foot up to the hill where the festival took place.

"I found it very difficult to see what everyone was so excited about when I first moved here," Vanessa had explained to Clare. "It seemed to me like the worst festival ever invented. It's not like the wine festivals held in various places around the lake in September. For a start, being in the middle of November the weather is usually horrendous, and as it's in the countryside it means freezing to death wading around muddy fields in wellies. Various associations and groups set up plastic tents all over the fields, with horrendous amplified music, and the gastronomic highlight is the tripe competition. The focus of the fair used to be the horses, with pony rides and other displays involving horses, but in the last few years I've seen fewer and fewer of them. To make up for that, cheap wine flows freely, and on the Monday in particular the whole village is full of drunks staggering around on their way back from the hill. There are market stands selling socks, Peruvian jumpers and nougat around the old church at the top of the hill, and a fairground with rides and bumper cars for kids back down in the village. Ah, and of course one should not forget the charity prize draw in the church hall."

"Well, you've really sold it to me," Clare had exclaimed "I don't see how I could possibly resist such an invitation."

"It's strange, but over the years I've warmed to it in a way, and both my son and daughter genuinely care about being there each year. It's an essential part of the autumn for them. If you come on Sunday we can walk up to the hill and have a risotto or something in the marquee, and then my son Ben can take you off to one of the tents where there's music and the younger people congregate. I'm sure you'll have a good time."

So on Sunday morning Clare had taken the bus from Verona to the village and she and Vanessa were now strolling leisurely towards the fair.

"My husband has stayed at home because he has some work to do, and in any case he's never been that keen on the fair," Vanessa explained as they headed up the hill .

"What about Janet? Is she coming?" asked Clare.

"She may do this afternoon, given that it's quite mild and sunny. She came two years ago, but did not have the best experience, because just as we got up to the top of the hill it started pissing it down and by the time we got back to my house we were soaked and had mud up to our knees! Anyway, she cheered up after we had a cup of tea and roasted some chestnuts over the open fire."

"I find her just slightly intimidating," admitted Clare. "I don't know whether it's embarrassment over the Marco situation, or because she's my boss, but she's rather detached and I never quite know what she's thinking. I'm always afraid she thinks I'm an idiot."

"I think you're reading her wrong. She told me that she thought you were doing really well at school, and if she seems detached that's just because that's the way she is. She didn't want to continue giving to lessons to

Marco because it was uncomfortable once they broke up, and that's why she passed him on to you. Ursula wasn't bothered who did the lessons so long as the money kept on coming in, and Marco finds the school convenient because it's close to his flat, I gather."

"I went there for the first time this week," said Clare. "We had been out together a few times after school, but the relationship only really took off when he invited me to go skiing last Sunday. I'd been on a couple of skiing holidays in the past, so I can get down to the bottom of the mountain one way or another, but he looks like a real pro. He was so gentlemanly, waiting for me all the time and helping me up when I fell flat on my face in a pile of snow. Anyway afterwards we went for dinner at a mountain hut and ended up staying there overnight. Since then I've been back to his flat a couple of times. I don't want to get too excited about it, but I do like him a lot."

"Well, I can certainly see why. He's good-looking, charming and intelligent, and what's more he's a doctor. A match-maker's dream! However, you should remember that he came out of a very difficult relationship relatively recently, and that tends to make people wary the second time around."

"I realise that," said Clare "and I'm under no illusions. Anyway, it's much too early to start thinking about a serious relationship. I'll just see how it goes."

Absorbed in the conversation, Clare nearly walked straight into a group of young people carrying wooden tankards lurching noisily across the road at the top of the hill. A series of market stalls marked the start of the fair, selling everything from woolly gloves to absurdly complicated vegetable shredding machines, while the smell of roasting chestnuts, candyfloss and fritters hovered in the air. The neighbouring field was dotted with transparent plastic tents and makeshift structures, while a row of horses were tethered along the hedge marking the boundary of the field. There was a largish enclosed area, where a number of not particularly obedient dogs were apparently involved in a demonstration of dog training.

"Well, here we are at the annual jamboree," said Vanessa. "Come on, let's go and get something to eat."

They jostled their way through the crowds to the marquee, where Vanessa paid for 2 risottos and half a litre of wine at the till. She handed Clare the receipt for the wine and pointed at the last of a series of rudimentary serving stations set up along the side of the tent. Inside the marquee there were rows of wooden tables, with families, groups of rowdy young people and equally rowdy pensioners squeezed onto precarious looking benches.

"Why don't you go and get the wine and then find somewhere to sit down, while I fight my way to the front of the risotto queue and join you when I've managed to get served," Vanessa suggested. "There's really no such thing as queuing in Italy, as I'm sure you must have realised by now, so I may be some time! It's partly a question of luck and partly about being sufficiently assertive to get yourself noticed, although I can't bring myself to be too pushy."

Clare exchanged the till receipt for a jug containing half a litre of wine and two plastic cups, and then wandered down the aisle between the rows of tables, looking for somewhere to sit. She managed to find a place on a bench towards the back of the marquee and sat down, pulling her coat around her and wrapping her scarf snugly around her neck. Once out of the sun, it was pretty cold, so she poured herself a generous cup of wine to warm herself up. Mulled wine would have been even better, it occurred to her, but perhaps not with risotto. She hoped that Vanessa wouldn't take too long to get hold of the food, because she felt slightly embarrassed at sitting there on her own, although the elderly couple on the same table had smiled in a friendly way as she sat down. Nevertheless, they were staring at her with unabashed curiosity, and she was afraid they might start up a conversation. While she could by now understand a fair amount of Italian, she had considerable problems with the local dialect, which differed quite radically from standard Italian and seemed to be spoken widely, particularly by the older generation. Fortunately, Vanessa appeared to have been successful in getting served, because she could see her making her way down the aisle, holding a tray with two steaming plates of risotto. She paused briefly en route to greet three or four groups of people sitting at other tables on the way, before plumping herself down on the wooden bench and handing Clare a plastic bowl filled with rice.

"Here you are: risotto with 'tastasal', a local speciality. Tastasal is the same mixture of roughly chopped raw pork used to make salami, and apparently the name originates in the custom of tasting the mixture for salt and pepper before it was stuffed into the casing."

"It really is tasty," said Clare, happily gobbling up the risotto, "and ideal for a cold day."

"It's one of my son's favourites. Fortunately it's one of the standard dishes at every local fair, because he can't get enough of it and he insists I don't make it properly. Ben's already here somewhere, by the way, and we agreed to meet up at the church after lunch so that he can take you around a bit and you can see how the other young people enjoy themselves."

"Are you sure he won't mind?" asked Clare. "I don't want to be in the way."

"Oh no, don't worry. His friends are a good bunch and they'll be happy to meet someone new. If they get too drunk and rowdy or you're fed up just tell Ben to bring you back to our house, or you can stroll back on your own if you prefer. I'm going to have a brief wander around and say hello to a few friends and then I'll go back for a cup of tea."

"I noticed that you seem to know lots of people."

"Well it's a village, so everyone tends to know each other, at least by sight, and the fact that I run the choir certainly helps. There are pros and cons of course. Like small communities all over the world, you can't do anything without everyone knowing and gossiping about it, but on the other hand people take an interest in each other's welfare and help each other out. I didn't have any trouble integrating in the community, despite being a foreigner."

"Are there many foreigners," asked Clare. "I don't notice that many immigrants here."

"When I first arrived there weren't many at all, but over the years that has changed radically and now probably about a quarter of the pupils at the primary school are the children of immigrants."

"Where do they come from?"

"There's a mixture really. Mostly Moroccans, Romanians and Albanians I think, but also quite a few from Sri Lanka and Brazil. At one point there were so many Brazilians that my daughter was starting to learn Portuguese at the playground, but then for some reason they all disappeared."

Vanessa paused to put her ear to her handbag.

"Is that my phone? I can't hear a thing with all this noise around us."

She opened up her bag and started grovelling around in search of her cell phone, finally spotting a glimpse of light at the bottom of her bag and triumphantly grabbing her mobile.

"It's Ben," she said as she stuck the phone to her ear. "Hello darling, where are you? OK we'll make our way to the church now. We'll be there in one minute."

The two women got up and began edging their way between the tables, eventually stepping out into the pleasant warmth of the sunlight. From here it was just a few yards to the small chapel at the top of the hill, surrounded by cypress trees and set in an olive grove.

Vanessa immediately spotted her son, standing around laughing and joking with a group of his friends. She waved to him, beckoning him over to meet her colleague.

"Hello, darling. This is Clare. I'm sure she'll have more fun with you than me, so can you take her off for a couple of hours and introduce her to your friends?"

Ben smiled at Clare, kissing her on both cheeks in the Italian fashion.

"Hi, nice to meet you," he said.

"Nice to meet you too," replied Clare, feeling immediately at ease with Vanessa's son. He was a slim young man with dark curly hair and bright blue eyes, dressed in black jeans and a green parka, the standard uniform for Italian youths.

"OK, I'll leave you to your own devices for a while. Clare's last bus is at 7.30, so you should bring her back by then. Unless of course you want to stay the night," she said as an afterthought to Clare. "We can always find a bed for you."

"That's very kind, but I think I'd prefer to get back."

67

"No problem. If the worst comes to the worst somebody can always drive you back to Verona. See you later then." Vanessa waved goodbye, confident that Clare would enjoy herself with the other young people. Clare's Italian had improved rapidly since she had arrived and she should have no trouble communicating in a mixture of Italian and English, while Ben's friends would be delighted to try out their primitive language skills on a pretty girl, In any case Ben was available as interpreter.

Vanessa headed back down the hill, already anticipating with pleasure a pot of Earl Grey tea and a plate of biscuits.

CHAPTER 10

Wednesday was the only day that Janet and Vanessa finished work at the same time in the evening, so after Janet had locked up the school they would often take the opportunity to go for a glass of wine, or a cup of tea, depending on their mood. Occasionally Vanessa would feel duty bound to go home to her family, but on the whole she was pleased to have some time to herself for a change, and quite frankly nobody seemed to miss her much when she wasn't there.

The temperature had fallen considerably since the beginning of November and the air was crisp. The two women moved cautiously over the marble pavement, because when wet or frosty it rapidly transformed itself into an extended ice-rink, and with the wrong footwear unwary pedestrians risked finding themselves flat on their backs. Janet shivered as they stopped for a moment at the crossroads to decide where to go, but they quickly settled for Mario's, one of their favourite haunts thanks to the cosy atmosphere, friendly staff and above all the lack of slot machines or loud music.

A few minutes later they were comfortably seated at one of the wooden tables, sipping their glasses of wine, and Vanessa had already practically finished off the accompanying bowl of crisps. She had chosen a Valpolicella ripasso, being a lover of soft, full-bodied red wines. "I can't have more than one glass because I'm driving" she had commented "so at least I want it to be something worth drinking". Janet, on the other hand, had opted for the inevitable Prosecco, the sparkling dry white by now as well-known in Britain as in the Veneto region. Given that it was a Wednesday evening at the end of

November, there were few other customers, and apart from a young couple hidden away in the corner and a solitary elderly gentleman propping up the bar who was chatting happily to the barman, they had the place to themselves.

Vanessa leaned back contentedly against the cushions on the wooden bench.

"It's always such a relief when I've finished teaching, and the effort seems to be getting greater over the years. How on earth do you manage to retain your enthusiasm?"

"Oh, I don't know. I've always enjoyed teaching, especially adults. I like seeing people's progress over the months. I like thinking about what to do with them next, what material to use and how to make lessons more effective. It's satisfying."

"I'm afraid I don't always find it satisfying. I like teaching some people; the intelligent, witty, interesting ones who have something to say, but when you get students who answer perpetually in monosyllables the lessons seem to drag on forever. Maybe I'm just a lousy teacher."

"You're not and you know it perfectly well, otherwise you wouldn't have lasted as long as you have at the school. Ursula gets rid of deadwood pretty damn quickly!"

"Well, whatever. I wish I were more like you," said Vanessa.

"Like me? You have to be joking! Apart from work, my life is pretty much a desert. You have your lovely husband and your children, your charming house and a dog. All I have is a rented flat, no stable relationship and most importantly no children."

"Children can be overrated. For a few years you are their hero, the magnificent super Mum who is never wrong, but after the age of about 11 it's all downhill and you become an irritating nag who relentlessly demands that they study, tidy up, eat healthily and behave like civilised people. There are exceptions of course, but as a general rule you can assume that they will never really appreciate you until they have children of their own, just as I never truly appreciated my mum until I became a mother."

"Oh, stop moaning! You don't really mean it anyway. You adore your kids."

"Of course I do", said Vanessa "but that doesn't mean I don't find it wearing being a parent, or get fed up of having to worry about other people all the time. In the family hierarchy the kids come first, then my husband and I come at the bottom, shortly after the dog!"

Janet's voice cracked slightly with emotion. "I never thought I wanted children, but now I find that I do. Desperately."

Vanessa looked at Janet in surprise. She had never realised that her friend craved motherhood so ardently. She had never seemed the type, preferring rather to concentrate on her career, enjoying an active social life and relishing her independence.

"It's not too late, if that's what you really want."

"I'm 35" Janet reminded her "and I don't have an available man at the moment, nor does there appear to be anyone on the horizon. That's really why I broke up with Marco. He was happy meeting two or three evenings a week and going off for the occasional romantic weekend, but he was definitely not looking for someone to set up home with in the near future and have kids."

"It's not indispensable to have a permanent man in order to have a child," said Vanessa. "There are lots of single mums around, and their children can be just as happy as those from 'ordinary' families, although I'm not sure I would recommend it, because it's already tough being a mother and having nobody to fall back on makes it even tougher."

"So what do you suggest? I can hardly just ask some acquaintance to father my child, and I am certainly not going to have a brief fling just to trick someone into getting me pregnant. Apart from anything else, given the importance of genetic factors I would want to be sure that there were no genetic diseases in the prospective father's family, and he would need to be reasonably intelligent, just in case it's hereditary!"

"Oh my God, you have actually considered it, haven't you?" exclaimed Vanessa. "Well if all else fails, I believe in America there are catalogues for artificial insemination, so you can choose sperm from donors with specific characteristics, not just in terms of physical traits like eye and hair colour, but also high IQ, artistic talent or sportiness!"

"Oh, good grief! So you can create a mail order baby? What a terrifying idea. Does that mean that graduate sperm is more expensive than uneducated sperm? Well, one thing that's certain is that I am not going to go in for artificial insemination. It's not even legal in Italy for single women."

"You could go abroad."

"Oh, don't be daft. I am most decidedly not going to have artificial insemination. What's wrong with sex anyway?"

"Nothing, if you can find a candidate with the ideal requirements. So what would be the ideal, given that you have obviously given this some thought?"

"Oh, I would say tall and slim with green eyes, intelligent, creative and with no physical or mental defects or history of genetic diseases and depression," laughed Janet "but don't you dare try and do any matchmaking!"

"I was thinking more on the lines of placing an ad online, with a questionnaire for suitable candidates."

"Great, if you want to attract sexual predators and social outcasts."

The women went through the merits of all the men they could think of between the ages of twenty and forty-five, giggling together at the absurdity of it all and attracting strange looks from the old guy standing at the bar.

"Oh God. I hope he doesn't understand English," whispered Janet. "Do you think he was listening?"

"No, and in any case who cares? He's way outside the age range!"

Janet snorted with laughter at the very thought, nearly choking on the last drop of her wine.

"Well thanks anyway, you've really cheered me up. Shall we have another glass before we go?"

"No, I'd better not. They have been tightening up on drink driving recently. In Italy they used to be rather relaxed over the whole thing, but recently quite a few people I know have been stopped by the police along the road to the lake. I know I probably wouldn't be over the limit with two glasses of wine, but I'm quite tired anyway, so it's best not to take risks. But you have another one if you like."

Janet considered the idea, but decided that she might as well get home and relax with a film or a good book. She could always have another glass of wine at home later if she fancied.

"No, I'm pretty tired too. Let's call it a day."

They got up and put on their coats. Janet pulled out her purse, walking over to the bar counter to pay the bill, while Vanessa wound her scarf carefully around her neck and donned her gloves, in preparation for the sudden drop in temperature. When they opened the door a blast of cold air hit them and Vanessa gasped with the shock of it.

"Well winter has certainly arrived. The temperature seems to have dropped even since we went into the bar an hour ago."

"Yes, the cold weather has got here just in time for the Christmas market in Piazza Bra," said Janet as they walked together towards the bridge. "It's fun wandering around and soaking up the Christmas atmosphere, but at the weekend there are too many people for my taste."

"I promised Clare we would meet up when they set up the Santa Lucia market next weekend, but I'm rather regretting it now. It'll be seething with people and it's practically impossible to find anywhere to park. But I have to admit that the atmosphere's always rather special. Ben wants to come too, which given that he never goes anywhere with me if he can avoid it can only mean that he wants an excuse to meet Clare again. I don't think she's very interested in him though, after all he's only a boy as compared to Marco."

"Well he's a very good-looking boy", said Janet "and closer to her age than Marco is."

"Yes, he's only two years younger than her, but you know how much more mature girls are than boys. I don't think Ben could be considered a serious rival. I just hope he doesn't take it too hard."

"Oh don't worry, I'm sure he has girls lining up for him."

Vanessa stopped as they reached the bridge. "Are you sure you don't want a lift? It's very cold and my car is just around the corner."

"No, don't worry. I enjoy walking, and it won't take me more than ten minutes from here," Janet marched briskly off over the bridge, calling over her shoulder "Thanks for the company. I'll see you tomorrow."

Vanessa waved goodbye, at the same time groping around in her bag in search of her keys. She couldn't find them and so went into her usual panic, rifling furiously through the multiple zipped compartments and swearing for the umpteenth time that she would get a smaller and more manageable bag, before realising that she must have already extracted the keys and had put them in her coat pocket.

"I *will* tidy out my bag. I *will* be more organised", she said to herself as she arrived at the car. As she got in she noticed that the car too was even fuller than usual of accumulated newspapers, crisp packets, old trainers, books and things to be taken to the tip.

"I will tidy up the car. I will tidy up the house. I will tidy up my life.... Oh for Christ's sake, who am I kidding." She turned the key in the ignition, backed out of the parking place and headed for home.

CHAPTER 11

After driving around Verona for ten minutes, Vanessa and Ben finally struck it lucky when Ben spotted somebody coming out of a car parking space in the mirror, slammed on the brakes and reversed twenty metres against the oncoming traffic before completing a manoeuvre that had Vanessa hanging onto the door handle on the passenger side like a leech. She would have been much happier driving herself, as when her son was in the driver's seat she found herself leaning away from obstacles an inch away from the passenger door, clinging onto the handle with her nails and desperately resisting the temptation to make use of the passenger brake. Unfortunately, he always insisted on driving when they were together, complaining that she drove like a geriatric tortoise, so she had reluctantly agreed to let him act as chauffeur, trying hard to talk in a normal voice and not to make it too obvious that she was on the verge of having a panic attack. At all events, she got out of the car with some relief and they walked down to the parking metre, with Ben fishing in his pockets for change and Vanessa feeling around the bottom of her bag to see whether any coins had fallen out of her purse. There was no point looking inside the purse itself, as any denominations larger than ten cents would undoubtedly have been stolen by her husband when looking for coffee money, or by one of the kids. However, between the two of them they succeeded in accumulating sufficient cash to pay for two hours' parking, so after leaving the ticket on display in the car, they walked purposefully up the road towards the gateway leading into Piazza Bra, with its characteristic clock and twin arches.

They had arranged to meet Clare there to visit the traditional market of Santa Lucia. Although the Christmas market lasted from the end of November until the end of December, the market dedicated to Santa Lucia only ran for a few days in December, leading up to the Feast of Santa Lucia on the 13th. During this time, over 300 vendors plied their wares in the shadow of the arena amphitheatre, selling sweets, decorative items and small gifts from around Italy. Ben managed to spot Clare among the crowds milling around the entrance to the square and ran over to greet her, kissing her on both cheeks and taking her by the arm, while Vanessa pushed her way through the tourists and local people to reach them.

"It's a few years since I last came for the fair" said Vanessa "and it seems to have become even busier. So much for the consumer crisis, although I suppose a lot of people just wander about without buying anything."

"I can see why people come though", replied Clare. "There is an amazing atmosphere, with all the lights, and that gigantic iron comet structure projecting out of the amphitheatre and down into the piazza."

"Yes, well you can hardly miss it; it's seventy metres high! Apparently it was only originally intended to be used for one year, back in the 1980s, but despite some criticism, it proved so popular that they have installed it at Christmas time every year since then. In fact it's become the symbol of Christmas in Verona, although personally I've never liked it much."

"You never like anything modern", grumbled Ben. "It's art. It was created by a famous architect."

"That doesn't mean I have to like it, although I have to admit that it is unmistakeably a symbol of Verona.

Christmas markets, on the other hand seem to be the same almost everywhere these days."

"But doesn't this one have something to do with Santa Lucia?" asked Clare.

"Yes, her Feast Day is on 13 December and that's when children in the Veneto region traditionally get their presents. I used to find it difficult when the kids were younger, because I would have preferred to celebrate Christmas, but all their friends got their presents for Santa Lucia's day, so we had to do both."

"I remember that all my friends got more presents than I did for Santa Lucia", said Ben.

"But then you got presents at Christmas as well" Vanessa protested. "Anyway since they've got older we've abandoned Santa Lucia in favour of Christmas."

Clare turned to Ben, "so who was Santa Lucia anyway? Is it a local tradition?"

"Santa Lucia was a Christian martyr who had her eyes gouged out, and not surprisingly she's the patron saint of the blind", explained Ben, clearly enjoying acting as a tourist guide and getting into his swing. "Legend has it that in the 13th century in Verona there was an epidemic of eye disease, and the people went on a barefoot pilgrimage to the church of Santa Lucia in December. In order to convince their children to come, despite the cold, they told them that when they returned they would find their shoes full of sweets. In subsequent years, the pilgrimage was repeated to thank the Saint for her intercession, but was moved to a church near Piazza Bra, so the traders got into the habit of setting up their stalls nearby, hence the origin of the market."

"The Feast of Santa Lucia is celebrated quite widely in the north of Italy", Vanessa continued. "She is traditionally accompanied by a donkey and dressed entirely in white, with her head veiled so you can't see her face, and she brings gifts and sweets to good children and coal to those who have been bad. Actually, quite a lot of kids are frightened of her, because their parents used to tell them that if Santa Lucia found them awake she would throw ashes into their eyes to blind them temporarily. She's a sort of scary version of Father Christmas."

"When I was younger I remember that somebody used to dress up as Santa Lucia and wander through the village, ringing a bell and handing out sweets to the children. Some of my friends were afraid of her, but I was just happy to get the sweets! Mum, do you remember when Spot managed to get out of the garden and was barking furiously at a terrified Santa Lucia backed up against the wall?"

"Oh God yes, I had to rush out and save her, and she didn't come back the following year! I have no idea who it was, because she, or possibly he, was veiled from head to toe. The only thing I noticed was that she was wearing trainers, which seemed just a tiny bit incongruous."

The three of them wandered around the stalls, breathing in the aroma of candied fruit and roasting chestnuts. Clare admired the many gastronomic specialities from all over Italy, from the olives and dried tomatoes of the south to zelten cake and cured meats from the German-speaking areas in the far north. She was pleased to have the chance to pick up some Christmas presents for her friends and relatives in England, and went to and fro from one stall to another, looking for inspiration in the annual challenge of finding cheap but appealing gifts. The school was closing for 2 weeks, giving her the chance to spend a decent amount of time at home, and she had already booked her plane ticket for the Christmas holidays. She chose a suitably festive candlestick for her mother and a woolly hat for her sister, but couldn't decide what to get her father. The obvious choice would have been a bottle of good wine, which would undoubtedly be appreciated, but with security regulations making it impossible to take any liquids in hand luggage, and the exorbitant cost of hold baggage, that option would have to be eliminated.

Vanessa bought some wild boar salami to take home, after which they stopped at a stand opposite the Arena, warming their hands on paper bags containing hot chestnuts and sipping cups of mulled wine, except for Ben, who preferred hot chocolate.

"There's an exhibition of nativity scenes in the tunnels of the Arena", Vanessa commented to Clare. "Have you been there yet?"

"No, It doesn't really appeal to me much. Do you think it's worth going?"

Vanessa shrugged, "I haven't been for years, but it's a very evocative setting. I agree though, I can't really get excited about nativity scenes either. Mind you, some people are really passionate about them. When the kids were at nursery school the mothers used to set up a nativity scene, with a different slant each year. So once it was all in wood, one year all the figures were made out of salt dough etc. Anyway, in agreement with the chief nun, one year it was decided that we would do a nativity scene with the Smurfs."

"Smurfs? You mean the little blue creatures living in mushrooms?"

"Indeed. It was a popular TV cartoon at the time. Anyway, we set up a woodland scene constructed with moss and bark and loads of Smurfs trailing across the wood towards the Holy Family (who were not Smurfs by the way - there are limits!). Suddenly one of the mums slapped her forehead and said 'But we've forgotten to do the desert!' I pointed out that a desert didn't really sit well in a woodland scene, but she insisted that it was absolutely essential, because the bible states that the Three Kings arrive from desert. At this point I reminded her that the bible did not envision dozens of little blue gnomes popping out from behind trees to pay homage to the baby Jesus. Unfortunately, she was not even faintly amused and she never really spoke to me again."

Clare laughed. "Yes, why is it that being religious appears to be incompatible with having a sense of humour?"

"Oh, I don't know. Maybe because religion means accepting authority, while humour means poking fun at it", suggested Vanessa. "From court jesters to stand-up comedians, humour is about pointing out human fallibility."

"The nuns were not renowned for their sense of humour", recalled Ben "but the priest was quite a laugh. Don Pietro once appeared at the Carnival party dressed as a cow!"

"Yes, well he was a rather eccentric individual. On one occasion I saw him walking up to the parish hall in his pyjamas! And when it snowed he could often be seen getting his skis out and skiing down the main street to the chemist. But he was an exception; none of the other priests I've met here have been anything like as amusing, or as committed to helping the least fortunate members of his flock for that matter." Vanessa finished off the last chestnut and turned to Ben "I think it's probably time that we headed back. The two hours must be nearly up and I really do not want to get a fine."

"I thought I might stay a bit longer and then take the bus, or I could come back with one of my friends who's got a weekend job in a bar in Verona. What do you think Clare? Do you have to go, or do you fancy going for an aperitif later? There's a happy hour with a buffet where my friend works and with a bit of luck we might even be able to scrounge a free drink!"

Clare considered the idea. She had nothing else to do, as Marco was at his mother's and her flatmates were away for the weekend. She couldn't say that she was attracted to Ben, but he had an endearing smile and she was sure they could spend a pleasant afternoon together.

"Yes, why not? That would be fun."

Vanessa was amused that her suspicions about Ben's interest in Clare seemed to have been confirmed.

"OK, you two have a good time then. Ben, I'll see you later". She stuffed the salami into her bag and took her leave, smiling inwardly. She still didn't hold out much hope for Ben's chances, but where there's life there's hope, she mused. Or should that be where there's a will there's a way?

Whatever. "Go for it Ben", she whispered under her breath.

CHAPTER 12

The following Saturday morning Marco picked Clare up in his Audi in front of the Castelvecchio. Given that it was such a beautiful sunny day, and that for once Marco was not on call during the weekend, they had decided to go for a walk along the lake, stopping off for lunch at one of the many restaurants looking out over the water.

For Clare it was a novelty having a proper adult boyfriend who could afford to take her out for lunch, with a car that could be trusted to do a 50 km round trip without the risk of breaking down on the way. Her previous relationships had all been short-lived affairs with university students, with whom being invited to dinner usually meant an improvised curry made with the previous day's leftovers, served up on plastic plates in a student bedsit. So now she was savouring the pleasures of playing the lady, accompanied by a man who opened doors for her and who would never have dreamed of allowing her to pay for a coffee.

She did her best to act like a sophisticated young woman, uncomfortably aware, however, that it was little more than an act and that she was about as refined as sausages and beans.

It was abundantly clear that Marco paid considerable attention to his wardrobe, so she made a supernatural effort not to dress like a student, pulling on a pair of jeans and the first sweatshirt that came to hand, but instead giving serious thought to previously unconsidered dilemmas such as colour coordination and choice of handbag. Christ, it was an uphill task though. How do some women manage to leave the house at 8 o'clock in the morning looking poised and immaculately elegant? For Clare even succeeding in getting up and leaving the house before 9 could be considered a miracle, let alone dealing with minor details such as washing, brushing her hair, getting together an outfit and blearily putting on eye make-up (foundation was not even part of her mindset).

On this occasion she had made an effort, and at 10 o'clock she had managed to present herself in reasonable order at the appointment, jumping into the car and leaning over to kiss the gorgeous Marco with his amber eyes. She relaxed back into the leather seat as they drove towards Lake Garda, although relaxing was perhaps not the right word, as Marco seemed to adhere to the principle of always travelling at the highest possible speed, weaving in and out of the traffic and occasionally cursing at elderly drivers clogging up the road, in the best Italian tradition.

Marco suggested they leave the car in Cisano, a small village on the lake, and walk to the larger town of Bardolino along the footpath. On this crisp cold morning the snow-capped peaks of the mountains stood out clearly on the horizon, acting as a backdrop for the reed thickets and quiet waters of the lake. Clare was amazed to see how close the mountains appeared, as on the previous occasion she had visited the lake the mist had almost completely obscured them, with the water melting into the sky in a monochrome palette of grey and blue.

Marco put his arm around her waist and they strolled at a leisurely pace along the path, with the self-absorption so typical of couples at the beginning of a relationship, barely noticing passers-by with dogs and children of assorted sizes. Clare was almost too scared to speak, frightened of breaking the magic and making some ghastly gaffe that would put Marco to flight. She didn't want to think about the future or admit, even to herself, that she was developing quite a serious crush on her pupil. She knew what she saw in him, but she couldn't quite understand what he saw in her (a bit like Groucho Marx thinking that there must be something wrong with any club that would accept him as member, she thought to herself). He was attractive, charming and intelligent, perhaps a little vain (but then who wouldn't be in his position?), and he radiated a charisma and self-assurance that made him eminently sexy.

When they reached Bardolino Marco pulled her towards him, putting his arms around her and kissing her at the base of her neck.

"So my little English girl, are you hungry? Shall we go to eat?" Although Clare's Italian had improved radically and she could now converse reasonably well, he liked to talk to her in English, insisting that she correct him when he made mistakes. She would actually have preferred to speak Italian, as she had enough of teaching English at the school and needed to improve her own language skills, but she wanted to keep him happy.

"Go *and* eat. Yes I'm always hungry, as you well know."

He steered her towards a restaurant overlooking the port, with an enclosed outdoor area making it possible to fully enjoy the view without freezing to death. They chose a table in the corner and ordered spaghetti with clams followed by mixed grilled fish, accompanied by a deliciously fruity bottle of Lugana.

Marco leaned back with a satisfied sigh.

"I'm glad that it is so nice today, because next week I must go to a convention in Rome."

"The whole of the week?"

"Yes, I will leave Monday and come back on Friday."

Clare was taken aback. "But that means we only have this weekend, because I'm leaving for England on Friday."

"Yes I know. I'm sorry."

"Oh well. At least we have today and tomorrow to be together."

"I am afraid tomorrow is not possible. My mother always expect me to be with her on Sunday."

"*Expects*", Clare specified. "Couldn't she make an exception?"

"You do not know my mother! Always she wants that I come to lunch on Sunday."

"She *always wants me* to come to lunch.... But there's still the evening, surely?"

"No, I must prepare everything for Monday. My flight is early in the morning".

"Oh .." Clare paused "couldn't I come for lunch tomorrow then? I'd love to meet your mother." She kicked herself mentally in the shins. That was way too pushy, but somehow it had just slipped out.

Marco looked uncomfortable.

"I do not think that is a good idea. My mother is still very...how you say ...attached to my ex wife. I don't tell her that I am seeing another woman."

"But it's been over a year since you separated, hasn't it?"

"Yes, but my wife still comes often to lunch on Sundays."

"*Often comes*. But that's a bit odd, isn't it? Why does she do that?"

"My mother likes it."

"Oh...". Clare dug her nails into her forearm to forcibly restrain herself, before saying anything that might do irreparable damage. "We'd better make the most of today then."

He smiled at her "Yes please Clare, I want to make today special."

They walked back to the car and then returned to Marco's flat in Verona. Clare did her best to be enthusiastic about the love-making, which was more than acceptable at a mechanical level, but at the back of her mind there was the feeling that this was the beginning of the end. She didn't understand why he had waited until today to tell her that he was going away next week, and worse still she couldn't escape the thought of Marco's ex wife.

Later in the evening he walked her back to her flat. As they stood in the doorway, he cupped her face tenderly in his hands and kissed her, looking into her eyes.

"Happy Christmas Clare. Time will pass very quickly, you see."

He put a small package into her hands, detaching himself and moving away before she had a chance to thank him. She looked down at the box and then back up at his retreating figure for a moment, before hauling herself up the interminable stairs. Once through the front door all she really wanted to do was to burst into tears and fling herself onto the sofa, but as it was already occupied by Astrid and Elsa she decided that a better option was to consume large amounts of alcohol. She gave her flatmates a forced smile, heading straight into the kitchen and pouring herself an exceptionally large glass of wine, before sitting down opposite them in the armchair to open Marco's gift.

Elsa glanced over curiously at the exquisitely wrapped box, "Ooh, what's that?"

"It's a present from Marco. I suppose it's his way of saying sorry that we won't see each other now until after Christmas." After a slight struggle, Clare succeeded in pulled off the wrapping paper to reveal a small navy blue box. Inside there was a polished stainless steel pendant on a chain.

"Very stylish", she commented "although I'm not sure that it's exactly what I would have chosen."

Elsa leaned over to look at it more closely. "It's lovely. What did you get him?"

"Nothing. I didn't realise that I wouldn't see him next week. I'll bring him back something from England I guess."

She sank pensively into the armchair, sipping her wine and barely listening to Elsa and Astrid gossiping away about their latest conquests. So is it better to ring him straightaway to thank him, she thought, or should I play it cool and wait until tomorrow morning? Should I hint at my disappointment that he didn't tell me earlier that he was going away or should I just pretend that it doesn't matter? She considered this Hamletian dilemma for a while, before deciding to call him briefly to say goodnight and thank him, but not until she had finished a second glass of wine.

CHAPTER 13

All teaching activities at the school had ended on December 20 and Ursula, who was not known for her unlimited generosity, had surprised everyone by providing an unusually sumptuous buffet and festive drinks on the last day of term. Chatting to each other over stuffed olives and vol-aux-vents, Clare and Janet had discovered that just two days later they would both be taking the same flight to London, from where Clare would head for her home town of York, while Janet would go to her elderly parents' house in a small village between Gatwick airport and Brighton.

"It's a bit like visiting a holiday camp for senior citizens, given that the average age is about 86", Janet had commented "and it's actually probably safer to walk down the middle of the road than along the pavement, because you risk being run over by a fleet of mobility scooters and powered wheelchairs. But my parents are happy there, because they have lots of friends and volunteer activities to keep them busy."

"So you're in for an exciting Christmas!"

"Well hardly, unless you consider OAP coffee mornings, jumble sales and carol concerts the height of entertainment. But of course Mum and Dad are delighted to see me, and it gives me a chance to catch up with some of my friends. It's doesn't take long to get into central London."

Clare and Janet had arranged to meet at the bus station in Verona to take the shuttle service to the airport. They were both travelling light, given the exorbitant cost of seasonal hold baggage on low cost flights, and Janet in particular had packing down to a fine art. Years of experience had taught her exactly how much she could get in a Ryanair-approved cabin bag, and her standard equipment also included a jacket with king-size pockets, into which she could stuff everything from books and camera to fossils and hairdryer.

"I only once nearly got caught out, on a flight back from Spain", she recounted. "At the gate they not only insisted that we insert our cases into the inevitable tubular blue metal case-measuring thing, having already obliged us to pack any additional handbags, but had also cunningly combined it with scales to weigh the cases at the same time. I had bought a paella pan, and unfortunately although I was OK on the measurements, the bag weighed in at 11.5 kg instead of 10. Well, there was no way I was going to pay an extra 40 euro, but I was nevertheless justifiably reluctant to abandon my 5 euro pan, so I withdrew to the back of the queue and started repacking, stuffing anything heavy into my pockets and piling on extra jumpers and scarves. As soon as they saw me doing it, heaps of other people in the queue started doing the same thing and we then waddled up to the gate for boarding again, sweating like pigs and looking like a group of obese Michelin men about to go on a trek to the North Pole. I was quite surprised by people's ingenuity; I saw one woman stuffing two pairs of jeans down the arms of her jacket! As soon as we got through the gate, we all stopped in the tunnel leading down to the plane and got undressed again, sticking everything back in our cases."

"Ah the joys of Ryanair!", exclaimed Clare "scratch cards, inexistent customer service and trumpeting 'on-time' jingles....".

"Outrageous call centre charges, sandwiches that cost more than the flight...." continued Janet, "although to be fair, they are still the cheapest and they do generally arrive on time. What's more, because you never have any hold baggage, you don't have to wait for it at the airport!"

"Except now sometimes you do, because they take away your cabin baggage and stick it in the hold anyway, if you're in the second half of the queue!"

"The trick is to arrive right at the very end, and then they usually allow it on anyway", suggested Janet "although actually I don't mind if they put it in the hold, because it saves hulking it up and down the stairs to the aircraft."

Given they had not booked together and the arbitrary nature of the automatic seat allocation system, they were uncertain whether they would be able to sit together on the plane, as neither of them had any intention of spending an extra 5 euro to select a seat, as a matter of principle. They had checked in online one immediately after the other in the hopes that they would be allocated adjoining seats, and this tactic had proved moderately successful, as they had ended up in the same row, across the aisle from one another.

They were now in the process of going through the security checks at the airport. Clare took off her belt and put it into the blue tray, along with her cell phone, handbag, assorted coins and the requisite transparent plastic bag containing liquids. The security guard gestured at her to also remove her boots, so she added these to the tray, pulling blue plastic bags over her socks, which made her feel a bit like she was at the scene of a crime. She walked through the metal detector, silently celebrating because for once in a blue moon it had not sounded, and retrieved her stuff on the other side of the machine, joining the usual group of slightly embarrassed passengers hopping around on one leg as if on pogo sticks, trying to pull on their boots while keeping an eye on their valuables, which were rolling down the belt as the plastic trays backed up. Behind her, Janet appeared to have been stopped by the female security guard, who not only frisked her, but then wiped a cotton swab over her hands. Testing for what? Clare asked herself. Drugs? Explosives? As a young blonde woman of Nordic appearance, Janet would not appear to be the most obvious candidate as a suspect terrorist or drug dealer, but maybe the staff were just told to carry out random checks. At all events she appeared to have passed the test, because she too had succeeded in making it past security control and was gathering up her things.

"Well, at least we're over the first obstacle", Janet said. "I always feel it's a bit like a video game with the final objective being to succeed in getting to the destination. Level 1: avoid strikes and traffic to arrive at the airport on time, either by public transport or by car, succeeding in finding the car park miles away you've booked online in order to have a cheaper rate. Level 2: getting through security checks and passport control. Level 3: getting through Ryanair checks without having to pay a supplement. Level 4: discovering whether the plane is actually scheduled to leave on time."

"After all that, the funny thing is that I've just remembered that I forgot to remove two cartons of orange juice I brought from home. It doesn't say much for security, does it?" Clare fumbled around inside her bag and extracted them. "Would you like one?"

"No thanks. I'd rather have a cup of tea. Let's check the departures board and then go to the McCafe. I'm not that keen on McDonalds but the McCafe's great."

They wandered over to the departures screen and saw that for the moment their flight was expected to be on time, which left them with an hour to kill before going to the gate. They made their way up the escalator and followed the designated route through the airport shops, ignoring the duty free, which was always twice as expensive as ordinary shops. Eventually they arrived at the cafe and sat down contentedly enough to enjoy a cup of tea and in Clare's case a slice of cheesecake.

Janet exhaled with satisfaction. "I drink so much tea that it might be easier if they just put me on an intravenous tea drip. I get withdrawal symptoms if I don't get at least 6 cups a day!"

"I've always been a tea drinker, but now I'm starting to get into the habit of drinking espresso coffee as well. I think it's Marco's fault. He keeps buying me coffee every five minutes", Clare responded without thinking. Bringing the subject of Marco up at the beginning of the journey was perhaps not the most tactful move. Why, oh why couldn't she connect her brain before opening her mouth? She flushed slightly.

"It's OK, you know," said Janet, sensing her embarrassment. "You don't need to worry about mentioning Marco. I mean, clearly we are not going to sit here swapping stories about what he's like as a lover, but you don't have to try and avoid mentioning him."

"It just feels really awkward. It's not as if I stole him away from you or anything, but for some reason I still feel slightly guilty. Maybe if I hadn't appeared you might have got back together."

Janet looked her straight in the eye. "That was never going to happen. We just weren't suited to each other, and above all I wasn't willing to hang around waiting for him to sort himself out. I admit I felt a bit strange about it when you first started going out with him, but it was just a momentary and completely illogical reaction. I really am over that now."

"So long as you don't have any regrets...."

"No, honestly I don't. I wish you all the best."

"Thanks, I appreciate it", said Clare. "Whatever happens with Marco, it's nice to know you don't resent me, or see me as some blonde bimbo who's elbowed her way in on your territory."

They sat for a moment in silence finishing their tea.

"OK. So now we've cleared that up, shall we go and see if it's time to head for the gate?" suggested Janet. A quick glance at the screen showed that their flight was due in on time, so they made their way down another escalator and through passport control into the international departures area. Here they joined the throng of people either heading home for the holidays, laden with children, Christmas presents and seasonal spirit, or at the other end of the spectrum, doing everything possible to escape the traditional family Christmas and all that goes with it. Clare had mixed feelings. On the one hand she liked all the traditional stuff; decorating the Christmas tree, carols in the Minster, bickering with her sister about who should help Mum out with the cooking, going to the neighbours for Christmas morning cocktails and staggering back half-pissed to eat turkey and trimmings at 3 o'clock in the afternoon, 101 recipes for turkey leftovers for the rest of the holidays. However, on the other hand she wouldn't have minded leaving everyone and everything behind her and heading for a tropical island with Marco.

When the flight started boarding Janet and Clare didn't rush to join the queue. Janet could never quite understand why some people were in such a desperate hurry to get on board, after all the plane wasn't going anywhere until everybody was seated and the seats were all allocated anyway. The two women sat chatting quietly until most of the passengers had gone through the gate, waiting until the last minute before pulling out their boarding cards and passports and strolling nonchalantly up to the counter. Ten minutes later Clare was staring out of the window, barely noticing the routinely strange choreography of the security demonstration.

It had been a truly momentous term. Her first time living abroad; first serious job; first time teaching; first love? Too early to say, really, but certainly it was the first time she had understood what people meant by a fluttering heart. Now she was heading home and was quite looking forward to temporarily relinquishing adulthood and abandoning all responsibilities for a couple of weeks. The next time she was in Italy it would be in the new year. She pressed herself back into the seat as the plane accelerated rapidly down the runway, savouring the exhilarating sensation as the wheels left the ground and the aircraft became airborne.

Part II – Spring Term

"Italy, and the spring and first love all together should suffice to make the gloomiest person happy."

Bertrand Russell

CHAPTER 14

Vanessa had managed to survive the Christmas holidays. Of course, she knew she should just be happy to have her family around her and in good health, but the rare moments when everyone was cheerful and collaborative tended to alternate with longer moments of tension and collective irritability. It was astonishing the speed with which an amicable family board game could degenerate into an argument about who had lost the remote control/spilt coffee on the kitchen floor /taken the spare set of door keys or failed to put the car in the garage the night before. When her children were born she had imagined Christmas as a warm, cosy occasion with a happy family standing around the piano and singing 4 part carols like a scene from Little Women, whereas now she was just happy if they could spend Christmas Day without recriminations, major upsets or anyone storming off in a huff. Why was it that some mothers had children who wrote disarmingly sentimental facebook dedications "to my best friend and the most wonderful mum in the world" on their birthdays or Mother's Day, whereas her own children certainly didn't want her as a facebook friend and hadn't had anything to do with Mother's Day since they were forced to write gooey letters at primary school?

The dog had also been a major cause for concern over the holidays. On Boxing Day they had all gone to bed late, after going out for a pizza with friends, but at around 4 o'clock Vanessa was awoken by the sounds of something bumping around in the corridor in the dark outside the bathroom. Assuming that no burglar could possibly be that clumsy, she got up to see what was happening and found Spot lurching around in circles like a drunken sailor, banging into the bathroom door, before his legs finally gave out and he was sick all over the bath mat. Horrified, she called her husband Giovanni and together they wrapped the dog up in a blanket and took him into the bedroom. His head was tilted over to the left and he was trembling violently. He tried to get up but didn't seem to be able to coordinate his limbs.

"What are we going to do? Do you think he's had a stroke? Where on earth are we going to find a vet at this hour of the night on Boxing Day", she whispered urgently, trying not to wake up the kids.

"I don't know. Is there some kind of emergency service?"

Vanessa crept into the spare bedroom, which also served as an office, and turned on the PC.

"I'll try looking up vets online to see if anyone is open 24 hours a day."

"Good idea. I'll clean up a bit in the meantime. He seems a bit quieter now."

Vanessa discovered that there was only one vet offering an emergency service, located around 20 km away. She went back to look at Spot, who now appeared to be asleep and was showing no apparent signs of distress.

"Do you think we can wait until tomorrow morning and take him to our usual vet?"

"I think so. It's almost morning anyway, but darling I think you need to be prepared. He's an old dog. I don't know if he's going to make it."

Vanessa's eyes filled with tears. Spot had been a part of their family for fifteen years, ever since they had moved into the house. However exasperating he was, however many times he had pulled the rubbish out all over the floor and however many cushions he had chewed, he was still an integral part of the household. What's more he was the only family member who was always and unconditionally happy to see her.

She lay down in bed and tried unsuccessfully to go to sleep for a couple of hours, but with every sign of movement from Spot she would lean over the edge of the bed to see if he was OK. She finally dropped off for a few minutes, waking up with a jerk when she heard the dog scrabbling around in the basket, trying to get up. She picked him up and took him downstairs and out into the garden, in case he needed to pee. Spot staggered about uncertainly, but he was walking and he did manage to relieve himself, although he couldn't cock his leg without falling over. It would have been comic if it hadn't have been so sad. His eyes were darting back and forth and he was definitely keeling over to the left.

Vanessa left Spot on a cushion in the living room and went upstairs to wake Giovanni. Together they took the dog to the vet, who carried out routine blood and urine tests and gave him an x-ray. Ready for the worst possible news, they were pleasantly surprised and relieved to discover that Spot stood a good chance of recovering totally, or at least substantially, his symptoms apparently being typical of a disease rejoicing in the name of canine idiopathic vestibular syndrome, which with a bit of luck should resolve spontaneously in the next few days. They took him home and Spot did indeed recuperate at remarkable speed, although his head remained slightly tilted to the left, giving him a somewhat quizzical air. His legs still tended to slide out laterally, meaning that he practically did the splits while he was trying to eat, so in the first few days Vanessa would stand with her feet on either side of his back legs, to stop them slipping gradually sideways. Nevertheless, within a couple of days he was trotting about reasonably happily, despite the fact that he could no longer jump onto the sofa, nor make his way down the stairs, although he could still manage to go up. This was actually a bit of a liability, because being almost completely deaf and half-blind, Spot would often go upstairs to look for somebody and then get stuck at the top, unable to come down again until someone came and rescued him. What's more he didn't seem to like being picked up, so when Vanessa tried to get hold of him he would run away and hide under the bed, only to reappear and whine again at the top of the stairs as soon as she had left. She had thus devised a strategy which involved her hiding just around the corner at the top of the stairs, or alternatively behind the bathroom door, and then leaping out to grab him before he had time to run away.

At all events, with the dog recovering and the holidays over, Vanessa breathed a sigh of relief now that her husband had gone back to work, her daughter to school and her son to university. Absurdly, the anticipation with which she looked forward to the end of the holidays was almost as great as her pleasure at the beginning of the holiday season.

Given that she was free to organise her own life for the first time in two weeks, she had decided to invite Clare and Janet over for lunch before the start of the spring term a couple of days later. They were both back from England by now and she looked forward to hearing their news and finding out how they had spent the holidays. What's more it would be a good opportunity to develop a short and medium-term strategy for coping with Ursula and the school in the forthcoming term, without her having to go into Verona.

Janet had arranged to fetch Clare and then drive to Vanessa's house, stopping off at the pastry shop in the village to pick up some cakes, confident that nothing could be guaranteed to ensure Vanessa's good humour more than cake. Janet had enjoyed her time in England, but although she was sad at having to leave her elderly parents, at the same time it had reminded her of the desolate landscape represented by her previous life in the UK and reinforced her conviction that she wanted to stay in Italy permanently.

Clare on the other hand was torn between two worlds. By now some of the novelty of living in Italy was wearing off and going back to England had made her realise how much she missed everyone at home. With the artistic and cultural treasures of northern Italy, the beauty of the landscape, Italian food and, although she hardly dared admit it, Marco on one side and the comfortable familiarity of friends and family on the other, the balance was still in favour of Italy, but the goodbyes had been tough and she was glad for the chance meet up with Janet and Vanessa, who might help her feel a little less homesick.

As usual, Vanessa knew that that her visitors had arrived a couple of minutes before they rang the doorbell, thanks to a series of strategically placed dogs left outside by their owners during the day in gardens along the road. A howling Akita warned of the approach of anybody from the left, while those arriving from the right were greeted by an Australian shepherd dog that barked desperately at anything that moved, rushing furiously backwards and forwards along the fence. While owning a dog seemed to have become fashionable lately, with an explosion of lap dogs in designer outfits, house-proud Italians still tended to leave larger dogs outside alone for much of the day, something which annoyed Vanessa considerably. After all, what was the point of having a dog if you just abandoned it in the garden all day? However, it did make for a convenient early warning system for the arrival of both wanted and unwanted guests.

Once in the house, Janet and Clare peeled off layers of outer clothing, scarves and woolly hats, presenting Vanessa with the pastries and a bottle of red wine and settling down in the kitchen around the wooden table.

Vanessa threw some pasta into a pan of boiling water.

"I thought I'd do some spaghetti all'amatriciana for lunch. Traditionally it should be made with 'guanciale', which comes from the cheek of the pig, but I've just used smoked bacon, because it's less fatty. Anyway, it's a nice warming dish for the winter".

"Great, It's one of my favourites", said Janet.

"Good, because I don't have a vast culinary repertoire. Now and then I try something different, but the family is usually so rude about it that I give up and go back to the old favourites."

Clare smiled at her.

"Well you can try anything out on me. I eat absolutely everything!"

They chatted for a while about what they had all done during the Christmas holidays while waiting for the pasta to cook. Vanessa waited until the spaghetti were 'al dente', with just the right touch of firmness, before tipping them into the sauce and giving them a good stir. Then she transferred the spaghetti into three plates using some ingenious serving tongs somebody had given her for Christmas and grated a little Pecorino cheese over the top.

"Here you are girls. Dig in."

As the least experienced spaghetti-eater, Clare was having a few problems coordinating fork rotation while avoiding spattering tomato sauce all over the front of her shirt.

"Mmm. It's delicious, but do you think I could have a spoon?"

Vanessa laughed. "OK, I can give you one if you like, but you really should make a serious effort to learn to eat spaghetti properly if you're going to stay in Italy. Look..." she proceeded to demonstrate. "You need to lift and separate (remember the old bra advert?), then wind the spaghetti around your fork while resting the prongs on the bottom of the plate and quickly shovel it into your mouth without trying to be too elegant!"

Clare made a few attempts, but always seemed to end up either with a single strand or a massive clump of spaghetti.

"I'm never going to get the hang of this! And it's not even as if I had never eaten spaghetti in England."

"Yes you will. It just takes practice. My husband eats spaghetti so fast that he practically vacuums it in rather than eating it. I've hardly had time to sit down and he's already finished."

Concentrating on the job in hand, Clare managed to finish off the whole plate and sat back with a sigh of satisfaction.

"Thanks Vanessa. That was delicious. I must try out your recipe when my cousin comes to stay at the beginning of March. He's doing a post-graduate degree in art history and he wants to come out for a couple of months to study Paolo Veronese."

"Oh, that's interesting" said Janet "but I thought Veronese worked in Venice for most of his life?"

"How well-informed you are! Yes, I think David's planning to spend some of his time in Venice and some in Verona to do his research. I was going to ask Ursula whether there might be a room free in my flat, as there's a constant turnover of students staying there. All my old flatmates left before Christmas and at the moment there's one room free and one rented to two German girls."

"You can certainly ask her. I doubt that the room will stay free until March, but Ursula has lots of contacts and I'm sure that she'll be able to find him somewhere to live temporarily, if she wants to of course", said Janet. "Try and get her on a good day."

"She doesn't have many of those", commented Vanessa "but so long as she can see a way of making money I have no doubt that she'll find something! More wine, anyone?"

They finished off the bottle and then started on the pastries. Vanessa offered to dig out a bottle of port that she had bought the previous year on a trip to Portugal, but Janet was worried about driving home and Clare avoided drinking too much at lunchtime because otherwise she was in a coma for the rest of the day, so they decided to move onto tea instead. Over a large pot of Earl Grey, Janet updated them on the amendments to the timetable for the forthcoming term at the school, with two new courses starting up at companies in Verona, directly at their premises. Janet arranged to take on the more advanced course and Clare would be teaching a group of office workers at the exhibition centre, while Vanessa refused point blank to take on any extra hours.

Having amicably sorted out the business side of things to their satisfaction, the three women spent a relaxing afternoon gossiping about the school and swapping stories about the most hilarious linguistic gaffes of their students, and their own equally cringeworthy cultural stumblings. Eventually, Janet decided that it was time to head back to Verona, preferring to leave before dark, so they said good-bye, promising to meet up the following week in the city for a drink.

CHAPTER 15

Clare had seen Ben and his friends several times since the day at the Christmas market in December. Spending time with them made her feel like she was back at university, enjoying the hang-loose lifestyle and sod-it-all attitude so typical of students, in the now distant days before she was expected to be a proper adult. She had introduced Ben to her new Teutonic flatmates, one of whom seemed to be quite keen on him, so she had phoned to invite him to the flat for a drink on Friday evening, thinking that they maybe needed a little encouragement to get to know each other better and rather relishing the role of match-maker. Unfortunately, she had neglected to inform Greta, the interested party, in advance and it turned out that she had already promised to be elsewhere that evening, while her friend Sarah had gone to visit a friend in Venice.

When Clare heard the doorbell ring, she went over to the intercom panel and told Ben to come on up to the fourth floor. She contemplated going down herself so that they could out for a beer somewhere, but frankly she was pretty wacked out, having only finished teaching an hour earlier, so she thought they might as well just have a beer at home and watch a film maybe.

Ben made the debilitating trek up the notoriously asthma-inducing stairs with comparative ease, stopping to check the name on the door before pressing the buzzer. This was the first time he had been up to the apartment and he was curious to see where Clare lived.

"Bloody hell, it's a long way up, isn't it", he commented as she welcomed him in.

"Yes, well at least it saves going to the gym. Apparently stair-climbing is one of the most effective forms of exercise", she smiled.

"I'm afraid I have to apologise for the lack of company, Ben. Greta and Sarah aren't here this evening. I feel a bit of an idiot, because I forgot to check with them before I asked you, and I only found out they couldn't be here an hour ago, when I got back from work. Would you like to sit down for a beer anyway, or would you rather go out?"

Ben plumped himself down on the lumpy brown sofa and grinned at her.

"That sounds great. Actually, I'm rather glad it's only you."

Clare went into the kitchen to get a couple of bottles of beer and a bottle-opener, then sat down beside him.

"Why's that? Greta's such a pretty girl, and she seems quite keen on you. I thought you'd be pissed off that she isn't here."

"She's a little bit predatory, if you know what I mean. I'm not sure I want to be eaten alive just yet. Anyway, can't you guess why I prefer to be alone with you?" He looked at her quizzically.

The suspicion had crossed Clare's mind, but she had dismissed it because she simply didn't see him in that light.

"But I'm going out with someone else. You know that."

"Of course, the famous Marco. Still he seems to leave you a lot of free time." Ben took a long swig of cold beer.

"He's a doctor, for heaven's sake. He doesn't have all that much leisure time. Anyway, what are you suggesting? That I have two part-time boyfriends, or are you just looking for a one-night stand? This may sound corny, but I'm afraid I'm not that type of girl! Oh God, I can't believe I actually said that."

Ben turned to look her straight in the face.

"No, it's not corny and I am not looking for a quickie or a part-time girlfriend, but I do think you should dump Marco and go out with someone your own age who might really care about you, namely me!"

Clare began to feel distinctly irritated.

"What makes you think Marco doesn't care about me? And you're not my age, you're two years younger!"

"Well, I'm a damn sight nearer your age than Marco. Don't you realise he's just using you? He gets free English lessons, and what's more free sex as well!"

"He pays the school for English lessons and we happened to meet there. The fact that I'm English has nothing to do with why he's attracted to me", Clare replied furiously "and what we do when we go out, or stay in, is certainly none of your business."

With a growing realisation that he had perhaps not been tremendously tactful, Ben backtracked and tried to be more conciliating.

"I'm sorry Clare. I didn't mean to be so blunt. It's just that I really like you, and from what you say Marco limits himself to seeing you once or twice a week and has somehow never got round to introducing you to his friends or family."

"He takes me to restaurants, for skiing trips or to exhibitions, not that's it's any affair of yours. He's a grown-up man, not a boy who's idea of a good night out is just going for a beer with his mates." Clare could not repress her mounting fury.

It was Ben's turn to get annoyed. "Oh, so that's it, is it? He's more interesting because he's got a posh car and can afford to take you out to restaurants?"

Clare jumped up, banging her beer bottle down onto the coffee table with a loud crash. She glared at him.

"OK, that's enough. I think it's time you left. I didn't invite you here to insult me. If you really think that I'm so superficial that I'd sell myself for a skiing weekend and a meal in a fancy restaurant then I don't think we have much to say to each other."

Ben got to his feet slowly. That hadn't gone at all like he planned.

"It wasn't meant to come out like that", he mumbled. "Clare, please...."

If she hadn't been so furious, Clare might even have felt sorry for him. He looked like a puppy who had just been told off for digging a hole in the lawn. But she was way past the point of being able to rein in her anger and all she wanted to was push him physically out of the flat (and preferably down all eight flights of stairs).

Tight-lipped, she turned her back on him, aware that tears that she had no intention of showing him were welling into her eyes.

"Just get out", she said "and close the door behind you."

Ben meekly placed his bottle of beer on the table and shuffled out of the flat. He halted for a moment just outside the door, wondering whether he should make another attempt to explain himself better, but concluded that nothing he could say or do was likely to go down well at this particular moment. It was a feeling he often had with women, starting with his mother. So with resignation he plodded down the stairs, muttering unhappily and wincing as the glass door slammed shut behind him, as if to emphasise his definitive exclusion.

Meanwhile, Clare was zapping between TV channels with the remote control, but found herself unable to concentrate on anything. Damn Ben! What did he know about anything? He was only twenty for Christ's sake, and everybody knows that boys of his age have the emotional maturity of a tomcat. Unfortunately, try as she could, she couldn't rid herself of the niggling feeling that the reason she was so angry was because there was just a hint of truth in his accusations. She did enjoy going to good restaurants and drinking posh wine for a change. Did that make her a superficial bimbo? And did Marco just see her as a handy part-time affair, with the added advantage of getting free English conversation lessons? Certainly, the fact the he had been out with another English teacher just before her was a trifle suspicious, especially as the said teacher had dumped him for being unable to commit. Maybe he had been out with a whole series of English teachers, moving from one to the next with each academic year! Worse still, maybe that had even been the reason for his divorce!

Clare tried to stop herself from dwelling on the worst possible outcomes. In effect, there was no reason to think that Marco's attentions, and intentions, were less than sincere. Naturally optimistic, Clare found it difficult to believe that his tenderness was completely feigned, but the few emotionally unsatisfying short-term relationships she had lived through with her peers at school and university had not really equipped her with the necessary tools and experience to deal with a man as mature and apparently expert as Marco.

She felt a burning need to speak to him, grabbing her cell phone on impulse, her index finger hovering over his name. Then, changing her mind yet again, she threw the phone down on the sofa. She needed to calm down first and not charge into things like a bull in a china shop, while she was still angry following the exchange with Ben. However much she wanted to clarify the situation, she was afraid that she might scare Marco off definitively, and the more she thought about it, the less she wanted that to happen. She turned off the TV and decided to go and read in bed, a nightly ritual that had always been an escape route for her since she was a child.

It occurred to her that the greatest literary love stories almost inevitably seemed to end badly, while modern day romantic Hollywood movies for adolescents appeared absurdly sentimental even at the grand old age of 21. Striking the right balance was clearly going to take some thought.

CHAPTER 16

Shivering slightly, Janet curled up in an armchair in the living room, equipped with a large roll of toilet paper and a plastic bag in case she should have a sudden desire to vomit again. Her head ached, her back ached, her joints ached and in fact she was pretty hard-pressed to find anything that didn't ache. It was probably just a bout of flu, but she hadn't felt this ghastly for years.

Realising that there was no way she was going to be able to teach that evening, she hauled herself up to look for her cell phone. Why did the bloody thing seem to have a life of its own and disappear at the most inconvenient moments? She wandered aimlessly from one room to the other, peering into bags and ineffectually lifting up cushions to search for it. Half an hour later, exhausted by the effort, she finally found her mobile in her coat pocket and immediately called the school.

"Ursula? It's Janet. I'm really not feeling well at all, so I won't be able to teach today."

"This is very inconvenient. You have three groups this afternoon."

"I realise that. You'll have to see if you can find a replacement. If all else fails, you'll just have to cancel the courses", said Janet rather sharply. "Thanks for the concern by the way. Now that I think about it, Clare may be free for the first lesson. I think she usually starts later today."

"So you phone Clare and Vanessa to organise replacement?"

"No Ursula, I'm ill. I'm sure you can manage to phone Clare and Vanessa."

"If you phone me, I think you can phone Vanessa and Clare. It's your job."

"I'm only phoning you to tell you I'm ill", replied Janet through gritted teeth "and now if you'll excuse me I'm going back to bed!"

With ill grace, Ursula agreed to deal with the problem, so Janet was finally able to suffer in peace, withdrawing to her bedroom and wrapping herself up in the duvet. She set her mobile to silent mode and concentrated on not being sick, eventually falling into a restless sleep.

In the meantime Vanessa was on her way to the headquarters of the electricity company. She rarely took on interpreting jobs, but the agency had called her up the day before, offering her a fee so much higher than her usual teaching rate that she felt she simply could not refuse, especially since it was not one of her teaching days. She left the car in the company car park and walked into the building, presenting herself as the interpreter at the reception desk. She was immediately accompanied into the conference room, where a fraught-looking PA greeted her.

"So where is your equipment?"

Vanessa was puzzled "Equipment? What equipment would that be exactly?" As an interpreter, she thought, what you see is what you get, a marvellously complete and self-sufficient unit.

"The equipment for simultaneous interpretation" replied the PA impatiently.

"Well, for a start the agency said the job involved *consecutive* interpreting, not simultaneous", said Vanessa "and secondly simultaneous interpreting normally involves working in a sound-proofed booth with at least one other colleague. It's a tiny bit difficult to carry a booth and full sound system around in one's briefcase. And I don't seem to see another interpreter anywhere."

The secretary considered the implications for a moment.

"OK, we'll just have to make do, I guess. Please sit down. The Germans will be with you in just one moment."

Vanessa experienced one of those moments when you just know that everything that can possibly go wrong is about to.

"Germans?" she queried.

The PA looked at her as if she were a complete idiot.

"The two managers you will be interpreting for, the Germans."

"There is just one tiny problem", Vanessa felt forced to mention. "The agency informed me that you required an English interpreter. Consequently, I'm English, not German."

"Well so long as you speak German....."

"But unfortunately I don't."

"You can't be serious?"

"I'm afraid I am".

"Oh my God!"

There was an uncomfortable pause as they looked at each other.

"OK. Wait here. I'll go and talk to the manager of the press office." The PA rushed out of the room, apparently on the verge of a panic attack, only to appear five minutes later with a middle-aged man in a grey suit.

He looked at her sternly "I understand you are not German."

"No, I'm afraid not". Vanessa had never previously felt the need to apologise for not being German, but obviously there was a first time for everything.

"And you do not speak German?"

"No"

"So we have decided that there is only one solution. Clearly, the Germans must do their presentation in English."

"Well that would certainly resolve the problem, so long as they are happy to do so", said Vanessa, trying to imagine the equivalent situation, with a pair of British managers, or Italians for that matter, suddenly being told that they had to give their presentation in another language, because their host had mistakenly arranged for the wrong interpreter. Thank God for the linguistic abilities of the Germans!

At this point the German managers were shown into the conference room and took up their seats on the platform. One of them was a youngish blond man of classically Teutonic appearance, while the other was a rather severe-looking middle aged woman in an immaculately cut skirt suit. Vanessa was sandwiched between the Germans and the Italian managers, while the participants at the conference began to file in and take their places in the rows of seats opposite them. As usual, Vanessa experienced the rush of adrenalin associated with the infinite opportunities for making a fool of yourself in front of lots of people.

Nevertheless, the rest of the morning went surprisingly well. The Germans turned out to be more than competent in English, but because it was not their first language they tended to speak more slowly and use simpler vocabulary than a native speaker, which in effect made things easier. There was one minor blip towards lunchtime, with Vanessa experiencing the interpreter's nightmare of getting out of sync and inverting her languages, meaning that she was translating into Italian for the Germans and into English for the Italians. Although surprisingly everyone was too polite to mention it, a row of completely blank faces alerted her to the fact that evidently her explanations were completely incomprehensible. She apologised, carried out a brain reset and set off again, concluding that all in all she had got away with it reasonably well.

Shortly afterwards the meeting broke off for lunch, and Vanessa seized the chance to go to the bathroom. Like many of her middle-aged women friends she suffered from 2-hour bladder syndrome, requiring regular pit-stops, especially if she had been drinking too much tea. While she was sitting on the loo she checked her mobile, immediately noting with some dismay that there were 4 missed calls from Ursula at roughly half-hourly intervals. She wondered what on earth the wretched woman wanted now, but was pretty sure that whatever it was, she wasn't going to like it. She seriously contemplated the idea of ignoring the calls, but ultimately decided that Ursula would probably continue calling until she did reply, so she might as well get it over with. She sighed and returned the call.

"Ursula, it's Vanessa. I see that you have been trying to get in touch."

"At last, why do you not answer the phone? I need you to teach this evening. Janet is ill."

"I'm afraid I can't. I'm doing an interpreting job in Verona and I don't finish until 5. What's wrong with Janet?"

"She cannot come, but it's OK. You can start at six. Clare will do the first lesson and you do the next two courses from six to nine", Ursula informed her.

"But Ursula, I'll be exhausted. I've been interpreting all day. I don't even have time off for lunch. Can't anyone else do it?"

"No. Nobody is free. It's very lucky you have time and are already in Verona. Thank you so much. I see you at six." Ursula rang off.

Vanessa couldn't work out how exactly that had happened. How did Ursula always manage to manoeuvre people to do exactly what she wanted? She thought she had said distinctly that she wasn't available, and with anyone normal that would have been sufficient, but when dealing with Ursula a significantly more emphatic approach was required. She was on the verge of ringing her back and refusing point blank to come, when the dreadful realisation came over her that if she knew her chickens (stupid expression really, why chickens?), Ursula would of course not answer her call, thus ensuring that she had no opportunity to refuse and confident that she would now feel obliged to come if she couldn't contact her. In any case, the conference speakers were waiting for her to interpret over lunch, so she could hardly spend time arguing with Ursula over the phone. Damn the woman and the whole bloody school!

Lunch was complicated, given that Vanessa was expected to act as interpreter for everyone while they ate. In effect, it proved practically impossible for her to consume anything, as she would take a bite but then not have time to chew it, because somebody would already be looking at her and waiting for a translation. So she would gulp the food down furiously in order to interpret, while in the meantime somebody else would say something requiring translation. In the end she gave up on food almost completely and sat there with her stomach grumbling, watching everyone else enjoy their food and occasionally trying to jam in a tiny morsel.

The afternoon session proceeded relatively smoothly, although towards the end of the day Vanessa was taking copious notes, aware that she was no longer able to remember more than about ten seconds worth of discourse. Not a great job for anyone over fifty, she thought, when the brain already seems to be giving out and major memory loss is looming. In any case, she was extremely glad when the session drew to a close, resignedly conscious however that her day was nowhere near its end. She still had to drive to the school, find a parking place and take two lessons with groups that she knew nothing about, with no preparation and no time to eat anything beforehand. Oh joy, oh rapture unforeseen!

She politely said goodbye to the Germans before launching herself out of the door and heading for the car park. As she trotted towards the car, she rummaged around in her handbag, hoping against hope that something edible, like a chocolate bar, could be found in the deeper recesses. Chocolate was the only thing that could make the thought of two extra English lessons bearable. She decided that even at the cost of arriving five minutes late, she would stop off at a cafe and pick up enough supplies to keep her going until nine. Forty minutes later, having parked the car and armed with a large Kitkat and a chocolate croissant, she was ready to face the enemy. "Once more unto the breach..." she said to herself as she headed up the familiar marble stairs.

CHAPTER 17

On the Thursday evening before the Carnival festivities were due to start in Verona, Janet suggested meeting up the following day to go and watch the procession of floats along the main road leading up to Piazza Bra, an event which marked the beginning of the celebrations in Verona. The school would be closed for the event, partly because of the difficulties linked to transport and parking, given the crowds of people coming to the city, and partly because none of the students were likely to turn up for lessons anyway, so the teachers were all given a more than welcome day off.

Clare was looking forward to seeing how people celebrated carnival in Verona, having never had the opportunity to participate in a similar occasion, so she welcomed Janet's suggestion, and the two women they agreed to meet at the fountain in Piazza Bra. Vanessa, on the other hand, flatly refused to come into the city.

"You must be joking. It's always absolute chaos and there's nowhere to park. I'll get stuck in the traffic on the way in and on the way back, just to see a load of floats with blaring music, ghastly bands and '70s style majorettes, with grown-ups using the excuse of Carnival to dress up in silly costumes. Why it is that so many men can't wait to dress up as women I'll never understand. Freud would have something to say about it I'm sure!"

"Oh, don't be such a killjoy", said Janet. "Carnival is a longstanding tradition; you have to remember that in the past it was the last chance to have fun before Lent began. In Verona specifically, 'Venerdì Gnocolar' is supposed to date back to the 16th century, when free food was distributed to the inhabitants to try and suppress a people's revolt after a long famine."

"Venerdì Gnocolar?" queried Clare.

"'Gnocolar' comes from the word gnocchi", explained Janet. "In Verona the ingredients necessary to make gnocchi were distributed free to the people on the Friday before Lent, and the Carnival celebrations officially begin on the Friday, ending on the following Shrove Tuesday, hence the name. Even today, gnocchi are traditionally eaten by families in Verona on Carnival Friday. They're often served with a sort of horse stew."

"Horse stew! That's gross". Clare shuddered. "I was absolutely horrified to find that the typical dishes of Verona include horse and donkey."

"Oh wait, I know the historical reason for that", intervened Vanessa. "Janet is the not the only one who knows anything about the local history and culture! The tradition is supposed to date back to a massive battle near Verona in the fifth century, when Odoacer, the King of Italy, was defeated by Theodoric, the King of the Ostrogoths. Thousands of horses died in the battle and as there was a major food shortage, the inhabitants took advantage of the unexpected resource, deciding to cook the meat by marinating it in well-aged red wine and spices so that it would keep longer."

"Well, I'm sorry but I still can't bring myself to eat horse meat."

"Neither can I. I know it's illogical, because it's there's no reason why it's any worse eating horses than pigs, cattle or sheep, but it's a sort of cultural thing for us Brits. In any case, I have no intention whatsoever of spending hours stuck in traffic just to eat gnocchi, with or without horse stew, and watch a lot of twats prancing about on floats. In the freezing cold, what's more. It would be different if we were in Rio!"

Janet and Clare had given up hope of convincing their colleague, but Clare's German flatmates came along the following day, together with one of Janet's Italian friends, a former pupil at the school. The two women shared a passion for running and would often meet up to jog along the River Adige in the early morning.

They pushed their way through the crowds to watch the procession of gigantic floats as they passed, surmounted by huge cartoon-like figures, and accompanied by hordes of participants dressed in every possible kind of costume, the music blaring out from loudspeakers. The spectators participated actively and enthusiastically, launching industrial quantities of colourful confetti and streamers. In theory, it was forbidden to spray shaving foam about, but this ban was taken fairly lightly by groups of over-enthusiastic young people, fighting their own personal wars armed with spray cans and large bags of flour. Innocent bystanders were frequently caught up in the crossfire, and after one particularly messy encounter Janet and her friend felt the need to retreat into safer territory.

"I think I'm getting a little too old for this", Janet shouted to Clare. "If you don't mind, Susanna and I are going to look for a cafe somewhere a bit quieter."

"No problem", Clare shouted back. "I'll see you at school on Monday then."

She watched as the two older women pushed their way out of the crowds lining the road, heading for the relative tranquillity of a side street. The final floats were passing and the procession was drawing to a close, beginning its tour of the city, so the crowds gradually began to disperse. When the last float turned the corner,

Clare turned to Greta, noticing that she was chatting to a group of boys who had arrived in the meantime, including Vanessa's son Ben. She hadn't seen him since they had argued two or three weeks earlier, and although she had calmed down since then, her feathers were still a little ruffled.

"Hi Clare. How are things?" Ben smiled at her slightly anxiously, in case she was still cross with him.

"Hi Ben. Everything's OK, but it's nice to have a day off from school." She smiled back, but just a little coldly, ready to forgive but not quite to forget.

"I've been busy too. I've had exams at university."

"How did they go?"

"OK I think, but I won't have the results until next week. Listen we're all going off to have mug of hot chocolate. Do you and your friends fancy coming?"

Clare looked at Greta and Sarah for confirmation. They seemed keen enough, so the group of young people moved away from the crowds, heading for a bar a little out of the centre, where the boys were fairly certain there would be space to sit down and get warm. When they got there, they all stamped their feet and emptied the hoods of their jackets before entering, to avoid leaving a trail of paper all over the floor. Clare ran her hands through her hair and scraped strands of pink foam off her jacket. The confetti seemed to have got everywhere, infiltrating down the back of her neck, into her boots, inside her pockets and even down her trousers. She didn't envy whoever had to clean up the city the following day, as the streets of the centre were submerged by piles of colourful paper flakes like multi-coloured snow. Thank God it wasn't raining, otherwise it would have turned into a polychrome slush, clogging up the roads and pavements.

The bar was busy, but they managed to find a table and cram themselves onto a couple of wooden benches, sipping mugs of hot chocolate and tea and sharing slices of apple strudel. Clare found herself next to Ben, at one end of the table, while her German friends were chatting to his mates at the other.

"It's good to see you", he said hesitantly. "I didn't mean to offend you the other evening, you know."

"I know you didn't. I suppose I was cross because there was a tiny element of truth in what you said", Clare admitted. "Let's forget about it and just stay friends."

He chewed his lip. "OK, although I would be happy to be a bit more than friends, you know."

"I do realise that Ben, but it's all I can offer you at the moment. You're a great guy and it's fun to be with you and your friends, so let's just leave it at that, shall we?"

"OK, but put me on the waiting list, in case you should happen to break up with Marco!"

Clare laughed. "Thanks. That's a great ego-booster. I've never had a waiting list before. In fact, I never really had that much success with men. I've never considered myself as particularly attractive and I certainly wasn't one of those girls who was hugely popular at school or university, not even with my own sex."

"Now you're fishing for compliments!"

"No I'm not. I'm just surprised that in Italy I suddenly seem to be considered more attractive than I was in England. It must be the blonde hair, I guess. The appeal of opposites".

"There are natural blondes in Italy", Ben said "but obviously there are more people with dark hair and Mediterranean looks. You are the archetypal Nordic girl though. Nobody is going to mistake you for an Italian. It's the same with my sister, who takes after Mum.

Everybody always talks to her in German at the lake, because they assume she is a foreigner, given that there are so many German and Dutch tourists. She gets really annoyed about it sometimes."

"You, on the other hand, look just like your Dad. Not English at all".

"Is that a good or a bad thing?"

"Oh, probably good I think. At least you won't break out in blisters after you've been in the sun for five minutes, like me. I have to smother myself in sun cream before daring to expose any skin".

"Yes, it's the same for Mum and my sister. They can't go out in the summer without a major creaming operation, whereas Dad seems to think of sun cream as completely unnecessary and somehow vaguely effeminate!"

Hearing them giggling, Greta turned around.

"What are you two laughing about?"

"Oh nothing", said Clare. "Just the difference between Italian and Nordic concepts of beauty."

"Well I think Italian men are very sexy", said Greta, wrapping her arm protectively around Ben's. Ben winked at Clare. "Well, as you said, opposites attract."

The evening was drawing in and it was almost dark. One of Ben's friends suggested that they all went back to his house, where they would have the place to themselves as his parents had gone to visit his grandmother. However, before leaving his mother had prepared kilos of home-made gnocchi, knowing that he would probably want to invite his friends back for dinner. The proposal was greeted enthusiastically, and the young people walked back to the district on the other side of the river, crossing the Roman bridge over the River Adige. They chatted together amicably, occasionally kicking up piles of confetti, and stopping to buy a few bottles of beer at the kebab house on the way. With supplies of beer and gnocchi guaranteed, the evening looked all set to be a success.

CHAPTER 18

The choir had been called on to participate at a local festival in a neighbouring village, singing first at the religious service in a small chapel and then at the jamboree afterwards in the church hall. Vanessa had concentrated on preparing some easy but energetic spirituals for the church and a couple of arrangements of Italian pop songs for the event afterwards. Over the years she had found that gospel music was the easiest and most entertaining thing to do with the choir and had the biggest impact on an Italian public. It was dynamic and exciting and usually had straightforward harmonies easy to teach people with little or no musical background. Above all, it made a change from the mind-bogglingly dreary stuff usually dished out in church, which had neither the beauty of classical music nor the dynamism of modern genres. The Catholic church seemed to work on the principle that anything even faintly inspirational interfered with the devotion of the faithful, and Vanessa's repertoire was not universally welcomed by local priests, many of whom however continued to call on the choir for local events, both liturgical and festive.

Recently Vanessa had lost some of her enthusiasm for the choir, despite being very attached to many of her chorists. They were a great bunch of people on the whole, but totally undisciplined. Getting them to shut up for long enough to actually do any rehearsing took more energy than she had left in the evening. An inordinately long time was then spent deciding what to wear at concerts, with the most acrimonious discussions in the past having concerned the need to find an outfit that was equally suitable for women with the slender physique of

Kate Moss and those with a body shape more closely resembling Aretha Franklin. After several years of activity there was also the normal turnover of people leaving because of family or work commitments, or simply because they needed a change. Vanessa had lost some of her old faithfuls and she was in a particularly difficult position in terms of male voices. If a couple of the key men fell ill simultaneously or couldn't come for some reason she was effectively in deep trouble. What's more, there was nobody who could substitute her. She had to do all the musical arrangements, take the rehearsals and conduct at the concerts, sometimes even accompany the choir as well. Realistically, she thought it was probably time to take a break, but it was difficult to abandon something to which she had dedicated so much time and enthusiasm.

They all met up outside the chapel, hoping to have time for a quick rehearsal before Mass. They trooped in, laughing and chatting to one another, but drew to an abrupt halt in front of what appeared to be a dead body in a glass box in front of the altar.

"What on earth is that", asked Vanessa.

"Ah, I think the priest mentioned that the ceremony was partly to celebrate the pilgrimage of the blessed somebody or other", whispered Grazia, who came from the village and had been asked to involve the choir in the festivities.

"Is he embalmed or is it a wax replica, do you think?"

The choir members gathered round to peer into the box, but keeping a respectful distance.

"I think it's a sort of statue."

"It's very realistic though, are you sure it's not real? Aren't Saints' bodies supposed to be incorruptible?"

"No look. It's peeling a bit around the ear. It's a bit off-putting though, isn't it?"

At this point the priest emerged from a side door. Grazia went over to ask him where the choir should station itself and where they should set up the keyboard.

"He says that we should stand on the steps on the left-hand side of the altar and put the keyboard next to the Saint", she said when she returned.

"I'm not sitting next to that thing", muttered the accompanist. "It's unnerving."

"Don't be daft, it's only a statue", Vanessa urged him. "Look we can move you over a bit further to the left so you won't be right on top of him. In any case we need to get a move on."

The faithful were already starting to arrive, sliding into the wooden pews and glancing curiously at the glass case.

Vanessa hurriedly organised the choir, distributing the twenty members over three rows to the left of the altar as requested, but moving the keyboard over to the far left, which meant she had to conduct standing uncomfortably close to the Blessed Whatshisface. It felt an awful lot more like a funeral than a festive occasion, and she was beginning to feel very uncertain about her choice of repertoire. Suddenly joyous handclapping seemed rather out of place.

Clearly the choir had come to the same conclusion, because when she raised her arms to bring them in with the first piece she could see the misgiving on their faces. She smiled encouragingly as the accompanist played the introduction, trying to infuse them with confidence and willing them on. For one ghastly moment she thought nobody was going to sing at all, but eventually a few hesitant voices entered, followed by the rest of the choir when she glared at them furiously, but with such an evident lack of enthusiasm that she wondered whether it was better to just admit defeat. Perhaps she could pretend to faint?

Somehow they made it to the end of Mass without totally humiliating themselves, despite a spectacularly uninspiring rendition of a number of gospel classics. The congregation departed and the choir couldn't wait to get out of the church. They gathered outside, uncharacteristically silent and looking slightly guilty.

"That did not go particularly well", said Vanessa with classic British understatement. "I felt like you weren't even trying."

The general consensus was that it just didn't seem right, given the presence of the corpse/relic/statue in the box.

"But singing badly didn't make it any better", Vanessa pointed out. "It just made us look like twats. Anyway, let's try and forget it for the moment and concentrate on entertaining people after the refreshments in the church hall. I really need you to give me some enthusiasm. We have to make up for the uninspiring performance in church."

Everyone agreed sheepishly to do their best and they all made their way over to the hall, cheering up after a few glasses of cheap Spumante and some pizza. Fortunately, many of those who had been present at the church were elderly, and with a bit of luck slightly deaf, Vanessa hoped. At all events, they were disarmingly pleased to see the participation of 'young' people at the traditional local festival and just glad for a break in the routine. The Spumante also had a curative effect and the choir later managed to give a passable performance of some Italian classics, sticking in a couple of numbers from the film Sister Act for good measure.

Feeling a bit better about the whole thing, Vanessa embraced the choir members one by one as they all said goodbye before setting off home. A little hesitantly, she seized the chance to suggest that as they didn't have any engagements booked for the forthcoming weeks perhaps they should have a break and meet up after Easter to discuss the future of the choir. Despite some protests, she sensed that nobody was suicidally upset and that maybe she was not alone in thinking that it was time to move on. The choir had enriched her life, the choristers had become her friends, they had enjoyed good times together and she had made them take on things they would never have dreamed of, but she didn't feel she had anything to give them any more. All things have a natural life cycle, and this particular one was coming to an end. Maybe she would recover her enthusiasm in the future, but for the moment she just wanted one less responsibility.

She drove back home feeling strangely light-hearted. Normally giving a bad performance gave her a grim feeling in the pit of her stomach, even leading to insomnia, but today she felt positively bouncy. It could of course be the alcohol, but she suspected not, two or three glasses of wine being an insufficient dose for euphoria. No, she was simply relieved; relieved to have one less thing to worry about, one less thing to organise and one less thing to go wrong. Perhaps she could apply this to other areas of her life? Abandon her job and her family and go and live on a beach in Cambodia? This was perhaps taking things too far, but nevertheless it had its attractions. Even just thinking about it made her smile blissfully.

Ten minutes later she was back at home. Everyone was still out, but all the lights were on, a clear sign that the last person to leave was one of the kids, with further evidence being provided by the dirty plates all over the kitchen. Cambodia was looking more attractive by the minute. Normally the dog at least would have been jumping up and down with excitement at seeing her, but since his last attack she usually had to go on a search mission around the house to find him. On this occasion he was stuck upstairs, peering desperately over the top stair and whimpering, having gone up to look for her and then been unable to come back down again.

She cleared the table, poured herself a glass of port and settled down contentedly on the sofa, installing the dog on a cushion beside her. Time to enjoy a moment of peace.

CHAPTER 19

Marco had decided not to continue having private lessons with Clare at the school. He had paid for a 30-hour course and once this came to an end they had both agreed that it didn't make any sense for him to continue paying over the odds to Ursula, when he might as well just give the money to Clare directly. They had therefore established that she would go to his apartment once a week on Monday evenings for an official 'lesson', but because they always spoke English together anyway, the boundaries between lessons and their private life were pretty bleary.

On the Monday before Shrove Tuesday and the end of the Carnival celebrations, Clare was at Marco's flat as usual. Once they finished the lesson he poured them both a glass of wine and they leaned back against the white designer sofa, listening to a CD of classic blues, one of Marco's passions.

"How about going out for a meal on Wednesday", suggested Clare tentatively, having tired of waiting for him to invite her out for Valentine's Day.

"I'm afraid I can't. I already have an appointment."

"Oh, that's a shame. Is it for work?"

Marco looked just the tiniest bit uncomfortable.

"No, I promised to help my ex wife with something."

Alarm bells were starting to go off in Clare's head.

"You have an appointment with your ex wife on Valentine's Day? I mean, I know it's commercial and all that, but I wouldn't have thought you'd want to spend Saint Valentine's Day with your former wife."

"I didn't realise it was Valentine's Day when she ask me."

"Asked me. Well can't you ask her to change the date? I'm sure she won't mind."

"I don't think that will be possible. I think that she invites another couple too".

Clare was beginning to feel distinctly hard done by.

"Think she has invited. You mean that you are spending the most romantic day of the year with your former wife and another couple in a sort of foursome?"

"Foursome?"

"A group of four. Well great. You just have a good time while I spend the evening alone."

"Are you being sarcastic?"

"That's very astute of you. Isn't it enough that you have lunch every Sunday with your ex wife and your mother? I don't understand why your mother is so keen on her anyway. It was your wife who left you, wasn't it? I would have thought that your mother wouldn't have been best pleased with her?"

"I really don't want to talk about that now."

"Well maybe I do. Why do you never present me to your friends or relatives, but you continue seeing them together with your wife? Are you thinking of getting back together by any chance?"

"No, I'm not. Please Clare. I don't want to argue. Valentine's Day doesn't mean anything and we can go out the day after."

Clare's suppressed a mounting desire to smash the large glass ashtray over his head. "You just don't get it, do you? I feel like you don't want anyone to meet me, because I'm not important in your life."

"Naturally you are important, but my friends and family are another part of my life. I like to keep you as something separate and special."

"So special that you only want to see me a couple of times a week."

Marco got up and walked towards the window, clearly irritated.

"Clare, I'm a busy man. I don't always have time."

"I notice you find time to have dinner with your ex-wife though", Clare said peevishly, unable to restrain herself, despite being aware that she was getting on his nerves.

"I think this is not a useful discussion. I like to be with you. You like to be with me, I think. Why must we argue?"

"Because I don't know if that is enough, Marco. I don't want to be your part-time lover cum English teacher. I want to be part of your life, and not a separate part, however 'special', on the fringes of it. I'm not even sure I always want to be your English teacher, at least not all the time. Has it ever occurred to you that maybe I want to speak Italian so that I can improve *my* language skills?"

"You want to speak Italian? We speak Italian. I am just happy when you stop arguing."

"When *I* stop arguing? Of course, it's all my fault. In a way you are absolutely right. You are perfectly happy with things as they are, so fundamentally I have a choice: I can either accept the situation or I can get out, is that it?"

Marco was silent for a moment.

"I don't know if I can give you any more Clare, not yet."

"Of course you can, but you simply don't want to. You're won't even look at me now; you're just staring out of the window."

"So what do you want me to say?"

"Oh for heaven's sake Marco! If I have to tell you what to say then it really is time for me to get out."

Clare downed the last drop of wine, slammed the glass down on the coffee table and got up, going over to the armchair to pick up her coat. She prayed desperately that Marco would stop her, put his arms around her and tell her it was all a terrible mistake, but he remained obstinately at the window, looking out towards the street. She couldn't work out how things had degenerated so quickly, and she was torn between the desire to hold on to him for dear life, whatever the cost in terms of personal humiliation, and the need to retain some semblance of self-respect. After a moment's hesitation her pride gained the upper hand. There was no way she was going to back down now.

"Don't bother to show me out. I know the way." Clare lifted her chin and strode towards the door, making a pathetic attempt at a theatrical exit. After all, one doesn't study drama for nothing. As soon as she was outside the flat however, all she wanted to do was burst into floods of tears and collapse in a gelatinous blob on the pavement. After seriously considering this option, she decided to hold back her emotions until she reached the flat, where she could sob out her misery in solitude, flatmates permitting. If the worst came to the worst she could always lock her door and hide under the duvet.

She walked back through the centre of the city. It was not particularly late in the evening and there were still a fair number of people around, but in any case she had never felt threatened, even when she was out alone at night. At worst you might be hassled by somebody begging for a few coins, asking for a cigarette or trying to sell you useless fluorescent gadgets. Was there any city in the world, she wondered where that doesn't happen by now? Anywhere at all where there are no beggars, nobody sleeping rough in doorways, no smiling Africans trying desperately to sell you everything from wooden elephants and friendship bracelets to fake designer bags and packets of paper tissues?

Right on cue, a man lurched out from a doorway, clearly the worse for drink, or drugs, or both, planting himself in front of her. He held out a dirty hand, demanding a couple of euro for something to eat. When Clare attempted to walk around him he made a grab for her, trying to get hold of her shoulder bag. Without even thinking about it, she swung her bag directly at his head and simultaneously kicked him in the shin. Not normally given to physical violence, she couldn't remember when she had last been so furious. It must be leftover rage from her argument with Marco. In any case, there was no way that she was going to let him have her precious bag. It had already been a bloody awful evening and it was not going to conclude with some filthy drunk stealing her money and documents. Then horrified at her idiotic bravery, she hung on to her bag for dear life and ran.

She could hear footsteps behind her and she turned, terrified that the man was about to grab her from behind, only to find herself face-to-face with a young Asian man holding a bunch of roses.

"It's OK", he said reassuringly. "I saw everything. The man ran away so there's no need to be frightened. Are you alright?"

Clare's heart was beating so hard that she thought it might be about to explode.

"I think so. Just a bit shaken that's all", she said. She looked at him for a second, then burst into tears.

The flower-seller gently pushed her into one of the few cafes that was still open at that hour, buying her a cup of tea and sitting quietly opposite her, looking at her with his head tilted slightly to one side and listening politely as she explained tearfully how she had broken up with her boyfriend just before the unfortunate encounter with the drunk. It was strange how easy it was to confess her most intimate secrets to a complete stranger, but he was the best listener she had come across in a long time.

By the time they left the bar Clare felt emotionally and physically drained, but was secretly relieved that he insisted on accompanying her to the door of her flat. Feeling guilty that she had taken up so much of his time, in her turn Clare then insisted on buying all his roses. He did his best to refuse, but she knew how difficult it was for people like him to make a living, and he deserved to be rewarded for his thoughtfulness.

She said goodbye to her Good Samaritan and trudged up the stairs. Greta and Sarah were sitting on the sofa, watching TV and drinking beer, a row of empty bottles suggesting that they had been there for some considerable time.

"Ooh, those are lovely", said Sarah, admiring the roses. "Are they from Marco?"

"No they most definitely are not", replied Clare succinctly, without offering any further explanation. She stuck a vase under the kitchen tap to fill it with water and stuffed the flowers into it randomly, before making directly for her bedroom. For once she was in no mood for chatting.

CHAPTER 20

It was a cold sunny morning and Janet had seized the chance to go for a run. It had been an uncharacteristically warm winter so she had been jogging regularly outdoors, rather than going to a gym full of sweaty macho men in tank tops, bent on demonstrating that they could lift bigger weights than anybody else. Sometimes she was joined by her friend Susanna, but on other occasions she preferred to be alone, appreciating the silence of her solitary expeditions along the River Adige. It was her favourite time for both thinking and for forgetting everything, the physical effort having the dual effect of concentrating and relaxing the mind.

This morning she really needed a break, after yesterday's pilgrimage to IKEA and her subsequent lengthy efforts to assemble a modest-sized chest of drawers. It was difficult to believe that such an unexciting and inconsequential piece of furniture could involve such an inordinately large number of parts, including screws of three different lengths, something she only realised after used the wrong ones to attach the drawer fronts, meaning that she then had to dismantle them all and start again. Even after solving this problem, the drawers obstinately refused to roll properly along the tracks, probably because trying to simultaneously insert both sides without the assistance of a partner was challenging to say the least.

As an independent-minded woman she flatly dismissed the stereotype that girls were incapable of coping with the challenge of flat pack assembly, although after a couple of hours struggling with misaligned drawers and with the chest having actually drawn blood,

Janet did admit that there were perhaps some occasions when men came into their own, with DIY, unblocking drains and the removal of spiders being at the top of this list. In her case, however, her former boyfriends had been more the intellectual type than the "let me put that shelf up for you" variety, so their usefulness as self-assembly companions had been debatable. What's more the advantage of doing it by yourself was that at least there was nobody to argue with. Janet still vividly remembered one occasion when she had turned up unexpectedly at Vanessa's house, only to find that her friend was in the midst of assembling some garden furniture together with her husband, and only a short step away from divorce.

At all events, after three and a half hours of determined effort and a great deal of cursing in assorted languages, the battle had finally concluded with Janet's victory over the chest-of-drawers. She had celebrated the conquest with a large glass of chilled white wine, a bowl of spaghetti and a romantic comedy on the TV.

Now, she was enjoying the chilly winter air in her face, as she jogged at a constant pace, maintaining an easy rhythm with comparatively little effort. She was not one for pushing herself too hard, but she nevertheless found that physical exercise, especially in the open-air, gave her a slightly euphoric feeling, making her forget her existential doubts about motherhood and failed relationships.

There were plenty of other people around, taking advantage of the pleasantly warm and sunny winter's day. Essentially they could be divided into two main groups: keep fitters and dog-walkers. In their turn the keep fitters could be sub-divided into various different groups, going from plump middle-aged women, usually in twos or threes, walking at a fairly relaxed pace along the path as they engaged in the more serious business of gossiping, to serious runners training for marathons and competitive races . Janet fell somewhere in the middle, in the solitary joggers category. The dog-walkers, on the other hand, were the most sociable. Even if they were on their own they would often stop to chat to other dog-owners with compatible pets, having first ascertained that their dogs were not going to bite each other's heads off. This involved an initial series of questions at a discrete distance - Is it a male or a female? Does s/he get on with other dogs?- followed by careful observation of the warning signs – tail up or down/growling etc. – after which the dogs were allowed to approach each other , heading immediately for the rear end for the sniffing ritual. Social interaction for dogs was so much less complicated, though Janet, although there was perhaps something to be said for human hand-shaking as opposed to sniffing someone's rear when you'd just been introduced.

Janet noticed that as in many other fields, fashions had changed in terms of dogs. In Italy Alsatians, Dalmatians and Poodles were out, while Chihuahuas, Maltese and other lap dogs were definitely in, along with a few more macho and exotic dogs, such as the bulldog, Akita Inu and Shar Pei. Italian women did not miss the opportunity to use their mini dogs as a fashion accessory, dressing them in absurd little pink outfits or tartan coats and diamante collars. Why on earth, she wondered, would a dog, especially a long-haired breed, need a coat in the Italian winter anyway? We're not exactly at the North Pole and they've already got fur!

At all events, while the birth rate in Italy had declined radically in the last few decades, there had been a corresponding explosion in the number of pets, possibly to compensate for smaller families. During the economic crisis of the last few years, one of the few categories of businesses to see an expansion had been shops selling pet supplies and products. Italians had finally embraced the idea of the family dog with enthusiasm, after decades of Italian mammas relegating the dog to the garden, or hunting dogs left outside in large cages, only to be taken out for occasional expeditions on Sundays.

As Janet jogged gently along the path she thought she saw someone looking suspiciously like Ursula up ahead with a largish dog, possibly a golden retriever, but the idea seemed improbable given that as far as she knew, Ursula did not have a dog. As she came closer, however, she realised that it was indeed her employer, so she came to a halt, bouncing up and down on the spot as she spoke so as not to lose her rhythm.

"Hello Ursula. This is a surprise. I didn't know you had a dog."

"Hi Janet. It is not in fact my dog, but sometimes I take him out for my friend when she is working."

"Well, he's a beautiful dog", Janet caressed the retriever behind the ears "and very friendly."

"Yes, he's gorgeous. I love dogs".

"You should get one of your own", suggested Janet.

"It is not really possible, with the school and so many engagements, but maybe in the future I will get a very small dog, like a Chihuahua or a Pomeranian."

Of course, thought Janet, you could count on Ursula to get the dog of the moment, and then naturally she could carry him around in a designer handbag. A leopard print one probably.

"Actually I really prefer Labradors, but the small dog he is so convenient, don't you think?"

"I've never had a dog myself", commented Janet. "We always had cats in our family. But I think that once you have a dog it probably doesn't make that much difference how big it is. You still have to take it out for walks every day. That's what I like about cats. They're more independent."

"Yes, but the dog he is so much more rewarding", said Ursula "and always he is happy to see you."

"Cats are happy to see you too. And so much more hassle-free!"

"But not a real friend, like a dog", insisted Ursula. "A dog he is almost like a substitute for a child, but much nicer, with fur on."

"Good grief Ursula. I hardly think you can compare a baby to a Chihuahua! Anyway I think I need to keep moving, otherwise I'm going to get cold. I'll see you later at the school." The two women said goodbye and Janet continued her run, arriving at the dam across the river, before turning around and heading back towards her flat.

As she jogged however, her mind kept returning to Ursula's words, churning around in a sort of loop. Ursula was right. In terms of the amount of care and attention required, on a scale of one to ten children were obviously a ten and a cat was probably around a one, while a dog probably came in at around a three or a four. So, Janet said to herself, if she was the sort of person who preferred cats to dogs because they are more independent, would she ever be able to cope with taking care of a child, or rather was she sure she wanted to? In which case, why did she desire a child so intensely? From a practical point of view the question was purely academic, as there was no man on the scene, nor did there seem to be any realistic prospects in the future, but there was still a small window of time in which she was sure if she really, really wanted, she would be able to find someone to have a baby with. It might not be anybody she actually wanted to live with, but there was bound to be somebody out there who could fulfil the mechanical function of getting her pregnant. The problem was that like so many before her, she didn't want to take whatever came along, just because she was getting close to her sell by date. She wanted the whole thing: the passionate love story, the life companion, the deep meaningful relationship culminating in the decision to have a baby together. Was she going to get it? The odds were against her, but she hadn't given up hope yet.

CHAPTER 21

Vanessa was on her way into Verona to meet her accountant. This did not rate particularly high on her list of fun things to do at the best of times, and on this occasion she was particularly irritated, because she had a lengthy translation to finish, instead of which she was obliged to waste most of the afternoon driving into the city, so that she could then be given some sort of device necessary to produce a digital signature. In their infinite wisdom, the authorities had decided that translations done for public sector clients now needed to be accompanied by a complicated series of forms, which then had to be signed digitally and returned via certified electronic mail. With each year that passed the bureaucratic procedures had become more difficult and more costly, ostensibly with the scope of discouraging tax evasion and money laundering, but effectively leading many self-employed workers to abandon a losing battle or else to go underground. It had now got to the stage that she sometimes spent more time dealing with the various administrative and invoicing procedures than effectively doing translations. It would indeed have been more profitable, and infinitely less hassle, just to do private English lessons at home and not declare anything at all, but the problem was that she unfortunately enjoyed translating far more than teaching.

She thought she had left plenty of time, but as soon as she got in the car, she realised that Ben had of course left it with a near-empty fuel tank, a problem well-known to parents with adult children living at home. This meant she was obliged to stop off at the very first petrol station she came to, given that with the extremely approximate fuel warning system of the Yaris there was no way of knowing whether she could make it for another 3 or 30 km. In theory, the last bar on the gauge was supposed to flash faster as you neared disaster, but in practice the difference was only noticeable if you happened to be watching at the precise instant it changed speed from 4 to 4.2 times a second. Having queued to fill up with petrol, she then got stuck at the temporary traffic lights, due to 'tree maintenance' work along the main road, which cost her another ten minutes. Once this obstacle had been overcome she made fairly good progress until she got to Verona, but here of course she had to match her wits against the one-way system. She had never been to the accountant's new premises, but as far as she could see on the map, she needed to turn off the main road before getting to the bridge over the river.

To make quite sure she didn't get lost, albeit with some qualms about the efficacy of GPS navigation, she stopped to set up the sat-nav before she got into town. This took another five minutes, but was better than losing far more time going round in circles. She proceeded cautiously, following the instructions imparted by the robotic female voice, calculating that she must be pretty near her destination and confident that she could still get to the office on time. The voice placidly instructed her to turn left at the next junction, so Vanessa carefully positioned herself in the centre of the carriageway and put on the indicator, only to discover of course that the next road was a one-way street in the other direction.

"I can't turn left, damn it. It's a one-way street." She was forced to continue straight on, the road transforming itself into a dual carriageway with a cement barrier down the middle of the road, thus ensuring it was impossible to take any of the subsequent turnings on the left.

"Turn around when possible", the robotic voice encouraged her.

"I would if I could, you bloody useless gadget" Vanessa shouted at her phone.

By this time it was too late and she had been channelled into the one-way system and over the bridge. Why was it, she wondered, that her husband and men generally, had such faith in GPS navigation, when in her experience one invariably ended up in the middle of nowhere, or getting a fine for driving through the restricted traffic zone?

Fifteen minutes and various complicated manoeuvres later she finally managed to drive back over the bridge in the opposite direction, having turned off the sat-nav and consulted a proper map. Now all she had to do was find a parking place. Rather than risking getting stuck in the system once again, she decided to park in the first free place she saw and walk to the office. There seemed to be several places free, but all limited to a sixty minute stay, so she parked in the nearest, fairly confident that she wouldn't be more than an hour.

Relieved to have finally arrived somewhere near where she was supposed to be going, she leaned back against the seat. Only ten minutes late, so not too bad. She noticed a bottle of mineral water lying on the seat and took a large swig before getting out of the car, only to snort with shock when the liquid hit her palate. To save money at the disco the previous evening, Ben must have filled up the half-litre plastic bottle with neat gin, not even gin and tonic! Taken totally by surprise, she automatically spat it out, spraying gin all over her coat. Great. She could hardly present herself at the accountant's office smelling overwhelming of gin, as if she had just consumed a bottle of neat alcohol at 3 o'clock in the afternoon. She quickly took off her coat and dumped it on the passenger seat, shivering in her flimsy top. It was, inevitably, one of the coldest days of the winter, but hopefully if she walked really fast she would warm up a bit.

Five minutes later she finally arrived at her destination, but discovered that the accountant had not yet arrived, being himself also stuck in traffic somewhere. She was ushered into his office by the secretary and left there, fuming slightly. There's nothing more annoying than rushing around like a lunatic because you're late, only to discover that the person you're meeting is even later than you, meaning that you could in fact have saved all the energy and anxiety you expended uselessly on worrying about being late. Her irritation mounted as each minute passed and she was close to boiling point when the door finally opened and the accountant walked in calmly.

"I'm so sorry I'm late. I hope you haven't been waiting long."

"Just a few minutes", she replied through gritted teeth, smiling forcedly. What she actually wanted to say was something quite different, involving a string of imprecations and quite possibly physical violence, but given that this would inevitably have led to her being forcibly removed from his office, she restrained herself by making recourse to superhuman control.

The accountant spent the next half an hour explaining how to adopt the USB device, insert the necessary codes and make use of the software in order to sign documents digitally. Vanessa tried to concentrate, but found her mind automatically switching off in an attempt to avoid the colossal boredom of the bureaucratic procedures involved. In any case, she was well aware that although everything seemed perfectly clear now, the moment she got home and inserted the device into her own computer, her mind would go completely blank and she would have to resort to her usual system, which involved clicking on everything available until something familiar popped up.

Her approach to technology was essentially based on trial and error, with the consultation of instruction manuals being considered only as a very last recourse, given that the relevant handbook had usually disappeared into the deep void created by her husband's occasional and random efforts at "organising our documents". This meant the only valid solution was to download the manual from the internet, not in itself impossible, but often requiring you to know exactly which version you were using. To find this out you would normally consult the handbook, something which of course you don't have, otherwise you wouldn't be trying to download it in the first place. Thus you enter a vicious circle of ignorance, the only possibility of interrupting it being to look up on the web how to find out which version you are using, so that you then download the instructions for whatever technological device you are trying to use at the time, by which time you have probably given up on the whole idea anyway.

"So is that all clear?" asked the accountant.

Vanessa rapidly returned to the present.

"Perfectly, thank you."

"Well, you can always call me if you need any help", suggested the accountant, somewhat rashly in Vanessa's opinion, as he handed her the USB key and card.

"Great. I'll do that." Vanessa stuffed everything into her handbag. "I think I really should be going, otherwise I may end up getting a parking fine."

They shook hands and Vanessa left the office, heading for the car as rapidly as an unfit middle-aged woman reasonably could, both in an attempt to arrive at her vehicle before the sixty minutes ran out, and to avoid freezing to death given that she had no coat. When she got there she had a moment of panic when she saw something yellow stuck under the windscreen wiper, but breathed a sigh of relief when she realised it was only a flyer advertising a new Chinese restaurant.

She planned out the next few hours in her head: stop off at the supermarket to get emergency supplies; mustn't forget to buy coffee; consider the idea of buying take-away sushi for the kids so it won't be necessary to cook; take advantage of cheap fuel at the supermarket to top up fuel tank; stop off in the village to pay the mechanic on the way back; stop off at the vet's to get prescription for heart medicine for the dog: go to chemist, if it hasn't closed already, to get said medicine; get back and prepare something to eat (take-away option appearing increasingly more appealing); finish doing translation, given final deadline of 9 o'clock the following morning. Yes, it could be done.

"I've got this", Vanessa said to the world generally. For some reason a line from a song - was it by Phil Collins? - kept coming into her head: "Oh, think twice, it's another day for you and me in paradise."

CHAPTER 22

Janet had kindly offered to take Clare to the airport to pick up her mum, despite her protests that her mother could easily have caught the bus.

"She's really quite independent, you know. She goes all over the place without worrying about it."

"I know, but it's always nice to avoid the hassle of getting public transport, especially when you're new to a place. Anyway, it's no problem. I'm not working until later and it'll be nice to meet your mother."

Janet dropped Clare off as close as possible to the arrivals hall of the airport, then driving off to wait in the road to avoid exceeding the maximum 15 minute period for free parking. Clare had of course offered to pay, but her friend refused to consider the exorbitant short-term parking charges.

She was a few minutes early so she made her way into the airport at a leisurely pace, wandering over to the arrivals screen to see when the flight was expected. She was surprised to see that the aircraft had already landed and hurried over to towards the automatic doors discharging arriving passengers, hoping that her mother had not been uncharacteristically quick through passport control. She was unlikely to have any baggage to pick up, being well-known for her ability to travel anywhere in the world for surprisingly long periods carrying only one small item of cabin luggage, mostly because her lack of interest in clothes was legendary.

Clare stationed herself midway between the two possible exits, a large opaque glass barrier making it impossible to see whether the emerging passengers were heading one way or the other. A young woman was greeted enthusiastically by a large welcoming committee, stopping directly in front of the exit so that nobody else could get past, with exiting passengers trying desperately to squeeze around the trolley and excited relatives, the family as a whole being entirely oblivious to the havoc they were causing.

Clare finally spotted her mum heading out of the other exit, wearing the inevitable black jeans and well-worn leather jacket, her shoulder length blonde hair tied back in a pony tail. Clare waved frantically, unable to get round the throng of people. As ever, her mother failed to see her and after peering briefly around, she started to move away, heading towards the doors out of the terminal building. Clare pushed through the crowd, shouting "Mum, Mum" as her mother made her way towards the exit, oblivious to her daughter's efforts to reach her. Clare finally managed to catch up with her as she was about to leave the building.

"Mum, where are you going? I told you I'd wait for you in the arrivals hall."

Her mother embraced her affectionately.

"Oh did you darling? I thought you might have forgotten, or I might have understood wrong and you meant outside the arrivals hall. Anyway, it's lovely to see you."

"And you. Did you have a good journey?"

"Yes thanks. No problems at all."

Clare pulled her mobile out of her pocket and rapidly sent a text to Janet, with the dexterity that distinguishes those who grew up in the era of mobile phones from the older generation, who take ten minutes to type in a telegraphic message with one index finger.

"I'm just letting Janet know that you've arrived. She's waiting round the corner, ready to come and pick us up."

"It's really nice of her. I do appreciate it. Maybe we could all go out for lunch somewhere in Verona."

"That would be good, because then I'll have to leave you to your own devices. I'm teaching this afternoon."

The two women stationed themselves in a strategic position opposite the building, waiting for Janet to appear with the car. When she drew up Clare flung her mother's case into the back seat and hopped in after it, inviting her mum to sit in the front seat. She introduced the two women, who seemed to hit it off immediately, and suggested that they all head for a wine bar or small restaurant in the centre of the city for a quick lunch before lessons started in the afternoon.

Despite being initially reluctant, thinking that mother and daughter might want some time to themselves, Janet gave in to pressure from the other two, and the three women were soon comfortably seated in a small trattoria, not far from the school. Clare's mum had the knack of putting people at their ease and Janet was uncharacteristically forthcoming, chatting away with a loquacity that made Clare think that perhaps she had misjudged her. Indeed Janet's presence made it almost easier, as it avoided her mother concentrating all her attention on her and asking her endless questions, something which for some reason always made her irrationally irritated. All in all, they spent a pleasant couple of hours swapping stories, enjoying a plate of pasta and a bottle of local red wine, although most of the wine was drunk by Clare's mum, as the only one not required to do any work that afternoon.

"I hope you don't mind", she said as she finished off the bottle "but it seems such a shame to leave it, don't you think? My generation was always taught to finish everything on the plate, and I really believe we should follow the same philosophy for wine. Waste not, want not!"

Later that evening Clare was tackling food and drink with the traffic wardens. They had indeed lived up to their reputation, not as the most difficult group to teach, but certainly as those making the least progress over the year, and by now she was fairly resigned to the fact that she was never going to succeed in making them fluent English speakers. There had been a perhaps predictable burst of enthusiasm when they had reached the lesson on giving directions, and Clare was fairly confident that by now they could all provide very basic walking or driving directions to foreign tourists, so long as the tourists asked the right questions. Even Giorgio I had made a superhuman effort and had actually succeeded in learning three phrases: go straight on, turn left and turn right. To ask any more of him than this, Clare felt, was putting unreasonable pressure on his single brain cell. He was a charming man and it was not fair to humiliate him simply because he was constitutionally unfit to undertake serious study.

One of the reasons why some of the others made so little progress was that they frequently skipped lessons. Human nature being what it is, as they hadn't had to pay for the course themselves, they were much less worried about attending, and to be realistic, given the overall level of the class, the brighter ones could easily recover two or three missed lessons with minimal effort. There were however a few assiduous participants who never played truant, including Fabrizio, Maria and another woman called Tiziana, who were regarded by the rest of the group as linguistic geniuses, acting as translators for the other participants.

This evening they were working on everyday situations involving food and drink, like ordering a meal at a restaurant, buying food supplies at the supermarket or just making conversation about food.

"What are your favourite foods?" Clare asked Fabrizio.

"I like meat."

"OK, what kind of meat do you like?"

"Beef, pig.."

"You mean pork."

"Yes, beef, pork and kitchen."

"I think you mean chicken," Clare smiled. Italians always had a problem with kitchen and chicken. To be fair, maybe all foreigners did, but she had only ever taught Italians. She had lost count of the number of times her students had told her that their mother was in the chicken. Of course the first time this was absolutely hilarious, but after a while it became like an old joke, wearing a bit thin.

"Now you ask someone a question", she suggested to Fabrizio.

He turned to Giorgio and Clare was already groaning inwardly; "What are your favourite foods?"

"Che?" Giorgio looked completely bewildered.

"What is your favourite food?" Fabrizio tried again, more slowly.

Giorgio looked hopefully at Maria, who whispered the translation loudly under her breath.

"Pasta", replied Giorgio with conviction.

"What sort of pasta?"

More bewilderment. More instructions from Maria.

Giorgio shrugged eloquently.

"Pasta."

"Pasta with meat sauce? Pasta with tomato sauce?" Clare tried stepping in to give Fabrizio a hand.

"Pasta". There was a long pause for thought, and more muttered explanations from Maria. Giorgio considered the question for some time, and then said with satisfaction "Pasta all'amatriciana".

Clare decided that this was as much as they were realistically going to get out of him, so switched her attention to Maria.

"So Maria, can you tell us how to make pasta all'amatriciana?"

This was a challenging one, but Maria made a decent attempt at describing how to make the dish and Clare spent the rest of the lesson swapping recipes with her students, sometimes in English, but more frequently in Italian, as people became more and more excited about the correct procedure and ingredients. They rapidly lapsed into their native tongue in order to urge their case, while Clare made occasional and generally unsuccessful attempts to get her students to communicate in English. There is nothing Italians take so seriously as food, except perhaps football, she thought. The British can spend hours talking about the weather, the Italians can spend days talking about food.

All in all it was a reasonably successful lesson, and Clare was pleasantly surprised when she looked at the clock and realised that it was time to wind up for the day. The students took their leave, still arguing passionately about exactly how to make an authentic pesto sauce, while Clare put away her books and turned off the computer. She put on her coat and headed towards the door, saying goodbye to Ursula as she left, before

155

making her way down the now familiar stairs and out into the street.

As soon she came out into the street she saw a familiar figure and her heart missed a beat. Marco was standing next to the entrance, as hellishly handsome and elegant as ever, wearing a long navy blue coat and clearly waiting for her to finish work.

"Clare, I try many times to call you, but you never answer your phone, so I come to meet you."

"I don't know about 'many' times. You mean three or four, maybe. Anyway I don't particularly want to talk to you." Clare lied. She was of course dying to talk to him, but only if he was going to admit that he was totally in the wrong and tell her that he was hopelessly in love with her.

"So we can go now and talk."

"No, we can't. I have to get back. My mother is staying in Verona and I said I would meet her for dinner."

"Can't she wait a little?"

"No, she can't. When did you ever keep your mother waiting? Anyway I'm hungry."

"OK, when can we meet then?"

"Oh I don't know. Mum's only here for a few days and I want to spend some time with her." Clare started to move away. She didn't want to risk Ursula coming down the stairs and finding them there.

"Can I at least walk with you to the apartment?" Marco asked.

"I'm just going round the corner to Mum's hotel, but you can come as far as there if you like, so long as you don't expect to come in and be introduced, after all I've never been introduced to your mother." Her remark sounded childish and petulant, even to her own ears.

Clare relented during the few minutes it took them to get to the hotel and agreed to meet Marco two days later, as she knew her mother was planning to go to Venice for the day. They stopped at the entrance and said goodbye, hovering slightly awkwardly before kissing each other on both cheeks, after which Marco turned away and headed back in the direction they had come from. Meanwhile, Clare pushed the heavy glass door of the hotel, to find her mother sitting directly opposite in one of the leather armchairs around the reception desk.

"Hello darling. Who was that you were speaking to?"

"Oh, just a guy".

"Well he was a very good-looking guy. Gorgeous, in fact." Her mother eyed her suspiciously.

"Mum, please!"

"OK, I promise I won't ask for any more details. Come on. Let's go and have something to eat."

CHAPTER 23

Two days later, Clare's mother had departed on a day trip for Venice, armed with a packed lunch and a thermos full of hot tea. The thermos made her feel a bit like she was going on an OAP outing, but given the notorious tendency of the Venetians to fleece visiting tourists, she was taking precautions, while nevertheless keen to revisit a city she hadn't seen since she was in her 20s and that she still recalled with affection. Its unique beauty more than made up for the disadvantages in terms of cost and mosquitoes.

Since she left, Clare had spent the morning worrying about the meeting with Marco, going through various scenarios in her head. They had arranged to meet in the early afternoon, once Marco finished work, but before she began, which only left them a window of about an hour and a half. They had chosen a neutral location, neither her place nor his, preferring a quiet cafe close to the English school. They sat opposite each other, neither quite knowing how to begin, with Clare staring blankly into her teacup and Marco hesitating before finally deciding to take the plunge.

"So why do you not want to speak to me?"

"Because I don't know that there is anything to say. The more I think about it, the more I realise that I don't want to just hang around waiting for you to find a moment to fit me in. It's almost as if you were still married and I am the bit on the side."

"Bit on the side?" Marco looked perplexed.

"Your lover, extra-marital affair."

"No. I am not yet divorced, but I do not live with my wife and you are not a secret."

"But I feel like I'm secret. I've never met your friends or family. Are you in some way embarrassed by me? Or just not sure whether it's serious enough to justify introducing me to them?"

"Of course I'm not ashamed of you. It's just difficult because my friends and family knew my wife very well".

"So at what point do you think I might be allowed to become a bigger part of your life? In three months? Six months? More than that?"

Marco shrugged. "I don't know. Can we not just wait and see how things develop?"

Clare paused for a moment before answering. "Of course we *can,* the problem is that I don't know if I want to. I may be young, but that doesn't mean I waste my time waiting for someone who is never going to make up his mind. I can't wait forever."

"It will not be forever, just a little time".

Clare looked down at her feet. It wasn't really the answer she had been waiting for. What she really wanted to hear, of course, was that he was madly in love with her, didn't care if he ever saw his ex-wife again and wanted to introduce her to his mother because he was certain that she was the love of his life. Maybe that just didn't happen in the real world. She was afraid that she was keener on him than he was on her, which was fundamentally rather humiliating. So it was a question of whether she accepted his terms and continued the relationship, hoping that it would develop in the direction she hoped, or cut her losses now, before she got too attached.

"I don't think that's enough for me, Marco. I'm not saying that you have to dedicate all your spare time to me, but I want to be more than a part-time girlfriend."

Marco sighed. "It's difficult for me. Why don't we go away for a weekend? Not this one, I am busy, but maybe the next one. No, I remember I have a conference. The one after that."

"I'm sure it would be lovely, but then it would just be back to square one; 2 evenings a week and a weekend every month or two."

"But I like being with you!"

"But evidently not enough to make any changes to your life! Look, we're just going over old ground. I think we need some time off to think about it."

"Time off? What is time off?"

"A break, a pause for thought."

Marco paused for just slightly too long before speaking, causing Clare to wonder whether he was really that bothered. He just didn't seem to have quite the right degree of enthusiasm.

"But I don't want a time off. I want to see you."

"Well, I'm afraid it's all or nothing. You can't have half." Clare looked him straight in the face.

Marco shifted about on his seat in silence, clearly uncertain how to answer and scrupulously avoiding her gaze. He looked down. He looked up. He looked anywhere but at her.

Clare decided it was probably the moment to beat a hasty retreat, before she embarrassed herself by bursting into tears.

"Well I think it would be a good idea if you took some time to consider it, and decide whether you really want to be with me," she said, trying desperately to be adult about it, but probably fooling no one. "I have to go to work anyway, so let's not see each other for a couple of weeks and then see how we feel, OK? She got to her feet energetically, in a hurry to get out of the bar as quickly as possible, before her emotions got the better of her.

Marco grabbed her hand for a moment, just as she was about to leave.

"OK Clare, but please you think about it too. I think you are too much in a hurry."

"Goodbye, Marco." She pulled her hand away and headed for the door, leaving him to pay the bill. He earned five times as much as she did anyway.

She didn't have enough time to go home, so she went directly to the school, wanting nothing less than to spend the rest of the day teaching, when what she really wanted to do was go home and cry properly. However, her state of mind was evidently clearer than she thought, because as soon as she got in Janet looked up from the reception desk.

"Are you alright Clare? You don't look very happy."

"No I guess not. I've just broken up with Marco", her mouth trembled.

Janet took one look at her and decided a cup of tea was necessary, steering her into her office and sitting her down in one of the fake leather armchairs.

"I broke it off and I'm not even sure why I did it. I think I've made a terrible mistake," wailed Clare,

"Oh believe me, I know how you feel."

That stopped Clare in her tracks.

"Oh God, I'm such a fool. I completely forgot. You're the last person I should be talking to."

"I don't see why. I'm probably the person who understands you the best."

"Why, did you regret it too when you broke it off?"

"Well, yes and no. Marco is handsome and intelligent and good company. How could I not regret leaving him?

But on the other hand, I felt really strongly that he wasn't ready for another serious relationship, and I'm too old to make do with anything less. Frankly, I'd rather be on my own."

"You're not old", said Clare generously but not entirely convincingly. "Anyway, I'm younger than you, but I still don't want to be a sort of zero-hours girlfriend, someone he can call on when he feels like it."

"I know exactly how you feel. But in some ways I also understand Marco. He had a pretty terrible time when his marriage ended, and now he finds it difficult to trust women, so he tries to keep relationships on a more casual level, to avoid getting hurt again. He'll get over it in the end, but I think it'll take him some time."

"Yes, I think you're right, but I don't want to hang around waiting for him to sort himself out!" said Clare. "The trouble is though, that I think I'm a little bit in love with him, so now I'm wondering whether it isn't better to have him part-time, rather than not at all. What on earth should I do? "

"Well, in this case you probably are asking the wrong person. Look at me. I'm still single at thirty-five, so probably not the best person to ask about relationships! However, if I were you I would wait and see for a few days. Maybe the fact that you aren't willing to be walked over will make him realise that he cares more for you than he thinks."

"Or maybe he'll just substitute me with someone else more accommodating".

"In which case he's not worth bothering about", concluded Janet.

"Oh, I don't know. You're probably right, but I feel quite jealous already. I don't want him to be happy with another woman. I want him to be madly in love with me!"

"Unfortunately Prince Charming doesn't always appear at the perfect moment, riding a white charger and behaving as he's expected to in romantic stories. I may be old and cynical, but in my experience people as a whole, and men in particular, are full of imperfections. They always carry a fair amount of emotional baggage with them and it's inevitably a question of weighing up whether their positive qualities compensate for their defects."

Clare looked up at the clock. "Oh God, it's nearly time for my pre-intermediate class. I must go to the bathroom and tidy up a bit before the lesson. Do I look totally crappy, like with mascara running down my face?"

Janet studied her. "No, you're more or less OK, although your eyes are a tiny bit red. Just go and sort yourself out a bit and nobody will notice. If you're really desperate, show them a short film for the first fifteen minutes to give yourself some time to recover your aplomb."

"OK. Thanks Janet, I appreciate it."

"You're welcome."

Clare gathered up her things and left the room, making a dash past Ursula at the reception desk in order to launch herself into the bathroom. Five minutes later she was ready for action.

CHAPTER 24

The lesson hadn't even started but Vanessa was already regretting the decision to try out Zumba exercise classes. The other participants appeared to be uniformly thin and suspiciously fit-looking, even those of her own age, with well-toned bodies encased in figure-hugging fluorescent Lycra gear. She, on the other hand, was wearing an oversized t-shirt, in a vain attempt to hide the worst bulges, and a pair of baggy black track suit bottoms. The instructor was a Brazilian woman apparently without a single gram of surplus body fat, her long black hair tied back in a ponytail that was so tight that it was almost an alternative to a facelift.

Vanessa had decided to make another of her sporadic attempts at doing physical exercise. She had never really enjoyed doing sport, especially team games, and although she liked going for walks she needed the perfect weather (not too hot, not too cold) and gasp-eliciting panoramas to really appreciate it. She had been a fat adolescent, although she had in fact between quite slim for most of her adult life, and she could date her dislike of sport back to her school days. She could still remember the humiliation of always being chosen last for the hockey and basketball teams, and the annual torture of school sports days, when everyone was forced to participate in relay races and she would arrive panting in last place, having inevitably and once again let down her team. Her chosen speciality in athletics was throwing the discus, not because she had any talent for it whatsoever, but purely she was allowed to retreat to the bottom of the hockey pitch to practice on her own. By the time she was fifteen or sixteen she had lost a lot of weight and there was no intrinsic reason for her to be worse than average at sport and games in general, but by this time she had channelled her energies into intellectual rather than physical activities, making a show of disparaging athletic and sporting prowess.

Vanessa placed herself in a strategically central position towards the back of the class, but not in the very last row, in case at any point the choreography involved turning around. That way she would always have someone in front of her to copy, whichever direction they were facing. This was a trick she had learned many years ago during dance classes, as she suffered from a chronic inability to remember choreographic routines. She had chosen Zumba because of the dance element, and because at least there was some music to relieve the monotony of exercise, and having studied dance for several years she was fairly sure that she would be able to keep up with the steps.

The lesson started off in a deceptively relaxed manner, with some simple stretching and mobility exercises, but the pace rapidly stepped up and after about fifteen minutes Vanessa was already perspiring heavily and out of breath. She was pleased with her ability to follow the routine, but as the minutes passed she was sweating so much that she was scattering droplets around her like the scene from Flashdance when the protagonist empties a bucket of water over herself, but in a decidedly less sexy way. Her hair was plastered to her face and her t-shirt was sticking to her in a sort of parody of a wet t-shirt contest. She would most certainly not have won a beauty pageant in her current state. However, her physical appearance was the least of her worries at the moment, as she concentrated on surviving until the end of the lesson, something which seemed increasingly unlikely with each minute that passed. There was of course nothing preventing her from dropping out, but although by nature somewhat lazy, she was also bloody-minded, and there was no way she was going to admit defeat and allow a simple Zumba class to get the better of her.

One way or another, although she was not really sure how, she got to the end of the lesson and retreated to the changing room to throw cold water over her face. It was not a pretty sight in the mirror. She was not so much red as completely puce, a sort of aubergine colour guaranteed to put anyone off for life. She slumped onto the bench and struggled to regain her composure.

Some of the younger women were looking at her askance, although it was not clear to Vanessa whether this was because they were concerned she was going to pass out, or because they were smugly enjoying their youthful superiority.

"Are you alright", asked one of the other class members in a concerned voice.

"I think so", she gasped. "I'll tell you in a few minutes."

"It's a really tough class. I had terrible trouble too at the beginning."

Vanessa looked up at her fellow participant with some incredulity. She appreciated her efforts to reassure her, but frankly she didn't look like the kind of person who ever lost her aplomb. Vanessa strongly suspected that she was the sort of woman who didn't even perspire, at most she glowed. There were no evident damp patches, her make-up was perfectly applied, and not a hair was out of place.

"I doubt it, but thanks for trying to make me feel better."

"No really, I was tremendously unfit, but it does get easier after a few lessons."

"I think it would take rather a lot in my case, and to be honest I don't know whether I can survive long enough."

"My name's Gilda, by the way. Nice to meet you."

"Like Rigoletto's daughter? It's a pleasure to meet you too." Vanessa was beginning to recover, at least sufficiently to realise that she was not going to die in the next 10 minutes.

"Ah, so you're an opera lover", concluded Gilda.

"I am indeed one of that rare species. And you?"

"I like going to the opera at the Arena in Verona in the summer, but I couldn't claim to be an expert. I don't really have anyone to go with."

"Well maybe we could go together. I usually manage to drag my husband along once, but any more than that is pushing my luck, so it would be nice to have some opera-loving companions."

"That would be great. We can talk about it nearer the time. Do you think you will be coming back to Zumba?"

"Well, I've paid for the first month, so I suppose I'll give it a go for a few lessons, but if things don't get easier I can't guarantee I'll continue", Vanessa sighed.

"OK I look forward to seeing you next time then", smiled Gilda, who had by this time changed out of her immaculate fitness gear into another impeccable outfit and was briskly making her way out of the changing room. She turned to wave goodbye to Vanessa, who was pulling on her clothes apathetically with the rapidity of an asthmatic sloth.

Vanessa took another look at herself in the mirror. She was now no longer puce, but still violently red. From experience she knew that it would take some substantial time before she returned to her habitual whiter than white, so she might as well get going. All the other participants had by now left and the next group had arrived for their course. This lot appeared to be even younger, slimmer and fitter than the last, so she was glad at least that she hadn't attempted to go for kick-boxing.

She made a mental note to drive to the gym next time, despite the fact that it was only ten minutes away from home on foot, because at least she would have been able to hide in the car, rather than having to walk past all her neighbours looking like a sun-burnt Miss Piggy, with lank hair dangling down the sides of her face.

When she finally got home, her husband looked at her in some alarm.

"Good grief. Are you alright? You look terrible."

"Thank you so much", she replied shortly. "It was a bit more energetic than I thought."

"You really should do more exercise, you know, and perhaps think about your diet more."

"I know your intentions are good", said Vanessa "but I strongly suggest that you don't say any more if you value your safety!"

Giovanni wisely shut up and retreated to the kitchen.

"Shall I make dinner?" he asked in a conciliatory tone.

"That would be very nice, thank you", Vanessa slumped onto the sofa, desperately desiring a large gin and tonic, preferably accompanied by a large packet of cheese and onion crisps, but decided that it would wipe out any possible advantage she might have gained from the sixty minutes of suffering endured at Zumba. Come on woman, a minimum of self-control is required if you don't want to look like a beached whale this summer, she thought to herself. It was a question of deciding whether it was better to accept with grace the fact that her body was apparently exploding out of control, convincing herself she was beautiful anyway, or to go on a drastic diet and subject her body to the torments of exercise, thus in theory resolving the situation. To all appearances, the answer was obvious; being thinner was healthier, made you feel better about yourself and meant you could get back into the clothes you wore a couple of years earlier and was in every possible respect a win win situation. So why did it feel so completely impossible? Why did the very thought of cutting back on completely unnecessary calories leave her feeling depressed before she had even started? Likewise, the idea of regular physical exercise had all the appeal of a cold bath in February. She couldn't even pretend it was because she didn't have time. She was of course very busy, with her teaching and translation work, family commitments and efforts to keep the house vaguely tidy, but if she was honest with herself she could always find twenty minutes to do the Sudoku in yesterday's newspaper, or an hour to read a book before falling asleep, so she could perfectly well go out for a brisk walk for half an hour, or do twenty minutes on the exercise bike. The reality was simply that while she both required and enjoyed intellectual stimulation, she hated getting hot, tired and sweaty in order to keep in shape.

"Want a gin and tonic?" shouted Giovanni from the kitchen. It was one of the few British traditions he had taken on board.

Vanessa hesitated only very briefly.

"Well…perhaps just a tiny one."

CHAPTER 25

Hearing the unmistakeable sound of a wheelie suitcase clonking over the marble floor, Janet looked up from the reception desk, to find a distinctly attractive young man with a red beard standing there. He was tall, slender and probably in his mid twenties, she estimated. His pale complexion and the way he was dressed suggested that he was very unlikely to be Italian, in fact Janet was willing to bet that he was British. It wasn't just the physical features, but also the cultural differences that were the giveaway. Italian men were inordinately careful about their appearance, just like Italian women or sometimes even more than their women, whereas British men tended to look like they had got dressed in the dark, grabbing the first thing that came to hand.

"Can I help you?" she asked.

"I was looking for Clare. I believe she works here. She told me to drop by when I arrived." He had a pleasant deep voice, and from the accent was most definitely English.

"Clare's teaching at the moment, but she should have finished in about half an hour. Are you the cousin?" Janet asked, recalling that Clare had mentioned that her cousin would be arriving today from the UK.

"That's right", he smiled at her. "My name's David. I've come to do a bit of research on Italian art."

"Nice to meet you. I'm Janet." They shook hands over the reception desk. "Clare said that you were coming here to finish your thesis on Paolo Veronese."

"That's right, although there are probably more works by Veronese in the National Gallery in London than there are in Verona, to be honest, despite the fact that he was originally from here. However, Verona is very strategically placed between Milan and Venice and there are various paintings that I want to see and archives that I need to visit", he explained. "Plus of course it'll be wonderful to soak up the atmosphere and improve my Italian a bit".

"Do you already speak Italian then?"

"Yes, I spent nine months in Florence when I was an undergraduate, with the Erasmus scheme."

"How wonderful! I didn't get to do anything as exciting as that when I was at university. I just spent three years in not so beautiful Birmingham."

"I guess it's one of the perks of studying art. The exchanges tend to be with places of considerable artistic and historical interest. They have to do something to make up for the complete lack of employment prospects", David grinned.

"Well, that's pretty much the same for any arts degree, I guess", commented Janet "and at least with Fine Art you get to study really interesting and beautiful things."

"Yes, I'm really looking forward to getting to know this part of Italy. I only really know Tuscany and Umbria, so it'll be great to explore the area. I've never been to Verona before."

"Really? There's plenty to see. Of course there's a lot of Roman stuff, like the Arena, the Roman theatre and the archaeological museum, although that obviously isn't your field of expertise. Maybe you should start with the Castelvecchio. That's really near here, only about a few minutes away from the school."

"Oh, I definitely need to go there", said David. "There are two paintings by Veronese in the museum."

"I must have seen them, but I can't really remember much. If you're not an expert you tend to just look at paintings and think 'I like that' or 'I don't like that'. It would be fascinating to hear what somebody who really knows his stuff has to say."

"You should come with me", suggested David. "Clare told me about your interest in Italian culture and monuments. I gather you took her Mum, who is my aunt by the way, around one day when she was staying last month. You can show me Verona and I'll give you the benefit of my expert knowledge of Renaissance Italian art!" He smiled at her disarmingly.

Janet felt an instinctive attraction to the young man. He was not exactly handsome in the conventional sense, but there was a warmth and spontaneity about him that was very appealing, and he was obviously intelligent. Shame he was so young. Nevertheless, he was someone she would enjoy spending time with, she thought.

"Why not?" she smiled back. "Let's make it a date!"

Janet glanced up at the clock.

"Clare should have finished soon. When she comes out we can ask her if she wants to come too. If you'll excuse me, I need to finish off a couple of admin jobs. Clare's group is the last lesson of the day and then thankfully I can close up the school."

David sat down in one the armchairs in front of the desk and glanced through a magazine, while Janet busied herself with the paperwork, although in truth most of the administrative tasks were computerised by now. Quite a substantial part of her job involved handling bureaucratic procedures, although Ursula dealt with invoicing and financial matters, but she was still responsible for student assessment, certification, booking people in for exams etc. It was an inevitable, if boring, part of being the director of studies. Nevertheless, she continued to prefer teaching, enjoying the day-to-day contact with her pupils and relishing the challenge of stimulating them to improve, thankless as the task was on some occasions.

At 9.30 prompt the door at the bottom of the corridor opened and a hotchpotch of participants came tumbling out of the classroom, immediately filling the corridor with their laughter and cheerful chatter. There's no doubt about it, Janet thought, Italians are loud. Whether they're teenagers or pensioners, they just can't resist being noisy. There's a sort of cultural decibel level built into their DNA, and trying to keep them below that threshold is simply a hopeless cause.

As the students passed her one by one on the way out she wished them goodnight, addressing some of them by name. There were certain people who returned year after year, aware that they were not making huge progress, but nevertheless keen to make the attempt, either because they needed to speak English at work, or simply because they liked travelling and had discovered that English was the lingua franca. Some of them had been in one of her own classes the previous year so she knew them well. Over the years several of her students had become good friends, and the relationship that developed between teacher and students could be truly rewarding, particularly in the case of adult groups. Many of the groups wanted to go out for a Christmas or end-of-term pizza and Janet and the other teachers often ended up with a whole series of dinners, particularly at the end of the year, given that in Italy celebrating anything invariably involved food.

A few minutes later Clare finally emerged from the classroom and spotted her cousin.

"David! How wonderful to see you. Have you been waiting long", she asked as she flung her arms around his neck.

"No, not long", he smiled, disengaging himself. "I chatted a bit to Janet here."

"Oh good, so you've introduced yourselves. I'm absolutely starving. I haven't had dinner yet. Why don't we go to the local pizzeria, or have you already eaten?"

"No, not yet", David replied. "That sounds great." He turned to Janet. "What about you Janet? How about a pizza?"

"That's very kind of you", she answered, suddenly noticing that he really had very beautiful blue eyes, "but I've already had dinner and anyway I have to close the school first".

"We can wait for you to close up", said Clare. "Do come, even if you only have a beer."

"Yes, please do", urged David.

Janet hesitated for a moment and then shrugged her shoulders.

"Oh, why not? Give me five minutes to turn everything off and then I'll be ready." She went round the classrooms, checking that all the lights and computers were off and all the windows closed. Then she double locked the old wooden doors and the three of them made their way down the marble stairs and out onto the street. The air was warmer than it had been for the last few weeks and you could sense that spring was on the way. It was that period of the year when the weather has not yet turned the corner towards the summer, but the imminence of warmer times ahead lifts the spirits. The lengthening days and shorter nights are evidence of the changing seasons, and the knowledge that summer will come soon makes you more willing to put up with the last vestiges of the winter.

The three young people arrived at the pizzeria, taking a seat at one of the wooden tables. They decided to go for a pizza 'by the metre', meaning that you could choose how long you wanted your pizza to be, then dividing it up between everyone at the table.

"God, I hope they're quick", said Clare, five seconds after they had ordered. "I'm absolutely starving."

In the meantime they sat sipping their beers, David's suitcase occupying the fourth chair around the table, almost taking on human status.

"So where are you staying?" Janet asked David.

"Well for the first few weeks I'm staying with Clare, because there's a room free in her house. Then I might go off to Venice or Milan for a couple of weeks and when I come back I need to find somewhere else to stay until the end of term, because the room in Clare's house is already booked for some language students."

"I'm sure you'll find somewhere. Ursula has lots of contacts, and it's not the busiest season. It's more difficult in summer", Janet said.

"Unfortunately I need to go back to the UK at the end of term to see my supervisor and make arrangements to submit my thesis, so I'll be gone by then." David turned to his cousin.

"I've convinced Janet to show me around Verona, and in return I have promised to dazzle her with my profound knowledge of renaissance art. When would be a good time for you two girls?"

"Saturday morning would be a good time for me", replied Janet. "What about you Clare?"

"Oh no, don't even think about dragging me around art galleries with David spouting on for hours about

Saints' attributes!" exclaimed Clare. "You don't know him, Janet. He can spend half an hour explaining the top right-hand corner of just one painting. What's more I've just been round all the galleries, museums and churches with Mum a couple of weeks ago. I like art, but enough is enough!"

"Looks like it's just the two of us then", grinned David "unless Clare has frightened you off!"

"Of course not. What could be better than having your own personal art historian as a guide?"

"Well don't say I didn't warn you." Clare wagged her finger at her cousin "And you, make sure you aren't too boring. Janet is much too polite to tell you how tedious you're being!"

"Rubbish." Janet smiled, "I'm really looking forward to it. Anyway, now we can forget art for a bit and concentrate on more substantial pleasures. I think I can see the pizza arriving."

Clare rubbed her hands together with glee as the waiter, who was bearing a wooden platter with a healthy half metre of pizza, arrived at the table.

"Art is good, but pizza is even better!" she exclaimed.

CHAPTER 26

Janet was surprised at how much she had enjoyed David's company during their visit to the Castelvecchio museum. She had felt completely at her ease, and was fascinated by his explanations and knowledge about renaissance art. They had inevitably spent much longer than they intended exploring the various rooms of the old castle, so it was nearly lunchtime when they finally left. They adjourned for lunch at a local café, before Janet in her turn showed David a little of the city, pointing out some of the main monuments in Verona. It was a long time since she had enjoyed a man's company so much and they truly appeared to be on the same wavelength, so much so that when he had suggested a trip to Tuscany the following weekend she had accepted without any hesitation. He had wanted to go by train, but she suggested that they would have a lot more flexibility if they went down by car, and there would be room for Clare too, if she wanted to come. Clare however had dropped out at the last minute, pleading other commitments, so it was just the two of them.

They left early in the morning, calculating that it would take them about 4 hours to get to Siena.

"Siena's about the right size for a short trip", David had suggested. "There's far too much to see in Florence in just two days. What's more I've got a friend in Siena who can put us up overnight, saving us a bit of money, which means I can maybe afford a nice meal on Saturday evening."

Thrifty by nature, Janet was more than happy to sleep on somebody's sofa, if it meant that she could spend more on the things she really appreciated. She felt no need for luxury, which was fortunate given her anything but generous salary, and she much preferred to squander her hard-earned cash on her true passions, like good food and travelling, rather than on posh clothes or hotels. In David she had obviously found a kindred spirit.

The journey passed quickly. Being to all intents and purposes complete strangers, they had a lot to find out about each other, and when they finally arrived in Siena they were genuinely surprised to find that four hours had gone by in a flash. Janet parked the car and they strolled down the medieval streets until they arrived in the magnificent shell-shaped piazza representing the heart of the city. It was a glorious spring day and Janet had a moment of genuine happiness that sprung up on her unawares.

"How beautiful", she turned to David, beaming at him with absurd euphoria.

He looked her straight in the eyes. "Yes, everything seems very beautiful at the moment. And nothing more than you". He put his hands on her waist and pulled her very gently towards him, almost fearful that she would push him away. However, caught up in the magic of the moment Janet had no desire to escape, so she simply turned her face up towards his as he kissed her delicately on the lips.

After a moment she withdrew. "I'm way too old for you, you know. Nobody blinks at a couple where the man is ten years older than the woman, but the other way round is practically unheard of, except among Hollywood stars, and I'm not exactly Demi Moore."

"You're nine years older than me, not ten, and in any case I don't care a fig. I've never met any woman I felt so instantly in tune with. Anyway, *carpe diem,* seize the moment!"

"I just have this horrible feeling that I might be mistaken for your mother!"

"Don't be daft. My mother is a plump middle-aged lady with grey hair. You are a beautiful young woman. Remember, women live on average seven years more than men, so ideally they should marry a man seven years younger, if they don't want to spend their old-age alone!"

"I think it's perhaps a tiny bit early to think about marriage", commented Janet. "I wasn't looking quite that far ahead. Nevertheless, I almost belong to another generation. I look at people in their 20s and feel old."

"You should worry", said David. "I was born old. Have you any idea how tedious young people find me? I don't like loud music, discos or getting drunk and my idea of a good time is looking at a renaissance pulpit!"

They giggled together, and Janet felt uncharacteristically frivolous. "Oh well, as they say, there's no fool like an old fool! For the moment let's just enjoy this day together", she concluded.

The rest of the day went past in a sort of idyllic haze. They held hands, wandered through the streets, visited churches and admired paintings. At lunchtime they sat on the ground in the main piazza, looking up at the clock tower, eating a slice of takeaway pizza and drinking cold beer.

"I came to the Palio here on July 2, when I was living in Florence", said David. "You know, the horse race they have twice a year in the summer around the main square. It was an amazing experience. Ten districts of the city compete in the race on each occasion and feelings run really high. You can see grown men bawling their eyes out when their horse loses, while those from the winning district go completely berserk."

"Yes, I've seen it on the television sometimes. The square is absolutely packed with people cheering on the horses and riders, but the actual race only lasts a few minutes. The thing that seemed to take the longest was the start."

"That's because the horses have to enter one by one between two ropes stretched out across the track", explained David. "When they've finally lined up properly in the correct order a gun fires, the rope in front of them drops and they're off. However, it usually takes several attempts, and in the meantime the jockeys negotiate among themselves, with major bribes apparently promised, either to help one district or to obstruct another, given the extent of the rivalry between them".

"It must be tremendously dangerous", commented Janet, looking around the piazza. "It's certainly not square, but it's not round or elliptical either and the shell shape means that there are two really sharp corners to negotiate. Plus the pavement is slippery. I can't see how horses can run over that."

"Yes, there have been protests from animal rights organisations for years, although they've tried to improve safety recently. Nevertheless, horses do occasionally die during the race or the trials in the days running up to the event. The pavement around the outside of the piazza is covered with packed earth to make the track, and there is heavy padding of the vertical sections around the first bend, where the horses are running downhill."

"I would really like to see it; I can imagine that atmosphere is amazing. Of course it's sad if a horse dies or is injured, but I can't help feeling that we do much worse things to animals, starting from eating them, or wearing their skins! The Palio has gone on for centuries and it's an integral part of the local culture, it would be really sad if it were to disappear for the sake of political correctness."

"I don't think that's likely", said David. "It seems to be more popular than ever, both with locals and tourists. It's practically impossible to find a room when the Palio is on."

"OK. If I do come this summer I guess I'll just have to sleep in the car."

"In that case maybe I'll have to come too in order to make sure you're safe!"

"Good Grief. You really were born old, weren't you? I'm not sure you were even born in the right century. Keep me safe indeed!" Janet snorted. "I'll have you know that I did karate as a child".

"I'm sure you're absolutely terrifying", said David "but couldn't you just pretend that I'm your knight in shining armour?"

"As you desire sire. Would you care to accompany me to the bar for a coffee? Methinks there may be cutthroats and bandits along the way."

"My lady's wish is my command". David got to his feet, stretching out a hand to pull Janet to her feet with mock solemnity. "By all means let's go and have an espresso, but then we should make the most of the afternoon while it's still warm; as soon as the sun goes down I think it'll get quite cold. Anyway I told my friend that we would arrive at his house at around half past six."

"That's fine by me. I put myself in your expert hands, but if we want to get to your friend's house on time we probably need to go and pick up the car around six, given that you appear to have forgotten your charger!"

Hand in hand, they grinned inanely at each other before heading for the nearest coffee shop. Fortified by a double dose of concentrated caffeine, they dedicated the rest of the afternoon to visiting the cathedral, the baptistery, the cathedral museum and the magnificent Piccolomini library. David waxed particularly lyrical about the pulpit by Nicola Pisano, but the thing Janet loved the most was the library, with its splendid frescoes by Pinturicchio and illuminated manuscripts. Her only regret was that much of the fabulous inlaid marble floor in the cathedral was covered up, apparently only revealed for a few weeks each year. Finally, drunk with culture, they emerged from the medieval Duomo with its black and white stripes to find that it was getting dark, uncomfortably aware that they needed to get a move on if they didn't want to be embarrassingly late.

They walked briskly back to the car park, with David attempting to programme the sat-nav at the same time without bumping into oncoming tourists.

"Riccardo lives in a village just outside Siena", he explained. "It's at the top of a hill, and once I'm fairly close I remember the way to the house, but I always have problems getting out of Siena and onto the right road. Thank God for modern technology. Otherwise we might spend ages driving round one way systems."

With the aid of the sat-nav they found the right route out of Siena surprisingly easily, and as soon as David recognised the village, he directed Janet down a long dirt track. She was forced to weave between an endless series of potholes, slaloming from one side to the other in a vain attempt to avoid the larger holes. She dreaded to think what the road must be like in winter, or in wet weather, but in any case she was relieved to finally arrive at Riccardo's house.

They were greeted by a large and aggressive turkey, which came rushing up to the car the moment they stopped, gobbling like a machine gun.

"I'm not sure I want to get out", said Janet. "They seem to have a guard turkey. You're the knight in shining armour. Why don't you do your job and chase it off?"

David looked slightly dubious, but to give him credit was starting gingerly to get out of the car, when they were saved by the arrival of Riccardo, who energetically shooed the bird off.

"Hello, come on in! I'm sorry about the turkey. The neighbour's rearing it for some dinner with his American friends and the wretched thing seems to think it has to defend its territory and terrifies all our visitors. Even my wife hates it and avoids hanging the washing outside because it keeps following her around. There will be celebrations all round when it finally gets the chop!"

Riccardo was a short, stocky man of around forty, with a thick mane of greying hair reaching down to his shoulders.

"Sonia's gone down to the shops to get a few things. She absolutely insists you have dinner with us this evening. She'll be back shortly, but in the meantime do you want to freshen up and dump your bags?"

Janet and David followed him up the stairs and into a smallish room with a double bed and an antique wooden wardrobe and dressing table.

"Will you be alright here?" asked Riccardo, noting David's slightly embarrassed expression. "I assumed you were together, but we can always make up the sofa for David".

Janet looked directly into his face and smiled.

"Oh no, don't worry. This will be absolutely perfect."

183

Part III - Summer Term

There is no world without Verona walls
But purgatory, torture, hell itself.
Hence "banishèd" is banished from the world,
And world's exile is death.

Shakespeare, Romeo and Juliet, Act 3, Scene 3

CHAPTER 27

Over Easter the language school was only closed for five days, corresponding with the school holidays in the Veneto region. For Clare in particular, a more recent immigrant and used to satisfyingly substantial breaks between one term and another in Britain, this was an unpleasant surprise.

"Of course I appreciate it means you get a really long holiday in the summer, when it's too hot to do any work anyway, but it's exhausting going from January to the beginning of June without even getting a full week off, especially given that there's no half-term either, just the occasional one-day public holiday", she complained to Vanessa, when they met for tea in Verona on Good Friday.

"It's tough on the kids as well, because they're totally fed up by the end of the school year", commented her friend. "By the time you get to the beginning of June they're completely brain dead and desperate for the holidays to begin, while the teachers are equally tired but forced to maintain a pretence of teaching them something over the last ten days."

"I bet the teachers are even keener to get to the end of term than the students. It's emotionally and physically wearing trying to impart knowledge to people who don't necessarily want to acquire it."

"Absolutely!" agreed Vanessa with conviction, "although teachers in Italy work shorter hours than their colleagues in the UK, which is perhaps fair given that they earn about as much as a road sweeper and that it can take decades to get a permanent job. The real advantage to being a teacher in the Italian education system is that most of them only work in the mornings and they have really long holidays in the summer, with almost three full months off."

"So what are you doing over the next few days", asked Clare, changing the subject. "What happens at Easter around here?"

"Well, obviously there are traditional events linked to religious festivities. A couple of years ago I rashly agreed to do the Easter Vigil with the choir in our church. I try to do my bit for the local community, but it seemed to be just a really long, drawn-out version of standard Mass, with singularly uninspiring music, in preparation for the resurrection on Easter Sunday. Given that I'm not Catholic, I'm afraid I decided it was one commitment I could do without. So I'm just planning to spend Sunday at home with the family, and on Easter Monday we'll go to the country with some friends and have a barbecue, weather permitting. The forecast appears to be good. What about you?"

"Well, I might go off for the day with David to visit Padua either tomorrow or Tuesday, but I don't think it's a good idea to go on Easter Sunday or Monday because everything will be closed. David was also talking about maybe going to the mountains with Janet on Monday, but I'm not sure whether to go along. You know, two's company...."

"So is there something going on between those two?" asked Vanessa with some curiosity.

"David hasn't said anything, but I have a fairly strong suspicion that there is. You know they went off to Siena together for the weekend a couple of weeks ago? Well, he came back unusually happy and was wandering about the place with a big smile on his face!"

"I have to say that Janet's keeping very quiet about it. She hasn't said anything to me. Mind you, she's a pretty reserved person so that's not entirely a surprise. She might be worried about the age difference."

"I know it shouldn't matter, and I do like Janet, but I still don't feel entirely comfortable with the idea of my cousin going out with an older woman, though of course I'm not going to say anything to him!"

"No, probably best not. Especially as you were going out with an older man…"

"Well that didn't work out too well either!"

"Anyway, if you don't want to go the mountains on Monday, you could join Ben and his friends for a barbecue in the countryside near the lake", Vanessa suggested. "When he heard I was meeting you this morning he told me to invite you. There's a biggish group and a couple of them are off to do the shopping tomorrow."

Clare considered the idea. The more she thought about it, the more appealing it seemed. "Actually, I might take him up on that. I hate being a third wheel. I'll give Ben a ring later today."

"I'll tell him when I get back, so they know to take you into account when they're calculating how much food to buy for tomorrow. It's a public holiday, so the Sunday bus service will be running; you can take the bus to the village and Ben can pick you up at the bus stop."

The two women lingered for a while chatting, before heading their separate ways, Vanessa towards the supermarket and Clare back to the flat to enjoy a meal prepared by David, who was always willing to act as cook so long as someone else did the washing-up.

***

Two days later Clare was lying on an old blanket under the twisted branches of an olive tree, watching a discreet fluffy cloud float across the clear blue sky. There were groups of people of all ages scattered around the olive grove, with improvised barbecues springing up everywhere like anthills. The aroma of roasting meat and crushed garlic wafted through the air, accompanied by the sound of laughter, children shouting, dogs barking and men of all ages discussing how best to cook sausages. It seemed to be universally recognised that barbecuing was a man's job, perhaps pandering to their childish fascination with fire, while the women busied themselves laying out checked tablecloths and opening up plastic containers full of olives and salad, or just sat back relaxing in the sun. A couple of Ben's friends were stringing up a rope between two trees to create a temporary volleyball court, while another was wheeling crates of beer up from the car at the bottom of the hill using a makeshift trolley.

They had been extraordinarily lucky with the weather and it was a perfect day, not so hot that it was unpleasant to sit in the sun, but at the same time warm enough to be able to lie around in short-sleeved t-shirts enjoying the outdoor life without shivering.

"Last year was a complete disaster", commented Ben. "It had rained all the previous day, so there was mud everywhere, and it was so cold and windy that we decided to relocate to the cellar of Tomaso's house. It was really cramped inside, while meanwhile outside the cooks couldn't manage to get the fire going properly for the barbecue and we ended up eating half raw spare ribs at 3 o'clock in the afternoon."

"OK, I'm glad I missed that one", said Clare. "So is it a tradition to have a picnic on Easter Monday then?"

"Oh absolutely. Easter Sunday is usually spent at home with the family, eating mostly, as for practically all important festivities in Italy, but Easter Monday is the day for going out to the countryside with your friends, generally horsing around getting filthy and roasting industrial quantities of pork sausages and spare ribs, accompanied by beer or red wine."

"That's great on a beautiful day like today, but presumably the weather isn't always so congenial."

"When I was a child, I always remember it being sunny", said Ben "but in the last few years the weather seems to have become much more unreliable. Still, this year it's perfect."

Having finally set up the volleyball 'court' to their satisfaction, Ben's friends called them over, urging them to come and play.

"Come on", urged Ben. "You need to work up an appetite."

"But I can't play volleyball", Clare protested.

"Don't worry. Nobody takes it seriously anyway. It's just for fun." He pulled her to her feet and she followed him slightly reluctantly, not overly eager to make a complete fool of herself. She spent most of the next quarter of an hour trying rigorously to avoid the ball, assisted by Ben who seemed on the contrary to be absolutely everywhere. Very occasionally she succeeded in getting the ball over the rope by some miracle, but it was blatantly clear that she was the least capable of the girls, who had probably all played at school she presumed. Apart from anything else the ball was harder than she expected and some of Ben's mates on the other side were perhaps excessively enthusiastic, or competitive, with their smashes. Seizing the chance of a break in play, she withdrew in good order and decided to go and get a beer and see how the barbecue was going.

"Wait", called out Ben. "I'll come too."

He seemed barely flushed, despite having run around like a lunatic for the last fifteen minutes, retrieving every ball that Clare had failed to reach.

"I did warn you that I can't play", she said "but you could have carried on. You were obviously enjoying yourself."

"Yes, I like sport, but I wanted a beer and anyway it's probably about time I gave the others a hand with the barbecue. Otherwise some poor sod gets stuck doing all the work, while everyone else just messes around having fun."

"Come on then, I'll do what I can to help too."

When they reached Ben's friend Tomaso he had already lined up rows of sausages, pork chops and spare ribs on the griddle in quantities sufficient to feed a small army. The partially cooked meat hissed as the juices dribbled onto the charcoal, and there was a sudden explosion of flames as the fat caught fire.

"Quick, grab the salt", ordered Ben, rushing to the aid of Tomaso and lifting the grill off the heat. Clare looked around desperately, rummaging in endless plastic bags and eventually locating the salt next to the olive oil and herbs by the griddle.

"Throw some on the fire. It'll put the flames out."

Clare scattered handfuls of salt over the charcoal, obtaining the desired effect, and they all breathed a sigh of relief. In the meantime others arrived to help out, laughing and joking as they helped themselves to bottles of beer from the array of cool bags.

When the meat was finally cooked they sat around in groups on the grass, absurdly satisfied with themselves as they gnawed on spare ribs like cavemen, indifferent to the comforts of modern life. They ate, drank and were merry, and afterwards some of them dozed off under the olive trees, while the more active continued an interminable volleyball game that had no beginning or end, but just a continuously rotating selection of players.

When it started to get cooler they began the process of packing up, collecting sacks of rubbish and carting all the equipment back to the cars at the bottom of the hill. Ben put his arm around Clare's shoulders.

"It's been a good day", he said. "I'm glad you came. I hope you had a good time."

She could see that he wanted to kiss her, but although she liked him and didn't find the idea objectionable, she just couldn't see him as anything other than a friend. She looked up at him apologetically and extracted herself from his embrace.

"I'm sorry Ben. I had a great time and I love being with you, but now I think I have to go and get the bus home. Can you take me to the bus stop?"

He sighed. "OK. Come on then. Let's go."

In the car they found they had little to say to each other. The bus was due in twenty minutes, so Clare had just time to stop off at Vanessa's house to pick up her bag and say goodbye, before Ben dropped her off on the main road to wait for the bus. She waved as he departed rather forlornly, heading for home.

CHAPTER 28

On the Sunday morning they had all agreed to participate in an organised walk/run through the vineyards on the hills of the Valpolicella area, just north of Verona. To Vanessa the early departure from the village at half past seven seemed masochistically early for a Sunday, but having been offered a lift by a group of friends belonging to the local club, she decided that for once she could make the sacrifice and haul herself out of bed. When she arrived at her destination she was astounded to see just how many participants apparently had no problems getting up on a Sunday morning: there were hundreds of people milling around, from young couples and sporty-looking types in track suits to groups of plump pensioners with granny perms and families with children, some even with babies stuffed into slings. It was a pleasant sunny day and the vineyards were still glistening with the early morning dew, but at this hour it was fairly cool, so most of the participants were dressed onion-style in several layers of clothing.

It was possible to opt for the 5 km, 10 km or 15 km route, and Vanessa and Clare had agreed to go for the intermediate walk, while predictably the more energetic David and Janet had chosen the longer route, planning to run for at least part of the course. As arranged, they all met up at the desk to pay the 3 euro registration fee, which included refreshments at stop-off points every 5 km and at the finishing line.

Vanessa greeted the other three enthusiastically, but was particularly happy to see Clare, who despite the age difference was essentially more similar to herself in terms of her attitude to physical exercise, at least so it seemed to her.

"Hi. I'm so pleased you came. Janet always goes much too fast for me and I've abandoned any attempt at trying to keep up with her. I hope I'm not too slow for you too. If all else fails you can go on ahead and we can meet up at the end."

"Oh, don't worry. I may be young but nobody could accuse me of being athletic. I only agreed to come because it's a nice day and I knew you were here too, as I certainly can't keep up with David and Janet. If you like we can even do the short walk."

"No, I feel I have to do at least the 10 km, otherwise it's hardly worth getting out of bed! It shouldn't take us more than two hours and in the meantime the other two will have arrived as well."

"Well I certainly hope so", intervened Janet. "We should be able to manage 15 km easily in a couple of hours, although in this area the route is not all flat and there are bound to be a couple of hills."

"I do hope you're not going to show me up by being much fitter than me", said David. "It's seriously humiliating for a guy to be unable to keep up with a woman."

"Don't worry. I won't damage your fragile male ego. If I see you're in trouble I will pretend to have a fainting fit and collapse in the middle of the vines, so that you can minister to me and get your breath back."

"Perhaps I should carry a little flask of brandy around my neck, just in case!"

"Like a St Bernard dog?" asked Vanessa. "I don't think the climate is quite right, but if you're planning on resuscitating anyone you should come with us. I'm far more likely to need it than Janet."

"I'm sure you underestimate yourself, but I can certainly come with you, if you like", said David politely.

"Don't be silly. I was only joking, and in any case I'm sure you would have much more fun giving Janet mouth-to-mouth resuscitation!"

David flushed disarmingly and Janet took him protectively under the arm.

"Oh leave the poor boy alone. You're embarrassing him. Come on David. It's time to get going if we want to get back before these two slackers." She set off smartly at a jog with a slightly surprised David following close behind, heading for the start of the 15 km route.

"Oh dear", said Vanessa to Clare as they started off, joining the long trail of walkers making their way between two rows of vines. "That just slipped out. I wish I could connect my brain to my mouth before speaking. Do you think Janet was annoyed?"

"No, I don't think so", replied Clare. "You didn't say anything inappropriate, and David isn't touchy at all. I think he was just embarrassed because he would like to be open about their relationship, whereas Janet seems more reluctant."

"I'm sure it's because of the age thing, but actually I think they go rather well together."

"Yes. I told you I felt a bit odd about it, but I'm getting used to the idea and it's true that they have a lot in common. Anyway, so long as David is happy then it's fine with me. I only have a sister and so in a way he's a bit like an older brother for me."

"You're lucky to have such a good relationship. I barely know my cousins", said Vanessa, already starting to get slightly out of breath as they started up the first hill. The slope was fairly gentle but the women nevertheless took it at an easy pace, with Vanessa not wanting to overstretch herself right at the beginning of the walk. At a certain point, however, she noticed that they were being overtaken by an excessively large number of walkers, many of whom appeared to be considerably older than herself. She glanced behind her and saw an elderly gentleman with a stick who looked about ninety, closing rapidly. Deciding that this was simply too much, she accelerated, lengthening her stride and trying to get into a rhythm. She managed to keep it up for about the next twenty minutes until they reached the next hill, but here she was forced to slow down, sluggishly planting one foot in front of the other as she plodded up the slope, breathing heavily like a tired old horse. The ninety-year-old sailed past with no apparent effort, smiling as he wished them a good day, and continued confidently up the hill.

Vanessa stopped for a moment to catch her breath. "Well kudos to him, but it's pretty pathetic when you're overtaken by someone that age. I did my best, but I just couldn't manage to keep ahead of him."

Clare laughed. "Don't worry about it. He has probably been active all his life, rather than sitting at a desk like us. Anyway it's not a competition."

"Just as well, as I clearly wouldn't even be able to win in the over nineties category!"

"Rubbish. I'm sure you could even win in the octogenarian class."

Vanessa looked suspiciously at Clare. "Is that genuinely the worst compliment ever or are you just making fun of me?"

"Don't be daft. Of course I am."

"Although to be realistic, I definitely wouldn't have a chance against some of the golden oldies participating here. I recognise a couple of them and they're well into their seventies. There are some frighteningly fit OAPs around on these occasions."

"You're not supposed to say 'OAPs' or 'elderly' any more in the UK. It's not politically correct", commented Clare.

"Oh good grief! I'm out-of-date again. What does one say now then?"

"Older people or older adults seem to be the preferred terms these days."

"Older than who, or what, for God's sake? Political correctness can be so tedious at times, and you end up not communicating anything at all. Thank heavens 'special needs' seems to have gone out of the window lately. It always seemed rather patronising to me, and gave you absolutely no idea what problems people actually had. They use the equally ghastly 'diversamente abili' in Italia, i.e. 'differently abled'. I hate it!"

The two women chatted away as they wandered along the path, following the trail of swifter fellow walkers and admiring the attractive landscape of the Valpolicella wine-producing area, with its rolling hills, vineyards and olive groves. They passed the half-way point, pausing for a cup of water and a biscuit before continuing along the route, through yet more vineyards and towards the finishing line. When they finally arrived, there were serious refreshments, with ham or salami rolls, soft drinks, cake and even wine, despite the fact that it was only half past ten.

"It does rather seem to defeat the object", commented Clare "if you've just been on a 2 hour walk or run and then you immediately stuff your face with everything available!"

"I find it very civilised", said Vanessa. "Having completed your exercise programme you are then entitled to consume your calories with minimal guilt."

In addition to refreshments, each participant was presented with a packet of pasta and a bottle of cheap wine, which could always be used for cooking if nothing else Vanessa concluded, and it was at the distribution point that the two women found their companions, flushed after the race but clearly satisfied with themselves.

"Isn't it a beautiful day", beamed Janet. "You always feel so refreshed after a run first thing in the morning, don't you?"

"Oh, absolutely!" Vanessa said with heavy sarcasm. In actual fact she felt pretty knackered, albeit glowing with a feeling of self-righteousness that she had got up on a Sunday morning to go for a walk.

"If you could just get it into your head that physical activity is pleasurable, and not just good for you, then you might be inclined to do more of it!"

"But the point is that for me it isn't particularly pleasurable. I see it as a means to an end, to keep fit, or to allow me to climb up a mountain in order to enjoy beautiful views, but I don't enjoy it in itself."

"You might, if you did more."

"Thanks Janet, but I think I have enough people telling me that I'm lazy and should do more exercise. You're all right, of course, but it's like telling someone who doesn't like reading that they should read more. They can force themselves to read a book, but that doesn't mean that they will enjoy it. Personally I adore reading and cannot imagine doing without it, whereas I can happily imagine doing without exercising."

"The two things are not mutually exclusive. I love reading but that doesn't stop me enjoying running. Stretching myself physically makes me feel more alive."

"Well, it makes me feel like I'm about to have a heart attack."

"Well you'll be more likely to if you don't do something about changing your lifestyle!"

Inexplicably, Vanessa suddenly wanted to burst into tears. She was so tired of trying to meet everyone's expectations. Tired of trying to be a good mother, a good wife and a good teacher and at the same time to take care of herself, remain attractive and not 'let herself go'.

With unusual sensitivity for a guy, David realised that the atmosphere was becoming uncomfortable and intervened.

"I don't know about you Janet, but I should probably be getting back to Verona. It's a beautiful day but I really must do some work."

"Yes, of course", Janet smiled at him. "I wouldn't want to be responsible for delaying the masterpiece. Vanessa, is someone giving you a lift back?"

"Yes, there's no problem", Vanessa waved at a group of people talking to the organisers behind the refreshment stand, now in the process of packing up. "My friends are over there. You go, I'll see you tomorrow at school."

She kissed them all goodbye, Italian fashion, and headed over towards the group of chattering walkers, while the other three strolled leisurely back towards the car park, now half empty.

CHAPTER 29

Having never been to the Vinitaly exhibition, Clare had hoped to visit the fair and maybe taste a few wines that she couldn't afford to buy, but when she discovered that this year the ticket had reached the outrageous figure of 80 euro, she discarded the idea.

"Of course I realise that it's really designed for the trade, but you'd think that there would be a section designed for the general public", she complained to Janet.

"I think that part's all been moved to the city centre. There are quite a few things happening here and there, so long as the weather holds out. Actually, I don't think you're missing much. I went last year, because one of my students gave me a free ticket, but understandably the exhibitors are only really interested in buyers and nobody particularly wants to hand out free wine. So either you wander aimlessly about, hoping that somebody will take pity on you and offer you something, or you pretend to be somebody important in the wine world, invent a plausible import/export company or pretend to be a buyer for a chain of supermarkets!"

"I don't think I have the gall to do that, and I'm probably too young to be taken seriously anyway. Still it would have been nice to be able to compare wines from lots of different regions."

"You might be able to get a job on one of the stands for the period of the fair. They're always looking for attractive young women who can speak English to act as underpaid interpreters."

Clare considered the idea. Since the beginning of the academic year her Italian had improved radically (not difficult given her point of departure) and she was now capable of speaking pretty fluently, although she still felt a bit flustered if she had to answer the telephone at school reception. For some reason it was so much easier when you could see people face to face. She also forced herself to read Italian newspapers in order to improve her vocabulary, although she usually skipped the political pages. However, she still did not feel truly confident about her ability in a professional situation.

"I don't know whether my interpreting skills are up to scratch yet, although I have to say I have made a lot more progress in Italian than my students have in English", said Clare "and anyway Ursula would never let me have time off to work for someone else!"

"You have a point. Oh well, I'll try asking around to see if anyone can come up with any free tickets, but they seem to have cut down on those this year. If all else fails, I think there's an organic wine fair in the old Hapsburg military depot, with street food trucks and accompanying musical events. We could take a look at what's happening there if you like, weather permitting of course."

"Actually that sounds quite fun. I'll give it some thought. I'm pretty sure that David would come too; it sounds like his sort of thing."

Janet offered to find out more about exactly what was on offer in the city and the two women agreed to meet up at some point at the weekend, confident that any event involving wine, food and music couldn't be a total washout, unless of course there was yet another massive storm.

Around Sunday lunchtime David and Clare were heading for the organic wine fair on board a clapped out

Vespa that Ben had agreed to loan them for a few weeks, as he rarely used it. They could perfectly well have walked, but David was excited to try out his new toy, after having suffered from male vehicle deprivation syndrome for the last few weeks, and so had insisted they went on the Vespa. Unfortunately, neither he nor Clare had ever driven in Verona and they spent a considerable time driving around in circles in the one-way system before finally managing to arrive within spitting distance of their destination. They were already ten minutes late for their appointment with Janet when Clare spotted a landmark she recognised and pointed up a street on their right.

"It's just up there", she yelled in his ear.

David wheeled rapidly into the narrow street, before realising that it was in fact one-way and all the parked cars were facing in the other direction, but as there was nobody coming he reckoned he might as well make his way to the top of the road and drop off Clare at least, so that she could go and look for Janet. Then he could take his time finding somewhere to park the Vespa. Unhappily, just as they reached the top of the street, a traffic warden was emerging from the bar opposite, noted where they were coming from and waved them imperiously over to the side of the main road. David groaned inwardly, outwardly and every which way, well aware that this was likely to prove unpleasant and distinctly costly, as well as making them even later for their appointment.

Clare, however, nourished some hope.

"Let me do the talking", she whispered to him in English as he drew to a halt. Although the traffic warden had not yet recognised her with a crash helmet on, she had immediately identified him as one of her students, non other than the notorious Giorgio, known to everyone at the school as George I, quite possibly the least improved pupil of the year. Clare lifted up her visor and directed her most dazzling smile at him, switching into Italian.

"Giorgio. How lovely to see you! This is my cousin David. You mustn't blame him, because it's all my fault. I told him to turn into this street because I've only ever come here on foot and I didn't realise it was one-way. We're so terribly late and we're supposed to be meeting Janet, you know, my boss at the school, so as you can imagine I didn't want to keep her waiting." For once Clare did her best to blatantly exert her feminine charm, praying that Giorgio would show mercy.

"Clare! I didn't recognise you." Making recourse to his limited vocabulary, he beamed at David and said in English "She, my English teacher". David nodded enthusiastically, but decided it was better to remain silent.

"We're trying to get to the Arsenale, you know, where the wine festival is", Clare explained. "Could you possibly tell us where we can park? I can't see any spaces for motorbikes."

Giorgio considered for a moment.

"If you take the second street here on the right, and then the first left, you'll find plenty of spaces to park, and from there it's only two minutes walk to the Arsenale." He lowered his voice and smiled conspiratorially, "but Clare, be careful. Not all my colleagues are so understanding!"

"Oh I will, we will. Thank you so much Giorgio. You are an angel."

David and Clare waved goodbye, breathing a massive sigh of relief, and ten minutes later they had finally managed park the moped and meet up with Janet at the fair.

Clare explained their narrow escape on the Vespa. "Thank God, for once I had a stroke of luck. We were stopped by George I".

"She was gushing all over him". David turned towards her, "I swear you were fluttering your eyelashes. I didn't know you had it in you!"

"Don't be stupid. I was sitting behind you, so you couldn't see anything anyway!"

"Well, whatever you did, it worked."

"You were very lucky", commented Janet. "You can get away with evading your taxes, taking bribes or swindling people out of millions of euro in Italy, but commit a minor traffic infringement and you can be in deep trouble!"

"Yes, I'd better be careful not to have more than two glasses of wine if I'm going to drive back."

"Otherwise you could leave the Vespa here, come back to my place for a coffee, and fetch it later this evening", suggested Janet.

"That's a great idea", said David, as they strolled around the stalls, looking at the different organic wines on offer.

It was a warm day, so Janet chose a fruity white Gewurztraminer, while David opted for a Valpolicella ripasso and Clare decided to try a Grillo, a Sicilian white wine. They sat down under an improvised canopy over a few wooden tables opposite the stage, where some kind of Italian swing band was performing with great enthusiasm, the middle-aged lead singer dancing from one side to the other and sweating profusely in the unseasonably hot weather. There were a series of food trucks scattered around the square, offering a range of specialities, from Chianina beef hamburgers and slow smoked American barbecue to Mexican food and Nutella fritters.

"Why don't you girls tell me what you want and I'll go and get it", suggested David.

"No, I'll come too, or it'll take you forever standing in different queues", said Janet. "But Clare you should stay here and save our seats, otherwise we're unlikely to be able to find anywhere to sit in the shade."

So Clare sat back contentedly sipping her wine, one eye on how the other two were doing in the queue and the other on the musicians. At times like this, she felt she could happily stay in Italy forever. The sun, the wine, the music; everything contributed to creating an idyllic atmosphere that made her forget the more negative aspects, like missing her friends and family. Her phone started vibrating in her pocket, although she couldn't hear the ring tone over the music, reminding her that she had suggested that Ben join them for lunch if he was in Verona. It was indeed Ben on the phone, wanting to know if they had arrived, so Clare explained where they were, in the meantime endeavouring to expand out over as large an area as possible at the table so that there was space for the four of them. Nevertheless, she was relieved when Janet reappeared, because it was becoming increasingly difficult to defend her space from assault by other shade-seekers.

Janet presented her with a smoked beef roll.

"You'd think that street food would be cheap, but actually it's a good deal more expensive than a kebab or a baguette bought at a shop", she commented. "Obviously, it depends on the quality of the ingredients, but even so I can't help thinking that food trucks have just become trendy and that's what has allowed them to bump up their prices."

"Yep, and how do we know whether they're really using Chianina beef instead of ordinary mince for their hamburgers, or rather beefburgers?" asked Clare. "I don't think many people could tell the difference. What is Chianina beef anyway?"

"It comes from a breed of cattle reared in Tuscany, I think. They're big and white."

"Well, it certainly seems to be the most popular option here. David's been in the queue for ages, but I think he's nearly at the front now. Oh, and by the way Ben has just called to say he's joining us."

At that very moment, Clare spotted Ben at the corner of the street, clutching a bunch of lamb skewers in one hand and a glass of red wine in the other, peering around in search of his friends. She jumped up and waved frantically, it clearly being impossible to call him given the noise made by the swing band and all the people milling around. Fortunately, Ben saw her almost immediately, raising one arm in recognition and nearly skewering a neighbouring woman in the ear with his kebabs. He made his way over, weaving his way through the crowd and arriving at the table almost simultaneously with David, who had finally succeeded in obtaining the coveted hamburger. The two men squeezed onto the wooden benches and the four of them sat there, drinking wine and biting into their rolls, trying not to let the sauce dribble out onto their t-shirts.

It was a happy carefree moment and they were all having a good time, but Janet couldn't help asking herself what the people sitting around them saw. Did they imagine they were two young couples? Or did they look more like a group of young people taken out by their older aunt, or worse still their mother? She sighed inwardly. She had the feeling it was too good to last.

CHAPTER 30

Vanessa was surprised when Ursula called her out of class ten minutes before the end of the lesson to answer the phone. She left the students reading a magazine article and made her way reluctantly to the reception desk, with a feeling that it was very unlikely to be good news. Her suspicions were fulfilled when she heard her daughter Elena's gymnastics coach on the other end of the line and learned that Elena had been taken to hospital in an ambulance after falling and hitting her head on the beam at the gym. The mother of one of the other girls had tried several times to call her, but obviously Vanessa had kept her cell phone on silent mode while she was teaching, and it was only when they arrived at the hospital that the coach had thought to ask Elena for the name of the school where her mother worked, so that she could contact her. She reassured Vanessa that her daughter was in no imminent danger, but obviously recommended she come as soon as possible.

"She says Elena lost consciousness for a few seconds and is bleeding from a slight cut on her head, but mostly she's just terrified", Vanessa explained to Ursula, in a bit of a panic. "God, it couldn't have happened at a worse time. My husband is away and my son has taken the other car. He was going to pick me up this evening, but he's bound to have turned his phone off because he has lectures at university. I have no idea how to get to the hospital quickly. I'll have to call someone. No, on second thoughts it'll be quicker if I take a taxi."

"I take you", said Ursula immediately. "One moment, I tell Janet to inform your next class that the lesson is cancelled, then we go."

"Really? Are you sure? That's very kind", Vanessa was completely astonished, but far too grateful to make any objections.

Ursula sped off to inform Janet, while Vanessa dashed back into her own class to explain that she would not be reappearing because of the emergency. The two women then half walked, half trotted to Ursula's car, fortunately parked relatively close to the school, and set off for the hospital, 15 km outside Verona, given that the ambulance had naturally taken Elena to the nearest hospital to the sports centre. Normally Vanessa found Ursula's driving style nerve-racking to say the least, but for once she was grateful that her boss drove like a maniac. She was too tense to speak much, and as soon as they screeched up outside the ER she jumped out.

Ursula stuck her head out of the car window, "I go park, then I come find you."

"Don't worry. I'm sure I can manage from here if you want to go back to the school…"

No, I wait see everything OK", Ursula communicated telegraphically, before driving off.

The waiting room outside the ER was full of bored-looking people, perched on uncomfortable metal seating. Some sat there resignedly, waiting for their turn, while others paced backwards and forwards, too agitated to stay still. Vanessa looked around for some sign of her daughter, but instead spotted Elena's coach in a corner, who jumped up to greet her as she approached.

"Don't worry, Elena's being taken care of. They wouldn't let me stay with her because I'm not a relative. She only has a small cut on her head but it was bleeding quite a lot, so they saw her almost immediately. If you go over there and ring the bell, they'll let you in, given that you're the mother and Elena is under 18, but I should probably be getting back."

"Thank you so much for accompanying her and waiting until I arrived. I promise I'll let you know how everything goes", Vanessa said. As soon as she saw her heading towards the exit, she walked up to the desk and rang the bell. She jiggled about from one foot to another, waiting for someone to appear, unable to control her nerves and anxiously tapping her fingers on the counter top. After what seemed an interminably long time, but was probably actually about two minutes, a bored-looking woman emerged from behind a screen.

"Yes?"

"I'm Elena Ferrara's mother. I believe you're treating her now."

The woman paged frustratingly slowly through a pile of papers.

"Yes", she concluded.

Wondering whether the woman was capable of communicating in anything other than monosyllables, Vanessa asked "So can I come in? I'd like to be with her."

"Minor?"

"Sorry?"

"Is she a minor?" the woman repeated slowly, as if dealing with someone intellectually challenged.

"Yes."

"OK, one moment."

The woman disappeared again behind the screen. There was no further sign of life for a time, while behind the glass doors Vanessa could hear two women animatedly discussing what they were going to cook for dinner that evening. Damn it, why couldn't they just let her in to see her daughter? Elena had always been terrified of blood and doctors. Taking her for vaccinations had been a nightmare, and she had nearly fainted when the school screened a film about first aid. Not being very fond of doctors, dentists and medical procedures herself, Vanessa sympathised entirely and knowing that Elena was not likely to be coping well on her own she desperately needed reassurance that everything was under control.

Finally the automatic doors slid open and a nurse gestured to her to come in, leading her into one of the small treatment rooms off the corridor. Elena was sitting on the couch with a large sticking plaster over her left temple. She was very pale and obviously not happy, but at least she was not completely hysterical, which was already an improvement on Vanessa's expectations.

The doctor turned towards her as she arrived.

"Ah, you must be the mother. We've just finished medicating your daughter. We had to give her a couple of stitches, but there are no signs of any serious problems. However, given that she lost consciousness for a few seconds we'd like to keep her in for observation tonight and maybe do a scan tomorrow morning."

"Yes, I understand" replied Vanessa, silently dreading her daughter's reaction. Secretly, she was rather relieved she had missed the stitching up. She would have done her best to be strong and supportive, but she could hardly bear to watch injections or blood tests, whether her own or other people's, so she couldn't guarantee that she would have remained standing.

"The nurse will take you through to the paediatric ward shortly, once you have filled in a couple of forms", the doctor said briskly, before turning on his heel and heading out of the room.

Elena looked up towards her mother, her face crumpling.

"Mum, I don't want to stay here. Please take me home."

"I know how you feel, believe me I do, but we have to be sure that you're OK before we go home. It's only for one night."

"I *am* OK. Mum please…"

"Now come along", the nurse interrupted, "get into this wheelchair and I'll take you to the ward. Have you got her health card?" she asked, turning to Vanessa. "I need it to complete the documentation."

"I think so", Vanessa pulled her wallet out of her bag and leafed through an ample selection of credit, cash and fidelity cards, until she finally located the right one.

Then, after completing and signing the form, she followed the nurse as they wound their way through a maze of corridors, into the lift, and then along further corridors at considerable pace, until they finally arrived at the children's ward. Here they were handed over to another nurse and Elena was assigned a bed in a three-bedded ward with only one other occupant, a girl around ten years old, accompanied by her mother. Vanessa was pleasantly surprised to learn that the armchairs beside each bed in the ward were actually foldaway beds and parents were allowed, indeed actively encouraged to stay with their children overnight; a far cry from her own childhood, when she had spent two weeks in hospital in an isolation ward after a bout of rampant impetigo, with her mother only being allowed to visit for an hour twice a day.

As soon as they arrived at the ward, Vanessa had called Ursula to let her know where they were, before then attempting unsuccessfully to get in touch with Ben and equally unsuccessfully to convince Elena that a brief stay in hospital would not be the end of the world. A few minutes later Ursula appeared at the door, striking as ever with her red hair and high heels. At that moment Vanessa felt her phone vibrating in her pocket, extracted it and saw with relief that it was Ben. She went into the corridor to answer the call, and from the door of the ward Ursula could see her walking backwards and forwards, gesticulating wildly.

"I can't believe it!" Vanessa exclaimed as she came back into the room. "Why does everything always have to happen at once? The car won't start. Ben thinks it's probably just the battery, but he's at a friend's house several kilometres outside Verona and everything's closed by now, so he doesn't know whether he'll be able to sort it out until tomorrow, and Dad won't be back until tomorrow evening from Milan either. Obviously I'll to stay here overnight, but I need to get some things for Elena from home. And arrange for someone to take care of the dog as well!"

"Is no problem. I take you home to get things and then I take you again here and then I go home", announced Ursula in her usual telegraphic style.

"Honestly? Thank you so much."

Although she had no desire whatsoever to be beholden to Ursula, of all people, Vanessa was desperate enough to take any help that was offered. So she reassured Elena that she would be back in an hour, at the latest, and the two women left the hospital and drove to Vanessa's house, about fifteen minutes away. Once there, they were greeted enthusiastically by Spot, who loved anybody who gave him enough attention. So Vanessa left Ursula and the dog to entertain each other and went up to Elena's room to pack a bag with wash things, pyjamas and a change of clothing, along with the only things specifically requested by her daughter: phone charger, chocolate and a book, in that order.

When she came down again, Spot was sleeping on the sofa with his head on Ursula's lap.

"Well, he's certainly taken to you!" commented Vanessa.

Ursula looked up at her from the sofa "I take him home with me. He is a very nice dog."

"Are you sure? I can probably ask a neighbour otherwise, because I don't know when I will be able to get someone to come and collect him tomorrow."

"No, no. I love dogs. I am happy he come with me."

More than a little surprised by this side of her employer that she had never come across, Vanessa then collected Spot's basket, lead and a bag of dog food and they loaded everything into the back seat of Ursula's car, along with the dog himself, who settled happily into his basket and seemed unperturbed by the unusual situation, or indeed Ursula's manic driving. When Vanessa got out of the car at the hospital, pushing forward the seat to grab the bag from the back seat, he jumped up and made an initial attempt to follow her, but sat down immediately when she closed the door, staring at her through the window with his head askew, as if a little uncertain about what was going on. Vanessa waved goodbye as Ursula screeched off, glad at least to have got the dog sorted out. She took a deep breath, summoned up her courage and headed back into the hospital.

CHAPTER 31

On Sunday morning Janet rolled over cautiously, trying not to wake David as she got up. She was not one for sleeping late, so she thought she might go out for a quick run, come back for a shower and then make them breakfast. It was one of the few times that David had stayed overnight and it gave her a slightly strange feeling to wake up with someone beside her, as she normally avoided having men come back to her apartment. It was if she wanted to prevent them encroaching on her space, which was a little absurd given that at the same time she yearned to find someone to share her life with.

As she was pulling on her leggings, sitting on the edge of the bed, David opened one eye and stretched out an arm to caress her back.

"Are you going somewhere?"

"I'm just off for a quick run. I'll be back in less than half an hour, so don't bother to get up." She leaned over to kiss him, barely brushing his lips with her own. "When I get back I'll sort out some breakfast. In fact I can pick up some fresh croissants on the way."

"If you like I'll get dressed and come with you", David said sleepily.

"No, don't worry. I'll be really quick."

"OK. Wake me up when you get back". He closed his eyes and rolled over onto his side, embracing the pillow.

Janet took a five euro note from her purse and slipped it into her money belt for the croissants. They weren't really croissants of course, as Italians prefer sweet things for breakfast, but they were the same shape. The local bakery offered them with jam, custard or chocolate filling, or else without filling, also in the wholemeal version, but always and inevitably sweet.

As Janet left the house, she asked herself why she was rather relieved that David had not insisted on joining her, when she enjoyed being with him so much. One reason was undoubtedly that she just liked being on her own for a while, but there was more than that. When they were together, she always had the feeling that people were looking at them, wondering why such a young and attractive man would choose to be with an older woman. Maybe it was just in her mind, and it didn't seem to bother him at all, but it made her uncomfortable and she tended to discourage displays of affection in public.

The twenty-minute run cleared her mind and left her pleasantly tired, but at the same time invigorated. Janet jogged up to the bakery and bought three assorted croissants, picking up an extra one in case David had a strong preference for one type or another, as she hadn't known him long enough to be certain about his culinary tastes. He was already up when she got back to the flat and was in the process of preparing the moka pot to brew coffee. He turned and smiled, wrapping his arms around her and pushing her hair back from her forehead.

"Hello gorgeous!"

Janet extracted herself from his embrace. "I won't feel gorgeous until I've had a shower. I'm all hot and sweaty."

"Can I come and wash your back?"

Knowing where this was going and not in the mood, Janet laughed it off "Actually, I'd rather you made the coffee! I'll be back in a flash." Then, seeing his slightly hurt expression she smiled, "I promise I'll make it up to you later!"

When she emerged refreshed from the shower, David had brewed the coffee and set the table for breakfast. Janet embraced him from behind and kissed his shoulder.

"Thanks, you're a treasure. Can I hire you?"

"No, but you can have me permanently if you like." David turned, suddenly serious, looking her straight in the eyes. He hesitated for a moment before speaking.

"You know I have to leave the room in Clare's flat in a few days, because it's already booked for some Iranian students? Well I had found another room, but that has fallen through. So I was wondering how you would feel if I came and lived with you, at least for a while, to see if it works out. I know we've only known each other for a couple of months, but you must realise I'm mad about you."

Janet was totally taken aback. "But David, honestly it's way too early to be thinking about living together. I think you're amazing, but I'm not sure we really have a future together. Anyway, don't you have to go back to England in the summer?"

"I have to go back to present my dissertation, but then there's nothing stopping me from coming back afterwards. I can always find work teaching and in the meantime I can do research. What is it that scares you so much, or do you just not care as much about me as I do about you?"

"Of course I care about you, but I want to be realistic about our relationship. You're so much younger than me, and in a couple of months you may look at me and see an older woman who no longer attracts you. I'm not sure I could bear it."

"You're talking as there were a gap of twenty years, not nine! There are plenty of happily married couples in which one partner is ten years younger than the other."

"Yes, but it's practically always the woman who is younger!"

David rolled his eyes. "Oh for heaven's sake! We're not in the 1950s. What kind of feminist are you? I really would never have expected you to come out with such a pathetic excuse!"

Janet started to get annoyed. "It's not an excuse, it's just a question of common sense. I'm a 35-year-old woman. If I want to have children I only have a few years, whereas you haven't even finished your studies, so there is no way you are going to want to settle down and have a family in the near future."

"How do you know? Have you asked me? Or are you just assuming that I will be immature and unwilling to commit because I'm a man?"

Janet stared at him furiously. "OK then. If I said I wanted to start trying for a baby next month what would you say? Are you ready to be a father?"

David drew in his breath as if about to speak, but then lapsed into silence.

"You see!" said Janet partly triumphant and partly horrified that she was deliberately frightening off the only man she had really considered as a possible soul mate for years.

"Now you're just being ridiculous. I said I wanted to move in with you, not start a family! There's plenty of time to think about that side of things."

"Not for me. The point is that you can afford to have a passionate relationship with a woman for a year, or a few years, before deciding whether you're truly meant for each other. And the reality is that you would probably eventually decide that the age gap was too big and be more attracted to someone closer to your own age."

"Good grief, so now you're anticipating what I will do in a few years time. Can't you just live in the present?"

Janet walked over to the table and poured herself a cup of coffee. She stared down at the now cold coffee and said softly, "no, I don't think I can."

"So what are you saying? That it's all off because at some point in the future I might no longer be attracted to you? Or do I have to sign a commitment here and now that I am willing to be a father?"

David stood there dismayed, waiting for some response from Janet, but she couldn't bring herself to speak. Eventually David went into the bedroom and started collecting his things. He packed everything into a bag and then returned to the kitchen, still hoping that Janet would throw her arms around his neck and stop him before he left the flat.

"I don't understand why you insist on ruining everything", he said finally, as he opened the apartment door. "Still, if that's what you want.....goodbye Janet".

As the door closed softly behind him, Janet walked over to the sofa and sat down. Was he right? Was she just ruining things out of pig-headedness? Or was she simply protecting herself from getting hurt in the future? In any case she felt empty and depressed.

In this situation her friend Vanessa would have drowned, or rather suffocated, her sorrows with a bucket of chocolate ice-cream, while Janet would normally have gone for a run, but as she had just got back from one she couldn't face going out again. Instead she sat down at the kitchen table aimlessly, drinking cold coffee and wondering why she always felt the need to sabotage her relationships before they even began. Was it control thing? Was she just afraid of getting hurt? Whatever the reason, it was about time she got her act together. Janet sighed.

Getting out her PC she decided that today she would do what she always did and take refuge in work.

CHAPTER 32

As Janet tended to keep very quiet on the subject, Vanessa was unaware of her friend's tormented love life. In any case she was having her own problems, while her family seemed completely oblivious that anything was wrong. They were so used to relying on her to remember everyone's appointments, organise family holidays, pay the bills and generally manage the household, while also working 3 days a week at the school and part-time from home, that nobody noticed that she was finding it increasingly difficult to cope. Vanessa found herself having frequent fantasies about escaping to a hippy commune in Asia, faking her own death or simply disappearing for a while. She had thought that it would get easier as the children got older, but somehow that did not seem to be the case, and what's more she now admitted to herself that she just didn't enjoy teaching any more.

Ursula was being even more obnoxious than usual and kept trying to push extra work on her, but as she had been so helpful when Elena had been taken to hospital Vanessa felt obliged to do everything possible to demonstrate her gratitude. For a brief time she seriously considered the possibility that she had misjudged Ursula, especially given the fact that Spot so clearly adored her. Weren't dogs supposed to understand these things intuitively? However, after the umpteenth example of Ursula's unreasonableness and total lack of sensitivity (when she charged into Vanessa's classroom to upbraid her in front of everyone for failing to complete some forms, forms that she only later realised she had never been given), she decided that Spot's discernment was evidently not to be trusted.

What made it worse was that Vanessa realised perfectly well that she was wasting her time and energy moaning about insignificant problems, whereas what she really needed to do was sort her priorities out. Elena's recent trip to the hospital had brought it home to her that her family's health was the only truly important issue. Fortunately Elena had been allowed to leave the hospital after a couple of days and had suffered no serious consequences as a result of her fall. She had complained of a severe headache for a couple of days and had been warned to take a rest from sport for a while, but apart from a lingering headache when she got overtired, she seemed completely back to normal. Nevertheless, Vanessa couldn't help being anxious about the possible long-term consequences and it seemed to be just one more thing to be added to the potential list of things to worry about.

Today, having got back later than expected from school, she was now sitting at the PC, trying to finish a less than fascinating translation about fungal pathogens, an article that she had promised send off to the author by 9 o'clock the following morning. Her train of thought was interrupted when Ben called up from the kitchen with the inevitable "Mum, what's for dinner?"

Vanessa glanced at the clock, realising that it was already 8 o'clock in the evening.

"Oh God, I don't know. What's in the fridge?" she yelled.

There was a moment's pause, during which Ben presumably checked out the situation.

"Practically nothing. Didn't you go shopping today?"

Vanessa counted to ten.

"No time. Can't you do some pasta?"

"What with?"

"I don't know. Tuna?"

"What?"

"OK. I give up. I'm coming."

As she came down the stairs, Elena looked up at her from the sofa.

"Mum, you know I can't eat carbohydrates in the evening, otherwise I'll never be able to keep my weight under control."

"Oh for heaven's sake. You won't get fat if you eat pasta for once in the evening."

"You always say that!"

In the kitchen, Ben was still inspecting the contents of the fridge. "There are two eggs, an old cucumber, four slices of salami and not a lot else."

Outside, on the patio, Giovanni was stretched out on a garden chair, sipping a glass of white wine and smoking a cigarette.

"I could nip down to the supermarket if you like", he offered, unenthusiastically.

"Too late, it'll be closed by now."

He shrugged. "We can do spaghetti with olive oil, garlic and chilli."

"Mum! Not carbohydrates please..." Elena shouted from the sofa.

"OK, I'll make you an omelette."

"I quite fancy an omelette as well", said Ben.

"There aren't enough eggs for both of you."

"So of course Elena gets them!"

"Well she was the one who said she didn't want carbohydrates", commented Vanessa. "You always like pasta."

"Well I wasn't in the mood this evening. But go ahead, make Elena happy. Everyone always does."

"Oh for heaven's sake! What is wrong with you, this evening? If you were so desperate for something else you could have done some shopping yourself."

"I haven't got any money, besides how was I supposed to know there was nothing to eat?"

"By looking?" suggested Vanessa sarcastically.

"Ah, so now it's my fault. Don't blame me if you forgot to do the shopping!"

"I did not *forget* to the shopping", said Vanessa between gritted teeth. "I was at school, and since I came back I've been working at the computer. Now do you think that between the three of you, you could manage to prepare dinner?"

"Why are you yelling?" shouted Giovanni, from outside. "I wish you two wouldn't argue all the time".

"And I wish that someone would give me a hand once in a while!"

"That's hardly fair. I've just got back from work."

"So have I, and I'm still trying to work, but I can't because nobody else can be bothered to do anything about dinner" said Vanessa angrily. "There are two other adults in this house, as well as one teenager approaching adulthood, but it never seems to occur to any of them to take the initiative to organise anything."

"Oh stay calm Mum" said Ben irritatingly. "You're just in a bad mood because you need a break."

"Exactly!" exclaimed Vanessa. "I never get one. Your idea of a break is a couple of hours playing video games, Elena is practically glued to the sofa watching the TV and Dad sits down calmly on the patio to have a glass of wine and read the online newspaper. My break, on the other hand, is usually doing the shopping, cooking or unloading the dishwasher. I am so bloody fed up I could scream! And now if you'll excuse me I have to get on with some work." Vanessa stormed up the stairs in a truly foul mood.

As she reached the top of the stairs she felt an excruciating pain at the back of her head. It had come on in a matter of seconds and it was so violent that she just dived onto the bed, clasping the back of her head with her hands. She lay there panting for a few moments, trying to breathe through the pain. She had always been prone to headaches but had never experienced anything like this before. She remembered that there were some painkillers in the drawer of the bedside table and cautiously reached out to get them, rapidly extracting two tablets from the blister pack. The prospect of moving in order to get a glass of water was simply too daunting, nor did she particularly fancy screaming for help, so she simply swallowed the pills without water (a practice perfected over years of taking the contraceptive pill in the dark in the middle of the night, having forgotten to take it before going to bed).

After a few minutes the pain was gradually wearing off and Vanessa felt almost human, if a little shaken. She lay there for a few minutes before daring to move, but finally pulled herself up into a sitting position on the side of the bed. She was relieved to find that the worst was definitely over, but she couldn't yet contemplate dragging herself to the computer to finish the translation, so she decided to rest for a little while and delicately lowered herself back down onto the pillow. She was woken by Giovanni's voice as he called up to her that the pasta was ready. For once in her life she was not hungry at all, so she told him to leave her plate in the microwave and she would eat it later, when she had finished working.

The dreaded translation could no longer be delayed, unless she decided to get up at 6 o'clock the following morning to complete it. Vanessa weighed up the pros and cons, but being the sort of person who required a considerable amount of warm-up time and at least two large cups of tea before being getting her brain into gear, she decided it was better to get it over with now. Sighing, she headed into the office, resigned to the fact that she needed to spend the next hour or two facing the intricacies of molecular plant pathology. For her, one of the things that made translating more interesting than teaching was the variety, but at the same time this was in itself a potential problem, as she was forced to deal with subjects about which she knew absolutely nothing. Thank God for the internet, she thought. She had no idea how translators used to manage before the era of digital communication, unless they had dozens of dictionaries and encyclopaedias available.

Vanessa was reading through her completed translation when Giovanni wandered into the office bearing a peace offering in the form of a cup of green tea.

"How are you love? Have you nearly finished?"

"Almost done now thanks", she gratefully accepted the tea.

"I left your pasta in the microwave if you want it", he said.

"Actually I'm not really hungry. I've got a bit of a headache. I might just have some fruit before going to bed, but thanks for getting dinner anyway."

"Actually Elena made her own omelette, and Ben even cleared the table before going out. We'll all try to help out more, I promise", he kissed her on the top of her head. "Just remind us if we're slacking!"

"It would just be nice not always to have to ask" said Vanessa resignedly, "but thanks anyway. I know you do your fair share. Maybe we just haven't trained the kids properly. Often it's such hard work getting them to do anything that it's easier to do it yourself."

"They're good kids, just a bit lazy," Giovanni smiled indulgently.

"Anyway, let me finish off this translation so I don't have to think about it anymore." Vanessa turned back to the computer as her husband left the office. Despite struggling to maintain her concentration, half an hour later she had finally managed to complete the job and send off the article via e-mail, breathing a huge sigh of relief as she turned off the PC.

Another long day over.

CHAPTER 33

One of the things that Vanessa truly hated was going to the dentist, and thus she was inevitably seriously overdue for a dental hygiene session. It was absolutely no use people telling her she was being childish, falsely reassuring her it was an utterly pain free procedure, because in her experience it was infinitely worse than having a filling done, probably not helped by the fact that she always put it off as long as possible. She realised that in a way this was counterproductive, as the longer she waited the worse it was, but this approach did nevertheless reduce the number of occasions she was forced to submit to the procedure, so it was a question of weighing up the best unpleasantness to frequency ratio. In any case, hygiene sessions came pretty near the top of her list of least favourite things to do, along with visits to the gynaecologist, obviously excluding serious events like having to take her children to the ER or going to funerals.

She had been terrified of going to the dentist for as long as she could remember; even accompanying someone else there brought her out in a cold sweat, so she was already anxious on the way to the surgery in the car, and the palms of her hands started to perspire as soon as she came through the door and recognised the unmistakeable smell she associated so clearly with dentists and hospitals. She forced herself to concentrate on breathing normally and sat down on the edge of a chair in the waiting room with that feeling of dread that often made the anticipation of going to the dentist worse than the actual treatment. After a few minutes the assistant called her into the torture chamber and invited her to take a seat in front of an array of hideous-looking instruments, tying a large bib around her neck. Catching her unawares, someone behind her reclined the chair so far back that she had to fight the temptation to immediately sit up and run off. As impotent as a beetle on its back waving its legs in the air, Vanessa looked up to see the dentist, already kitted out with mask and goggles, making her feel that she was radioactive, or an extraterrestrial about to be examined by a curious scientist.

"So how are we today?" he said, his voice dripping with that false cheeriness typical of medics who are about to do something unpleasant to you.

"OK thank you," Vanessa responded with minimal conviction, far too nervous to contemplate a witty response.

"Shall we get on then?"

She nodded as he turned on the descaling machine, the sound already enough to set her nerves on edge. He had barely started on the first tooth when she felt the headache hit her like a mallet on the back of the head. She tried to resist for a couple of seconds, but it was only getting worse, so she gestured wildly to the dentist to stop.

"Did I hurt you?" he asked in some surprise.

"Not you. It's my head," she managed to blurt out, pulling herself up into a sitting position and clasping her hands around the back of her head. The pain was even worse than on the previous occasion, three days earlier, and she was sweating profusely.

"Do you want to lie down?" the dentist asked.

"I don't think so. No. Oh God...." said Vanessa desperately, clutching her knees to her chest.

"A painkiller?"

"Yes, anything."

The assistant disappeared behind a screen and reappeared shortly with a glass of water and a couple of pills, which Vanessa gulped down rapidly. Initially she was unaware of what was going on around her, but after a few minutes, too soon for the pills to have taken effect she realised, the pain began to wear off and she felt well enough to sit by herself in an empty surgery for a while and recover her aplomb. After a further 15 minutes she was ready to go home. The assistant looked at her with some concern.

"Are you sure you're OK to drive? Would you like me to call somebody?"

"No, it's fine thanks. I feel much better."

She couldn't wait to get home and lie down, crashing out on the bed the moment she arrived, but after sleeping for an hour or so she felt considerably revived. She was a little shaky, but well enough to once again resume her normal activities. She was however forced to recognise that this second episode had really frightened her, realising she needed to go and see the doctor at the earliest opportunity, however much she disliked the idea.

The following week Vanessa was telling Clare about her experiences during a tea break between lessons.

"Unfortunately I couldn't get an appointment for a few days, and when I did my usual doctor was on holiday and his substitute seemed to think I was just neurotic. She told me to go home and relax and prescribed some tranquillisers, but I have no intention of taking them without knowing whether they're really necessary. She did give me a prescription for a specialist visit with a neurologist, but I can't get an appointment at the hospital for at least a couple of months".

"Have you had any more attacks?" asked Clare.

"Only one milder episode, when I got up to speak at a meeting. It seems to be connected to anxiety or intense emotion in some way. The trouble is that I'm so terrified that I'm going to have another attack that I'm frightened of doing anything."

"What about seeing a specialist privately?"

"Yes Giovanni is insisting that I do that, but the only neurologist I know is Elena's and he's away for over a month as well. I don't know where else to go."

"I think I do. Did you know that Marco's a neurologist? And a good one, I gather."

"Really? It's a shame he's not one of my students. I've seen him around once or twice at the school but I've never spoken to him."

"I could ring him if you like. We're still on speaking terms, even if we're not seeing each other any more." Secretly, Clare rather relished the idea of having an excuse to call Marco.

"Would you really? I would feel so much happier if a specialist reassured me that nothing is seriously wrong. I'm essentially an optimist, but at the same time there is still that niggling doubt at the back of my mind that I have a brain tumour or I'm about to have a stroke!"

"Don't be daft. Anyway, I'll ring him this evening and see whether he can manage to see you in the next few days, or at least recommend somebody else."

"Thanks. That would be great."

True to her word, Clare phoned Marco later that evening. He seemed pleasantly surprised to hear from her and was more than cooperative. When he heard about Vanessa's symptoms he immediately suggested that she should come and see him the following morning at the hospital, so Clare phoned her fellow teacher straight away, urging her not to miss the opportunity to set her mind at rest.

The following day the two women saw each other at the school in the evening between lessons and Vanessa rapidly updated Clare on developments.

"Marco was really kind and understanding, but hardly reassuring. After I explained everything to him he gave me a note for the doctor ordering an emergency CT scan in order to exclude anything serious, presumably the possibility of an aneurysm. But what really got me worried was when he said I should avoid any major physical effort or getting agitated and overexcited until I had the results. It made me feel there was a danger that my head might explode at any minute! There was a sort of surreal moment when he started explaining how to go to the loo without straining; that was really embarrassing."

"So have you had the scan?"

"Not yet. I'm going tomorrow morning and to be honest I can't wait. At least maybe then I'll have some answers."

Clare looked at her watch, "I'm afraid I have to go now. The next class is due to start, but please let me know how it goes."

"Of course. Will do."

In the morning Vanessa left early for the hospital, allowing ample time to look for a parking place, always a challenge at the local hospital. In the end she decided to park in the supermarket opposite and walk to the clinic; it was less hassle and didn't involve strenuous negotiations with self-appointed car-park attendants. Even after making her way to the reception desk, picking up a ticket and waiting to pay the fixed charge for the visit, she was still early, so she sat down in the waiting room with the other patients to await her turn.

She was not particularly anxious about the scan itself. She had had an MRI scan before, and although it was a bit claustrophobic being shunted into the tunnel, from her point of view it had the big advantage of not involving any invasive procedures. In this case she knew that she would have contrast material injected into her arm, but this was the sort of thing she could just about cope with without major trauma. No, what really bothered her was the possibility of getting another headache while she was inside the machine, given that they seemed to be triggered by stress. She knew you had a panic button while you were inside, but would they be able to get her out quickly enough before she went completely berserk? Aware that the fear of getting another headache might itself trigger another attack, she was trying, with little success, to breathe slowly and stay completely calm, something which was not her forte at the best of times.

When they finally called her in for the scan Vanessa was pleased to see that the machine was different from the one used for the MRI, more like a ring than a tunnel and definitely less claustrophobic. The nurse had already stuck a needle into her arm in preparation for the injection of contrast material, so now all she needed to do was climb onto the couch and be wheeled into position with her head under the ring. She had been warned that she would feel hot when the contrast was injected, but she was not entirely prepared for the strange sensation when this happened. She had imagined a sort of overall hot flush, not unfamiliar to menopausal women, whereas what she actually felt was a sudden heat in the genital region (for a moment she almost thought with horror that she had wet herself), with a warm glow that then shifted about to different body parts; weird but not in any way painful.

Once the examination was complete Vanessa was extracted from the machine and invited to come and collect the results in a couple of days. This was in itself reassuring, she decided, as she was moderately certain that if there had been a major problem they would have said something immediately. In her experience the health service in Italy was excellent in terms of the diagnosis and treatment of serious health issues. Where it tended to fall down was in terms of humanity. Doctors and nurses did not seem to be trained to deal with patients, and thus tended to treat them as an inconvenience, with pain relief being considered an unnecessary extravagance. Of course there were plenty of compassionate and caring professionals, but largely because they were by nature like that, not because they were trained to consider the psychological as well as the physical wellbeing of patients as a priority.

At all events Vanessa was so relieved *not* to have had another violent headache that she was unjustifiably cheerful and self-satisfied. How absurd was it, she wondered, to feel proud of herself simply for not becoming hysterical while doing a perfectly routine examination? Whatever the reason, she walked back to the car with a new found bounce in her step, reasonably confident she was not going to die in the next week and finally feeling that the oppressive sensation in the pit of her stomach was lifting. Of course, she wouldn't really be able to relax until the results came in and the doctor confirmed that there was nothing fundamentally wrong with her brain, but at least she felt that she had taken some action towards finding out whether a major disaster was imminent. As someone who had always placed more emphasis on intellectual rather than physical activity, she was absolutely terrified of any impairment to her mental faculties. It frightened her far more than the idea of a heart attack or some disease affecting her physical capabilities.

As she walked back to the car she made a promise to herself that she would make a serious effort to lose weight and take more exercise, even if the results of the test were negative, or rather especially if the results were negative. If she was graced with another chance, she owed it to herself to make the most of it.

CHAPTER 34

The sunlight bounced off the waters of the lake as Clare and Marco strolled down the promenade towards the centre of Sirmione, the swallow-tail merlons of the castle's tall tower standing out against the azure blue sky. Representing a rare example of a medieval port fortification, the fortress was located in the old town at the end of a long narrow peninsula jutting out into Lake Garda, offering a spectacularly picturesque setting, amply justifying the huge number of tourists visiting throughout the year. On this balmy Sunday evening Clare was instead pleasantly surprised by the lack of crowds and the total tranquillity of the place, presumably because it was still low season.

When she had phoned Marco to thank him for seeing Vanessa so quickly, she was genuinely touched that he remembered it was her birthday the following week. He had insisted that they should go out to celebrate, and had suggested going to the famous spa in the centre of Sirmione, where they could enjoy the magnificent views while relaxing in the sulphurous waters of the hot springs. Clare was aware that she was at risk of falling back into the same pattern with Marco, but frankly she didn't care. She had missed him, and given that she was planning to go back to England in a few weeks she decided she might as well enjoy her remaining time in Italy.

Now, as they walked through the narrow streets, heading for the spa, she could already feel the attraction between them, although they hadn't even touched each other, apart from a peck on the cheek when Marco had picked her up in Verona.

They separated at the reception desk, making their way to the changing rooms and emerging on the other side, dressed in identical white towelling robes provided by the spa. Clare immediately spotted Marco, who even managed to look elegant in a bathrobe and flip flops, and they made their way outside, leaving their robes on two loungers overlooking the lake and slipping into the warm waters of the outdoor pool. There was the usual array of hydromassage jets and water features to be found in spas around the world, undoubtedly pleasurable and relaxing, but what really made this spa special were the sulphurous waters of the natural hot springs and the spectacular views.

The most popular feature was a row of hydromassage beds with pressurised water jets in one of the swimming pools, looking directly out towards the lake. There was only one free when Clare and Marco arrived, but they were wide enough to accommodate two people, so they squeezed in together, reclining blissfully amidst the bubbling waters. Clare felt strangely shy, as if it were the first time he had seen her in a bikini. In effect, it *was* the first time he had seen her in a bikini, although he had seen her in much less, but for some reason she felt more embarrassed about being partly dressed than about being completely unclothed. She was vividly aware of the contact along their thighs and of Marco's arm around her shoulders.

After a few minutes she turned her head to smile at him. "It is a truly special place. Thank you for bringing me here."

"I'm glad you like it. I wanted to take you somewhere beautiful to celebrate your birthday."

"There are so many beautiful things in Italy. I shall really miss them when I go home."

"Why? Are you planning on going back to the UK?"

"Yes, I think so, although I haven't decided definitively yet. I only intended to come for a year and I miss my friends and family."

Marco was clearly taken aback. "That's a shame." He paused, "I've missed you, you know. I was hoping to have the chance to spend some more time with you."

Although her heart was beating faster, Clare was unwilling to admit that nothing would have pleased her more. She was deeply attracted to him, but she had enough sense of her own worth not to show her vulnerability to someone who perhaps considered her principally as a temporary diversion. She decided to play it fairly cool.

"I shan't be going for a couple of months anyway, so if you like there's time for you to play the tour guide!"

She slid off the Jacuzzi bed and into the swimming pool. "Come on. Let's go and try those water jets over there." She swam off, leaving him to follow her, and incidentally discovering that she was probably a better swimmer than he was, as he struggled to catch her up.

"I'm impressed," he said when he reached her. "You're a really strong swimmer."

"Oh, years of swimming courses at home. It's the only sport I'm any good at, probably one of the few things I'm good at in general!"

"Hardly! And if you're you fishing for complements, I must say that your Italian has improved tremendously. You've made more progress in a few months than I have in years."

237

Clare realised with surprise that without even noticing it, for the first time in their relationship they had been conversing in Italian.

"That's normal. You can't help learning a language when you live in the place. I only speak English at school, and with my cousin David, but he's moved out of the house now and got his own place. I even think and dream in Italian now!"

"And of course you're so young! I forget. Your mind is still so flexible."

"Ah, there speaks the neurologist!"

"Or rather a man who is eleven years older than you and probably already in cognitive decline!"

"Rubbish! You've just never spent any time living in an English-speaking country."

"And probably never will, by now."

"Maybe you could have a sabbatical year."

"Possibly. But it's fairly unlikely I fear."

Changing the subject Marco pointed towards the lake.

"Look, the sun's going down. How glorious are those colours?"

"The sunset is just beautiful. Shall we get out of the pool and watch it from the wooden deck?

They climbed out of the water and wandered over to the row of loungers facing onto the lake, so close to the water that it was almost like being on a boat. Wrapped in their white bathrobes, they lay back, holding hands and watching the sun fall behind the horizon. It was a magical moment, thought Clare, a moment when it was almost impossible not to be romantic, one of those occasions when she seriously called into question her intention to return to the less than fair climes of northern England. Still, it would take more than a glorious moment to change her mind about going back. There were so many things she missed at home, even though she was well aware there would be many other things she would miss if she left Italy. Was Marco one of them? He probably was, but she couldn't make him take her more seriously. A line from a song came to mind "I can't make you love me if you won't", and childish as it was, she wanted the fairy tale ending, not just a passionate love affair.

In the meantime, however, it was a wonderful evening. Clare and Marco tried out the different saunas and 'emotional' showers. They improved their circulation by walking through the hot and cold tanks, flushed toxins out of their bodies in the Finnish sauna and relaxed in whirlpool baths. When they had had enough of wellness treatments they sat down on the terrace of the bar and ate melon and Parma ham, accompanied by a glass of cool white wine.

"This is extraordinarily civilised", said Clare. "I feel like a proper VIP. Not at all what I'm used to!"

"And just think, people have been doing the same thing in this very place since Roman times!"

"What? Exactly here?"

"Well, in Sirmione anyway. There's an archaeological area on the tip of the peninsula with a huge Roman villa called the 'Grotte di Catullo'. There were undoubtedly thermal baths there. We could go there if you like sometime."

"That would be really interesting. So did the villa belong to Catullus?"

"I think that's debatable. The name was attributed to the villa as a result of one of his poems entitled 'Return to Sirmione', but the ruins you can see now actually date back to a later period."

"Well, whoever's residence it was, the Romans certainly had the knack of choosing beautiful places for their villas, and with all mod cons as well!"

"Yes, underfloor heating, thermal baths; it was a good life, so long as you were rich of course!"

"So nothing much has changed then", commented Clare.

"Oh, I think we can safely say that life is a bit better for most people now than it was two thousand years ago, certainly in Europe."

"Perhaps", said Clare thoughtfully.

Once they finished their meal they sat for a little longer, enjoying the atmosphere, although by now it was almost completely dark. They could see the lights of the towns on the other side of the lake, across the gently rippling black water.

They adjourned to the respective changing rooms to recover their clothes, before meeting up in the foyer. Clare didn't bother to dry her hair, as it was a warm evening, and she didn't want to leave Marco waiting for too long. In actual fact she was ready before he was; she had forgotten to take into account how careful Italian men are about their appearance. So he inevitably emerged looking immaculate, while she looked like a foreign tourist on her way back from the beach.

They came out of the spa and walked back through the town towards the car. As they approached the bridge over the canal Clare noticed Marco stiffen slightly, and followed his gaze towards a strikingly beautiful woman with black hair in a white linen dress, who was approaching with two women friends. She was tall and well-proportioned, probably around thirty years old, her classic Mediterranean beauty carefully enhanced by accurate makeup and perfectly-cut clothes. Everything about her screamed money, from the long gold earrings and stylish haircut to the designer shoes and handbag. Furthermore she had that air of overwhelming self-confidence that goes with being both rich and beautiful.

The woman drew to a halt and smiled coolly when she saw Marco, revealing her pearly white teeth.

"Well, what a surprise! What are you doing here?"

"We have just come from the spa."

"How nice." The woman cast an appraising glance at Clare and was clearly underwhelmed. "Aren't you going to introduce me to your *friend*?"

"Of course." For once Marco seemed distinctly ill at ease, turning towards Clare, who had remained half a step behind. "Clare this is Marina," he said succinctly.

"Pleased to meet you", said Clare, holding out her hand.

Marina briefly offered her a limp hand, with just a hint of a curling lip. "The pleasure is mine. Another English teacher perhaps?"

Clare felt her colour rising. "Yes, I teach English in Verona."

"I thought you might. I do hope Marco is making good progress." Marina turned towards him. "Darling, I can only say that your commitment is commendable!"

"Yes, he is an excellent student, although no longer one of mine", retorted Clare.

"I can imagine."

Despite the warm evening, the atmosphere was decidedly frosty and Marco clearly could not wait to get away.

"Well I think we really should be going, if you will excuse us." He politely said goodbye to Marina and her friends and gently took hold of Clare's elbow, steering her over the bridge and towards the safety of the car. Once away his relief was almost tangible.

"I'm sorry about that. When I suggested we come here I really did not expect to meet my former wife, although she doesn't live far from here. Marina can be rather intimidating."

Clare raised an eyebrow.

"Well she certainly intimidates me! She's very beautiful though."

"Oh yes, there's no doubt that she's beautiful."

They lapsed into a slightly uncomfortable silence as they reached the car. Clare couldn't help but ask herself whether Marco was still in love with Marina. She knew that it had been Marina's decision to leave him, but obviously she had never inquired into the exact circumstances of their divorce. Perhaps he still secretly hoped they would get back together. Certainly having seen his ex, Clare couldn't plausibly consider herself as a rival. Marina was in an altogether different league, and even if she was no longer in the race she set such a high standard that Clare was instantly demoralised.

Just before they reached Verona Marco turned to smile at her. "The night is young. Won't you come in for a coffee?"

Maybe it would all end in tears, but despite her best intentions, Clare nevertheless found herself accepting. "Yes. That would be lovely."

CHAPTER 35

As the gates opened, those spectators with unnumbered seats poured through the entrances at the back of the amphitheatre, making their way up the steep stone steps in an attempt to reach the most sought after places, closer to the front or even more importantly, with the chance of leaning back against the step behind. It was a generally well-behaved crowd, 19th century opera undoubtedly attracting a different kind of audience compared to the one Verona Arena was originally designed for two thousand years earlier.

Vanessa had warned the others to bring cushions and bottles of water with them, as spending three or four hours sitting on marble steps that had been absorbing the heat of the sun all day was inevitably hot and uncomfortable, as well as potentially haemorrhoid-inducing. In any case, inside the venue there were vendors selling everything from opera librettos and CDs to wine and ice-cream. Depending on the weather, they extended their range of goods to include plastic raincoats or blankets, but on this torrid summer evening it was unlikely that such merchandise would be required.

Of the group, Vanessa was probably the only genuine opera-lover, but given that Ursula had access to cut-price tickets for the summer season, she had also managed to convince her two colleagues to come along with her, and at the last moment David had decided to join them as well. They had the very cheapest seats, the unnumbered upper terraces on either side of the stage, but this did not detract from the unique atmosphere of the place, while the acoustics of the amphitheatre ensured that everybody inside could appreciate the music.

The four friends had arrived fairly early in order to ensure they got reasonable places, although they were a fair distance from the stage and it was a bit like having a bird's eye view of the performance. Janet was kicking herself for not having brought her binoculars, while Vanessa had a sort of Mary Poppins bag from which she kept extracting an endless selection of food, plastic bottles of wine and water, and photocopies with a summary of the plot for her friends. There was a pleasant holiday atmosphere among the crowd, largely made up of foreign tourists, but with plenty of Italians as well, while every couple of minutes a vendor would climb up or down the steps, loudly hawking his wares. After battling with complicated tiny cardboard candle holders as intuitive as Ikea flat-pack assembly, the spectators sat clutching the candles distributed at the entrance, ready to light them when the sky began to darken and the performance began.

"I just love the moment when the sun is setting and the walls of the amphitheatre are silhouetted against the sky, while the moon emerges from behind the amphitheatre", said Vanessa. "You can see the lights of hundreds of tiny candles twinkling for a few minutes, just as the orchestra sets off with the overture. It's worth coming just for that."

"Yes, I definitely wouldn't have wanted to go home without experiencing an opera in the Arena", replied Clare "although I'm really more of a theatre person."

"Have you definitely decided to go home then?"

"I'm really torn. I love it here, but I'm a bit homesick too. It's even more difficult because I've started seeing Marco again, but I don't know whether it's serious enough to justify changing my plans. In any case I will have to make a decision before the end of year meeting with Ursula in two weeks' time."

The group lessons at the school had drawn to a close two weeks earlier, with just a few private lessons and the Italian courses continuing until the end of July. After that the school would close completely in August, to re-open its doors in September. The meeting in mid-July was intended to plan the staffing for the following year, so that Ursula and Janet could then sort out the courses.

"Yes, I have my own decisions to make about how much teaching I want to do next year", said Vanessa.

"Hold on a minute. I hope that you aren't both going to abandon me simultaneously!" said Janet with horror.

"Oh don't worry! I'm sure you'll find a solution," smiled Vanessa, as the final gong announced that the performance was about to begin and the crowd grew silent.

She had always had a fondness for Verdi's "La Traviata", because of the contrast between the intimate and touching moments and the more spectacular scenes; plus of course it was a really good story, being based on a novel by Dumas. The opera lacked some of the more theatrical moments intrinsic in Aida, staged every single year at Verona Arena by popular demand, but from Vanessa's point of view it was more satisfying musically.

On this occasion, a Russian soprano was making her debut at the Arena in the title role - the 'Traviata', translatable as a morally corrupt woman, namely Violetta - and doing a good job of it in Vanessa's opinion, while the tenor was slightly disappointing, even though he nevertheless received his share of applause. Italian audiences, even when including a substantial share of foreign tourists, tended to start clapping every time the music stopped, Vanessa found. At amateur level this was an advantage, as it meant that unless you made a complete cock-up of the performance people would applaud enthusiastically anyway, but at professional level it did tend to interrupt the dramatic flow. The set, always a challenge in a venue the size of the Roman arena, was made up of a series of gigantic picture frames, literally framing the scenes in the different houses. The audience gasped as Violetta sang her aria at the end of the first act perched precariously on top of the frame, which rose up until she was at least 5 metres off the ground, and she concluded to thunderous applause. As she was lowered gently to the ground Vanessa was relieved to see that she was in fact belted on, detaching herself to acknowledge the well-deserved acclaim.

It was a relief for all of them to be able to stand up and stretch their legs during the interval, especially for David, who had not heeded Vanessa's advice to bring a cushion. Leaving their coats and bags behind on the stone steps, all four of them headed down the stairs and into the Piazza. Before leaving the Arena Vanessa took one look at the queue for the loo and decided she would be better off going to a bar, so they made for the slightly less obvious one around the corner, in order to avoid the crowds.

When she re-emerged, the others were enjoying a cold beer, but Vanessa reluctantly decided to give it a miss, justifying her refusal as part of her new-found attention to her diet.

"I've been meaning to ask you how all the tests went" said Janet. "Were all the results OK then?" "Yes, there was nothing serious, but some narrowing arteries and high blood pressure mean that I need to make lifestyle changes."

"I've been telling you that for ages! But anyway it must have been quite a scare."

"Oh God yes. It was the most enormous wake-up call, and quite apart from realising that I need to be serious about losing weight and doing more exercise, it made me want to spend more time doing what I really enjoy doing. There's nothing like thinking you might die for making you realise how much you want to live!"

"I can believe that", David broke in, looking at Janet. "You have to take the opportunities life offers. Not worry about everything that might go wrong in the future!"

"He's absolutely right", said Vanessa. "You can't analyse everything all the time. Sometimes you just have to go with what you feel."

Janet glanced from one to the other. "Why do I feel as though I am under attack here?"

Vanessa smiled. "You're not under attack, but you can't deny you're a bit of a control freak."

"Rubbish!" She paused to reflect. "OK, well maybe just a bit! Anyway, it's getting late. We should go back or we risk missing the second act of the opera."

The four of them made their way back to amphitheatre entrance, arriving at their seats just in time for the final gong. They made themselves as comfortable as was possible on two thousand-year-old stone steps and settled down to enjoy the performance. However, by the time the next interval was approaching David was seriously regretting his decision not to come with padding. He had stuffed his coat underneath him to partly alleviate the discomfort, but he was nevertheless secretly relieved when it was time for the second interval, and got to his feet as soon as possible, tilting his head back and stretching his arms out wide in a sort of salute to the moon.

As the second interval was only fifteen minutes long, they decided against leaving the amphitheatre, but all of them took the chance to stand up and stretch out their legs for a few minutes. Janet decided to brave the loo queue, heading off down the steps, while the others stood around chatting. Prompted by discussions around them, the three friends were also talking about the Brexit vote, the results having taken them by surprise that morning.

"When I went to bed at 1 a.m. all the polls were predicting that the voters would decide to remain, so when I got up and found out that people had voted to leave I was totally taken aback. I couldn't quite believe it", said Vanessa.

"Yes, it makes it even more annoying that I wasn't able to vote, because my postal vote didn't arrive in time," complained Clare. "The same thing happened to you David, didn't it?"

"Yes it did. I was really fed up, especially when I discovered that the vote was in favour of leaving. I was a little shell-shocked. Practically everyone I know was in favour of remaining."

"I wasn't even allowed to vote, because I've lived out of the country for over 15 years" commented Vanessa "so in the end, of the four of us the only one who actually got to express their preference was Janet, because she voted by proxy."

"What do you think will be the consequences? Will it make much difference to us personally?" asked Clare.

David stroked his beard pensively. "Probably not in the short term. It'll take a couple of years before we leave anyway, but in the longer term it's certainly not going to help international mobility, and I fear the British economy will suffer, and perhaps also the Italian economy."

"I have dual nationality, as do my children, so it probably won't make any difference specifically to my family" said Vanessa "but I can't help feeling that it's not going to be positive for either the EU or Britain. And what about Scotland, for example? They've just voted to stay in the UK, but will they want to now, given that Scottish voters also voted to stay in the EU?"

David shrugged "I've no idea. Only time will show, but in any case it's bound to be a period of uncertainty."

The gong sounded again to mark the end of the second interval as Janet charged up the stairs, arriving panting just as the lights went down for the final part of the opera.

"Sorry. There was a huge queue outside the ladies loo. I thought I wasn't going to make it back in time", whispered Janet, as she slipped into her place.

It was after midnight when the opera finally ended and the audience swarmed out of the various exits, like bats out of a cave. The four friends stood around for a while outside, amused by the enormous opera sets for other performances positioned incongruously around the piazza, with gigantic knights in full armour set against the background of the Roman amphitheatre, while tourists queued up to take photos of themselves with sphinxes and warriors.

David suggested going for a drink, but Vanessa was keen to get home and Clare claimed that she was too tired, so they said goodbye to the others and headed off in opposite directions, Vanessa towards her car and Clare to her flat, leaving the other two on their own. In actual fact Clare knew that David was still very taken with Janet and would relish the chance to spend some time with her alone, so she thought she would make a strategic withdrawal.

As she arrived at the edge of the Piazza, Clare turned around to look back at her cousin, smiling quietly to herself as she saw him reach for Janet's hand.

CHAPTER 36

When the other two women made their excuses, leaving them standing alone in the middle of the square Janet was not sure whether she was relieved or irritated. She felt surprisingly nervous, as if she were an adolescent waiting for a boy to make the first move, rather than a mature woman who had calmly decided to break off a relationship for which she saw no future.

No sooner had his cousin departed than David smiled at her, stretching out his hand shyly for hers in the hopes that she would not immediately withdraw.

"Come on. Let's go and get that drink. I'm sure some alcohol would make us both feel more at ease!"

Janet hesitated for just a fraction of a second before taking his hand. Oh what the hell, she still enjoyed being with him.

"Sounds good. There's a bar looking out over the river specialising in of gin and burgers. Do you fancy that?"

David raised one eyebrow. "Sounds like an unlikely combination, but I'm game if you are!"

"Trust me. I think you'll like it. It's a few minutes' walk, but I could do with a bit of exercise before sitting down again."

"Yes, I didn't want to admit to Vanessa that I wished I'd brought a cushion as she suggested, but the marble seemed to get harder by the minute. I couldn't wait for Violetta to die so that I could get up!"

"Ah well, they do tend to take their time dying in opera, I find", laughed Janet. "Anyway I'm sure the stone steps were one of the reasons that everyone was so eager to get to their feet and applaud at the end."

"Still, I wouldn't have missed it." David suddenly turned serious, his eyes fixed intensely on hers as they wandered along the street, swinging their arms. "Being there, with you, under the moonlight, listening to music in a Roman arena; it was special."

Janet fell silent for a moment. She couldn't quite hold his gaze, because the truth was that it was special for her too. It was a memory she would cherish; one of those rare unexpected moments in life when for a few moments she had felt at complete peace with the universe.

Finally she glanced up at him. "You're right. It was."

It was David's turn to hesitate. "Janet. I have to go back to England soon to submit my dissertation, but I could be back by October. All it would take is a word from you, you know."

"We've been through all that. I'll miss you, but I don't believe it can work."

David let go of her hand. "Because of the age difference? This is so frustrating. Why can't you just stop analysing everything and trust yourself for once. OK so maybe it won't work and we will break up in five or ten or twenty years' time, but lots of couples do that anyway. Why do you insist on throwing away something potentially wonderful just because we might not make it until our golden wedding anniversary?"

The terrible thing was that he was right, Janet realised. She was so busy trying to find the perfect match and analysing all the possible obstacles that she was denying herself the opportunity to be happy.

"I don't know, because I'm scared I imagine", she said quietly.

David put his arms around her.

"Scared of what? There's nothing to be frightened of. Please, please don't throw away what we have, or what we might have, out of fear, or just pigheadedness! I care about you and I want to be with you."

Janet smiled at him ruefully. "I think I may have developed pigheadedness into an art form. You should be aware of that before you offer yourself up as a sacrificial lamb."

"I'll take my chances. I'm a grown man you know."

David was literally aching with the desire to kiss her, but he didn't want to risk her pushing him away, perhaps ruining his last chance of convincing her. She still felt slightly rigid in his arms, ready to retract at any second, so he released her and after a second they resumed their walk towards the river.

When they reached the bar, they sat down at a small table overlooking the dark, swirling waters of the River Adige. They both ordered a gin and tonic, sipping it gently while they talked and talked, for what seemed an eternity, essentially oblivious to everything around them. They talked about their families, about their past and their future dreams, about art and music. It was if the whole world was conspiring with David; the warm balmy summer night, the sound of the water, the beauty of their surroundings. And when at last it was apparent that the waiters were trying to close the bar, clearing up around them after everyone else had left, Janet realised that David had won and that she was incapable of sending him away. She couldn't deny it any longer. She was just as crazy about him as she was about her and she no longer cared whether their relationship lasted for a month or a lifetime; she wasn't going to give up her chance of happiness.

As soon as they got up she pulled him towards her and kissed him, and this time there was no chance of her withdrawing. The two of them just seemed to merge into one. When they finally detached themselves they turned towards the bridge, making an automatic beeline for Janet's flat on the other side of the river without even realising it, and for the first time that evening there was no need for words. They both knew where they were going and what they wanted. In silence they crossed over the bridge and walked through the by now abandoned streets, until they arrived at the door, giggling like teenagers as they entered the flat and abandoning items of clothing almost before they had closed the door behind them.

When Janet woke up later that morning, she lazily stretched one arm out to where she expected David to be, only to find an empty bed. For one ghastly moment she thought he had changed his mind and sneaked away during the night, frightened off by the thought that she was finally ready to commit. She sat up hurriedly, but realised she could hear the sound of activity in the kitchen, so she fell back onto the pillows with relief, assuming that David had got up to make himself a coffee.

She couldn't explain to herself exactly what had happened the previous night, but it was a like a revelation on the road to Damascus. She had suddenly realised that the biggest obstacles to her happiness were her own reluctance to accept her feelings and her desperate attempt to keep everything under up control. Now, from one moment to another, she was ready to embrace the relationship and accept whatever came out of it. She couldn't quite believe her luck in finding a man like David, and still couldn't rid herself of the idea that it might all be an illusion and come to an end at any minute.

At that moment David pushed open the door with his foot, entering the bedroom with a breakfast tray balanced on one hand.

"Oh my God", said Janet. "Breakfast in bed. You are definitely a man worth marrying. You have so many virtues that I'm surprised you weren't snapped up even before university!"

"Rubbish. It's just that you haven't had time to find out about the defects yet. For the moment I'm on my best behaviour."

"I don't care about the defects. They can't be any worse than mine anyway." Janet pulled herself up into a sitting position, propping up the pillows behind her, as David precariously balanced the tray on her legs. She sat sipping her coffee and nibbling her toast, contemplating how radically things had changed in her mind. Before, she had always been slightly relieved when he left the house and she had the place to herself again, now suddenly she couldn't wait for him to move in so that she could spend as much time as possible with him.

"We have a lot to talk about", she said cautiously.

"So long as it's not just talk", he grimaced.

"Oh, I'm sure we can find time for other things as well." Janet put her arms around his neck and pulled him towards her, risking upsetting the tray all over the bed.

In between lovemaking, cooking and eating, all shared passions, they spent the rest of the day planning out their lives for the next few months, trying to work out how long David would need to be in the UK and when he could come back to Italy, what he could do when he returned and whether they would both stay on in Janet's flat or look for something a bit bigger. They were both in agreement that for the moment at least, they wanted to stay in Verona, the birthplace of the artist to whom

David's thesis was dedicated and the place where their own love story had begun.

"It somehow seems that it was meant to be", said David "so maybe our destiny is linked to Verona."

"You're such a hopeless romantic," sighed Janet. "But that's fine by me…despite the city's unfortunate record for star-cross'd lovers!"

David grinned. "Don't confuse literature with the real world! Whether it was fate that we met or coincidence, our future will depend on us."

Janet threw a pillow at him "I sometimes think you're too mature for me!"

"You see", he smirked. "I told you."

CHAPTER 37

The following Sunday Clare was on the phone to Vanessa and was dying to tell her all the latest gossip.

"You know we left David and Janet in the Piazza after the opera? Well, I saw David the following evening, and he looked like the cat that had got the cream. He couldn't stop beaming, and it didn't take an enormous of imagination on my part to figure out why he was so happy. In fact he couldn't wait to tell me that he and Janet are back together again!"

"That's great news! I think they make a really good couple, but isn't he about to go back to the UK?"

"He is, but then he's planning to come back in October and …wait for it ….move in with Janet."

Wow, that *is* news."

"I'm really happy for them. I know I was initially dubious, but I can't fail to see how completely smitten he is, and apart from the age thing, they are perfect for each other."

"He's very mature for his age, and Janet looks younger than she is anyway. I don't see why it shouldn't work out, but what's he going to do in Verona to earn a living? He definitely won't want to live off Janet, because that would put too much strain on the relationship."

Clare considered the question for a moment. "Oh, I don't know. He may have some freelance writing work, and if all else fails he can do what all well-educated Brits do abroad when they can't find work – teach English!"

"Tell me about it! Actually, he might be rather good at it. He's very patient, and in my experience male teachers are popular with female students."

"Janet might not like that!"

Vanessa laughed. "I don't think she's the jealous type; too logical. Anyway I'm sure he'll find something. So that leaves you. Have you decided whether you're staying?"

Clare groaned. "I keep changing my mind. One moment I decide to go and the next I think I'm crazy to abandon everything, especially now that Marco and I are seeing each other again, but I know it's silly to base my decision purely on that. Actually he's coming to pick me up later this morning. I think he's planning on taking me out to lunch somewhere, so I should probably go and get ready. He's always so immaculate that I feel I should at least make some effort to look my best."

"I have much the same problem with my husband", commented Vanessa "but I think that by now he's abandoned all hope of ever turning me into a polished and appropriate companion. I am most definitely not a trophy wife! Anyway I'll let you get on. Have a good time!"

Clare rang off and turned her attention to the delicate question of her wardrobe. It was stiflingly hot, but she knew that if she wore shorts she would be unequivocally identified as a foreign tourist, so she decided to play it safe with a pair of navy blue linen trousers and white tank top. She regretfully discarded her beloved Birkenstocks (regarded with complete horror by Marco), in favour of a slightly more acceptable pair of sandals with cork wedge heel. Never very skilful at applying make-up, she limited herself to a quick swipe of lip gloss, because she found that she tended to forget she was wearing eye make-up and rub her eyes inadvertently, while mascara inevitably seemed to smudge or run at the most inconvenient moments, the waterproof variety failing conspicuously to live up to its name. Having tied her long blonde hair back in a pony tail, she took a quick look at herself in the mirror and decided that she was presentable overall. Just in time, because at that moment the doorbell rang. Picking up the door phone, Clare told Marco she would be down immediately, grabbing her bag before closing the door behind her and launching herself down the marble stairs with more caution than usual, given her heels.

When she reached the street below, Marco greeted her with the usual peck on both cheeks. She could tell he was surreptitiously appraising her attire, but she seemed to have passed the test because he smiled as he took her by the hand and led her towards the side street where he had parked the car.

"Where are we going today?" asked Clare. "A restaurant?"

"No, today you will have the chance to taste some good home cooking. I have a surprise for you. My mother is expecting us for lunch."

"Marco! You should have told me. I might have paid more attention to my appearance. And I could have got some flowers or something!"

"You look fine, and I have some cakes from the pastry shop in the car."

"But why didn't you tell me?"

"Precisely because I didn't want you to worry about it. Come on. We don't want to keep her waiting."

Clare climbed into the car and they made the short journey to the northern side of Verona, where Marco's mother lived in a relatively modest apartment on the second floor of a modern block of flats. Most of the furnishings seemed to date back to the 1970s and it was definitely a world away from the sophisticated

contemporary atmosphere of Marco's small flat in the city centre. Clare was a little surprised, because she had assumed that he came from a fairly wealthy family, given his lifestyle and love of beautiful and costly things. His mother was equally down-to-earth, a short plump woman who welcomed Clare with a kiss on both cheeks and apparent enthusiasm. She had prepared enough food for a rugby team and was clearly delighted that her guest appreciated it, heaping second portions onto Clare's plate despite her protests. By the end of the meal she was so full that she had to loosen the button of her trousers, and when they finally left in the early afternoon, she felt she had been stuffed like a goose destined for foie gras production. Nevertheless, she had felt surprisingly comfortable with Marco's mum, listening to her stories about her son's childhood, much to his embarrassment, and chatting away with no particular effort. Since the evening at the spa in Sirmione, Marco had always spoken to her in Italian and after ten months in Italy Clare was now sufficiently fluent to converse in her second language without even thinking about it.

Once they had said goodbye to Marco's mother, they decided to go for a short walk in a nearby park before heading home, so they wandered hand in hand until they found a free bench in the shade under a tree.

"Your mother's lovely Marco. I know you say she's very attached to your ex wife, but I didn't feel that she was hostile in any way. She seemed genuinely pleased to meet me."

"Yes, she took to you surprisingly well, which is a relief, because she can be very direct if she doesn't like someone! You have to understand, for my mum Marina was a sort of Goddess. She's beautiful, extremely charming when she wants to be and she comes from an old aristocratic family, whereas my mother's origins are quite humble. She saw our marriage as a chance for me to rise up the social ladder, a sort of reward for all the sacrifices she had made to allow me to study and become what I am today."

"I can see that, and I'm afraid I can't offer quite the same advantages. Believe me, I understand why it's so difficult to get over your ex!"

"Oh I am totally over Marina, if that's what you're worried about. She is the most manipulative, calculating woman I've ever met in my life. I admit I was initially dazzled by her beauty and her extraordinary self-confidence, but I soon realised she only married me because she saw me as a rising star in the medical field. In any case, she was quick to dump me when she got a better offer!"

"Nevertheless, she's a hard act to follow."

Marco put his hands on top of Clare's and looked her directly in the eyes.

"You have so much more to offer than Marina. You're an attractive, intelligent and charming woman, so don't ever put yourself down!"

Clare paused for a moment, before blurting out impulsively "Marco, do you want me to stay in Italy?"

"Of course I do."

"Then why on earth don't you say so?"

"Because I want you to decide for yourself. I don't want to push you to make a decision you might regret."

"That's all very well, but it would help me to make a decision if I knew you really cared about me."

"I do care about you Clare. I think you're amazing and I'm doing my best to show you how much I like you, but I'm not quite ready to make a declaration of undying love. I've already burned my fingers once and now I

261

want to take things one step at a time. I know that's probably not what you want to hear, but that's how I feel."

Clare pondered for a moment. It wasn't quite the great romantic finale of Hollywood films, but given how she felt about him she would be crazy not to give him a chance. He had taken the first step by allowing her to meet his mother. She could take the next by staying in Italy for another year. In any case it wasn't exactly an atrocious sacrifice.

"OK. I'll stay. Maybe it won't work out, but even if it doesn't I'll still be happy to have spent another year in Italy. Just promise me that you'll be honest about your feelings."

The way his face lit up convinced her that she had made the right choice. She could see he was genuinely delighted that she had said she was staying.

"I promise I'll always be honest with you", he said, embracing her. They sat entwined in silence for a while, each with their own thoughts. Clare rested her head on his shoulder, relieved to have finally come to a decision and confident that it was the right one. She stared at the sunshine filtering through the leaves of the trees and smiled to herself, happy to be where she was.

CHAPTER 38

Ursula had scheduled a meeting with all the staff of the school in the second week of July to talk about the plans for the following year. The teachers responsible for the intensive Italian courses for foreigners, which also continued over much of the summer, had already met up with Ursula in the morning, whereas the encounter with the English teachers was organised for the afternoon. In addition to the three friends, the teaching staff included two other teachers who did occasional courses and made themselves available in emergencies, but neither of them would be present that afternoon.

Clare and Janet were already at the school when Vanessa arrived, as Clare was helping out for a few hours a week at the reception desk now that the English courses had terminated for the summer to make a bit of extra money, while Janet had been busy printing off timetables and end-of-year reports. Vanessa, who would normally have appeared bearing the customary tray of cakes, had steadfastly resisted the temptation to stop off at the pastry shop, well aware that if she was serious about changing her habits she had to make some sacrifices. She wasn't sure how long she would be able to keep it up, but she assumed that it was just like any other addiction and all she could do was take it one day at a time.

Clare came bounding out from behind the reception desk, greeting her with genuine affection. Over the year Vanessa had become very fond of her, almost inevitably becoming a sort of substitute mother figure because of the age difference. They often met up before or after work for a chat and a cup of tea or a glass of wine and she was the first person Clare had called once she reached her decision to stay in Verona.

Vanessa responded to her hug with enthusiasm. "Well hello. You're full of energy today. Has Ursula arrived yet?"

"No, but she should be here at any moment. Janet's already making tea in her office and thought it would be best if we had the meeting there."

"That's fine by me. I might as well go through then. There are a couple of things I wanted to say to her before Ursula gets here."

"Great. As soon as she arrives I'll close the door to the school and put the answering machine on. That way we won't be disturbed."

Vanessa made her way to Janet's office. She had already spoken to her on the phone in the last few days to let her know her plans, but she hadn't had the chance to see in her person since the evening they had gone to the opera. However, she had barely had time to get through the door and say hello when they heard the unmistakeable sound of Ursula clattering up the stairs, followed by distinctly unexpected squeals of enthusiasm from Clare.

"What on earth is going on", asked Janet. "She's not usually that delighted to see Ursula. Nobody is."

Curious, the two women poked their heads around the door, to see Clare embracing a tiny white wriggling bundle of fur on a long pink lead.

"Oh my God" said Vanessa. "It's the most adorable puppy; a Jack Russell. I can't believe it."

She rushed out of the office to take her turn cuddling it. "Is it yours Ursula, or are you taking care of it for someone else?"

"No, she is mine. I take her two days ago."

"She's gorgeous. What made you decide to get a Jack Russell?"

Ursula stared at her as if to suggest that the answer was perfectly obvious. "But you know. I love your dog, so I decide to get one like it. She has very good pedigree."

"I was never in any doubt. I'm sure she'll be a wonderful companion. What's her name?"

"Jackie."

Nobody commented on the predictability of this and in any case, Vanessa thought, she was in no position to plead the cause of originality when she herself had a dog called spot!

After a further ten minutes dedicated to discussing the merits and problems of terriers, Janet coughed discreetly from the doorway.

"Well, if we're all ready perhaps we should get on with the meeting."

Clare went off to close the main door and the women sat down around the desk in Janet's office. Vanessa poured herself a cup of tea and took a deep breath before broaching the subject she had been dreading.

"Before we start Ursula, I have to tell you that I have decided to abandon teaching and concentrate on translation, so I won't be coming back to the school next year."

Ursula looked at her with complete horror and disbelief.

"But you must! You are teacher here now for fifteen years!"

"Sixteen, and I've decided that's enough. I simply don't have the same enthusiasm and I need to do something different."

"But I need you. We already change one teacher this year and now we need to find another!"

"Well you've seen how quickly Clare has settled in. She will still be here next year, and as regards my replacement I might have a suggestion. You've met Clare's cousin David. He's planning to come back to Verona in October and will be looking for work, so he could take on my 3 days of teaching and still have time to dedicate to his artistic interests."

Ursula considered the issue for a few moments.

"No, I don't think this is so good. I prefer to have an experienced teacher. Why don't you stay for one more year and then we will have all year to decide what to do?"

"I don't think you quite grasp the situation Ursula" said Vanessa with quiet exasperation. "It is not a question of choosing between be me and David, because I am leaving in any case, but of deciding whether to seize the chance to take on David or to look for someone else. Personally, I think you would be silly not to take him into consideration."

There was a longish pause, as Ursula considered the issue, the cogs of her business mind turning almost visibly. Having apparently weighed up the possible options in her mind, she eventually broke the silence.

"Maybe it is possible. It is also good to have a man for teacher. If Janet thinks he is suitable."

"Oh don't worry. Janet thinks he is very suitable", Vanessa said, her mouth twitching just slightly.

Janet intervened, resisting the temptation to kick her under the table.

"As we were meeting today, I took the liberty of speaking to David informally a few days ago, and he would be interested in taking up the position, if you approve. However, if I might also make a suggestion, as David is an art historian, what about offering courses on Italian art and Verona's artistic and cultural treasures to the students coming here for Italian courses? As he would only be teaching English part-time he could also offer art courses a couple of mornings a week. I think there might be quite a market for it. We already do cooking courses in association with a local restaurant and it would be a way of extending the school's activities."

It was clear that Ursula was interested. Never one to miss out on a potential money-making scheme, she could undoubtedly appreciate the advantages of having a member of staff with a dual function.

"In the meantime, I could be available to cover the first two or three weeks of the term in the event that David is unable to get back from England for the beginning of the school year, or to help in the transitional period", said Vanessa.

Again the three English teachers found themselves holding their breath as they waited for Ursula's response. Of course there were other potential solutions, and nobody could force Vanessa to stay on if she didn't want to, but the proposal seemed to resolve all their problems amicably in one go.

Ursula drummed her long, perfectly-manicured nails on the top of the desk.

"I think it is good. If Janet says he will be a good teacher he can take Vanessa's place and then maybe we see if there is request for art courses in the autumn. Then later we can think about including the proposal on the web site and in the publicity material that goes to new students."

From here on it was plain sailing, with nothing more demanding to discuss than timetabling and the allocation of courses to the different teachers. The only slight bone of contention was when Clare tried to pass on the traffic wardens' course to David, on the grounds that as he was the least senior member of staff he should get the naffest group. However, Ursula flatly refused, because the group was always made up largely of men, and she was convinced they would feel defrauded if she gave them a male teacher.

When the meeting came to an end around an hour later, Ursula had one of her moments of rare and unexpected generosity and insisted on taking them all out for an aperitif at the neighbouring bar as a sort of leaving party for her oldest teacher, and to celebrate the end of the academic year. As she walked out of the school Vanessa was aware that it was unlikely to be the last time she crossed the threshold, as she had agreed to be available at the beginning of the next academic year until David settled in, but nevertheless she felt as if a big weight had lifted off her shoulders. No more teaching commitments, no more battles with Ursula and no more commuting in and out of Verona; the prospect was distinctly appealing and she counted on being definitively out of the school by half-term. What she was going to do with herself afterwards was another question, but having a life seemed like a good start.

It was only a couple of minutes' walk to the local bar, where they all sat down at an outside table, sinking comfortably into the wicker chairs. In her usual fashion, Ursula ordered Aperol Spritz all round without bothering to consult anyone, but the three teachers tacitly agreed that there was no point looking a gift horse in the mouth. In the meantime Ursula extracted Jackie from her bright pink puppy carrier and put her on the ground, where she bounced around happily, receiving an inordinate amount of attention and admiring gazes from passers-by. She was perhaps less popular with the waiter, who kept nearly falling over her every time he passed with a tray of drinks, but she was definitely a hit with the general public and Ursula took every compliment as if it had been made to her personally. After half an hour she made her excuses and dashed off to her next appointment, stuffing Jackie back into her bag and embracing everyone enthusiastically as if they were all long lost friends, before taking her leave noisily.

Once whirlwind Ursula had moved off, the three women breathed a sigh of relief and decided to order another round of drinks, this time of their own choosing.

"I think that all went rather well, wouldn't you say?" said Vanessa, blissfully clasping a glass of cool white wine.

"Absolutely", Janet confirmed. "Better than I could have hoped."

Clare too raised her glass.

"Well here's to us! It's been a life-changing year for all of us."

They chinked glasses.

"To friendship!" said Janet.

"To friendship and love!" added Vanessa.

"To friendship, love and the city that made it all possible: Verona!" concluded Clare.

The three women smiled at each other. Maybe in a year's time everything would have changed, but for the moment they knew their place in the world.

Acknowledgements

First of all, I must thank my friend and fellow writer/translator William George for encouraging me to write this book in the first place, and for his support throughout the process. In addition, I must express my gratitude to Linda Combi, another long-standing friend and a talented illustrator, for the cover. Thanks also go to my brother Ivor for his invaluable editorial assistance, and to various friends for their comments and suggestions. Finally, I must recognise the contribution of my husband and two daughters, without whom this book would probably have been finished much earlier, but who are nevertheless my raison d'être. Thank you for existing!

All the characters in this book are fictional, although the descriptions draw on many people I have known during the course of my career, while all the places and festivals mentioned are real.

17882949R00156

Printed in Poland
by Amazon Fulfillment
Poland Sp. z o.o., Wrocław